UNDAUNTED BY DANGER,
MEN OF DREAMS AND WOMEN OF PASSION
ANSWER FREEDOM'S CALL.

GHONKABA—Mighty Seneca warrior, grandson of the great white Indian Renno. His courage in battle has already made him a legend, but his smouldering hatred for the British can make him betray his own people even as he becomes a hero in the white man's war.

TOSHABE—Dusky, passionate wife of Ghonkaba. Her loyalty to her husband takes her away from her Indian world—and leads her into a dangerous liaison with a handsome American rogue.

COLONEL ALEXANDER HAMILTON—A dashing leader of the American cause. His sexual appetite for the delicious charms of another man's wife could endanger his country—or cost him his life.

ENA—High-spirited daughter of Ghonkaba. As skilled as any Seneca brave at stealth and scouting, she will take a terrible risk to prove herself a true inheritor of the White Indian's fighting spirit.

GENERAL GEORGE WASHINGTON—Supreme Commander of the Colonial Army. Even his military genius is no match for the superior British forces until his wisdom leads him to trust a noble Indian, who is branded a traitor by his own people but called a great American hero by generations to come.

The White Indian Series
Book IX

SENECA

Donald Clayton Porter

Created by the producers of
**Wagons West, Children of the Lion,
Stagecoach,** and **Saga of the Southwest.**

Chairman of the Board: Lyle Kenyon Engel

BANTAM BOOKS
TORONTO · NEW YORK · LONDON · SYDNEY

SENECA

A Bantam Book / published by arrangement with
Book Creations, Inc.

Bantam edition / April 1984

Produced by Book Creations, Inc.
Chairman of the Board: Lyle Kenyon Engel

ISBN 0-553-23986-4

Published simultaneously in the United States and Canada

Bantam Books are published by Bantam Books, Inc. Its trademark,
consisting of the words ''Bantam Books'' and the portrayal of a
rooster, is Registered in U.S. Patent and Trademark Office and in
other countries. Marca Registrada. Bantam Books, Inc., 666 Fifth
Avenue, New York, New York 10103.

PRINTED IN THE UNITED STATES OF AMERICA

H   0 9 8 7 6 5 4 3 2 1

SENECA

Chapter I

The usual early-afternoon quiet following the midday meal in the main town of the Seneca was broken only by the war chief's stride as he made his way to the most holy place of his people.

The Seneca, with their fellow nations of the Iroquois League, lived in the upper lake region of the New York Colony. Universally regarded as unparalleled in the art of making war, they were feared by colonists and fellow Indians alike. Their granaries were filled, as were their warehouses. Women had harvested the vegetables. Hunters had gathered huge quantities of venison, buffalo, and other meats. Stocked as well were tons of fish, now thoroughly smoked. In the late autumn of 1773, the main town of the Seneca was ready for the approach of winter.

The war chief who disturbed the afternoon's quiet was Ghonkaba, a renowned warrior whose lineage was unique. His father, Ja-gonh, was the Great Sachem of the entire Iroquois League, and his uncle, No-da-vo, was the sachem of the Seneca. Ghonkaba was the grandson of Renno, the renowned white Indian, and the great-grandson of the great Ghonka, founder of the Iroquois League and the first member of the family to become a close friend of English colonists.

Today Ghonkaba was sore at heart and deeply troubled.

He made his way to the Room of the Great Faces, where unnumbered generations ago medicine men had constructed fearsome masks out of leather, wood, and feathers. These represented the faces of the manitous, the intermediaries between the nation's gods and the mortals who currently made up the Seneca nation.

It was an ancient custom of the Seneca to go to the Great Faces and ask for their help with difficult problems that affected the entire nation. So it was that Ghonkaba was presenting himself to the Faces.

He desperately needed some word, some sign, that would point the path for him to take in order to solve his terrible dilemma. He had thought about the problem day and night for many weeks. Having been unable to come to a conclusion, he was following the only remaining path open to him as an honorable Seneca who believed in the ways of his people.

Afternoon sunlight flooded the empty building and highlighted the grotesque figures that looked down from the walls on mere men. Then the door closed, and the Room of the Great Faces again was enveloped in darkness.

Taking a firm stance and folding his arms, Ghonkaba bowed his head, content to wait. With his eyes partially closed, he gradually became acclimated to the darkness, and the Great Faces on the walls began to take shape once more. Finally, he was ready.

At last, he broke the sepulchral silence and softly caressed the figures on the walls. "Great Faces, which have guided the Seneca nation since the beginning of time, hear my plea," he said. "Great Faces, which have guarded the Seneca and have brought the nation to greatness, help us now in the supreme trial that we face. I ask you, Great Faces, to show us a sign of the will of the gods in this matter that tears us to our roots.

"For many years," he continued, "the Seneca and the other nations of the Iroquois have been the staunchest allies of Great Britain and of her colonies. Now a dispute threatens to disrupt the peace between Britain and these colonies. What should the Seneca do if a war breaks out between them? Do we abide by the terms of our treaty with England, or do we join the Americans, by whose side we have fought in so many battles? These Americans have been deeply influenced by us and are more like us than like the English."

Ghonkaba waited patiently as the silence grew longer and more tense. He could expect no reply in words; that would be asking far too much. On several occasions of great crisis, the Great Faces had responded to his appeals with signs that he could easily interpret. They had shown him the way that he should go. Now he was trusting again that they would offer a sign, such as creating a physical reaction within him that would be plainly revealing.

The silence continued and grew more oppressive. The Great Faces remained impassive. Ghonkaba neither felt nor saw any result of his heartfelt appeal. It was both disappointing and surprising to him.

At last he concluded that he would receive no

supernatural assistance with his problem, and he withdrew from the Room of the Great Faces. Then, with a shake of his head, he squared his shoulders, adjusted the tomahawk hung from his belt, and walked rapidly to the council lodge, where, he knew, his father and uncle were conferring. All the members of the older generation—El-i-chi and Walter, Ba-lin-ta and Deborah—were gone, and Ja-gonh and No-da-vo were now the elders of the nation.

Reaching the entrance to the council chamber, Ghonkaba could see Ja-gonh seated cross-legged on the ground within, illustrating his remarks by making drawings in the dirt floor with a stick. No-da-vo, his brother-in-law, sat beside him, listening eagerly and not interrupting.

Ja-gonh was tall and distinguished in appearance. His light brown hair and blue eyes clearly marked him as a son of Renno, the original white Indian, and his American colonist wife, Betsy. Like his late father, he was slender and appeared to be no match for the heavier, full-blooded braves of his tribe, but actually he was endowed with prodigious strength. His valorous deeds as a warrior and a war chief had gained him the renown that had led to his selection as sachem of the Seneca and then Great Sachem of all the Iroquois.

No-da-vo was far more typical of the Seneca. Dark and burly, he had a thick chest, long arms, and a powerful torso.

As Ghonkaba crossed the threshold of the lodge, his shadow fell across the light cast by the fire. The two older men looked up and saw him standing rigidly, his back straight, his left arm extended in a formal greeting.

Coming into the presence of the supreme leaders of the Seneca, Ghonkaba was careful to observe tribal amenities.

Ja-gonh beckoned him closer.

"We have no need for formality when we're alone, my son," he said mildly.

Ghonkaba seated himself on the far side of the fire. "Do I interrupt an important discussion?" he asked. "If so, my news certainly can wait."

"We've been engaging in idle speculation, Ghonkaba," No-da-vo said. "We've been wondering just how battles would be fought if England and the colonies went to war."

"Frankly," his father added, "it is difficult to imagine such a war. The idea that the English and the Americans would kill each other is beyond my ability to understand."

Ghonkaba said, "It is easy for me to understand how hard feelings can grow between colonists and those who represent the mother country. Ever since you sent me to England as your emissary to the monarch, King George the Third, I have been telling you how difficult a man he is to know and to like. King George knows virtually nothing of the colonists and their ways, and has no desire to learn. Yet they are expected to obey him unquestioningly and to look up to him as their earthly lord and master."

"So you have said many times," No-da-vo replied somberly.

Ja-gonh sighed and took his time removing a live coal from the fire and lighting his pipe with it. "If war breaks out between the British and the colonists," he said, "our family will suffer more than most. Renno, my father, surely had many relatives in Massachusetts Bay, and although we do not know them, we do have blood kin there. Betsy, my mother, came from one of the leading families of Virginia, and therefore we have cousins who are prominent in the military and in politics. What they will do in the event of war, I cannot predict. But I know what I must do, and what the Seneca are obliged to do."

Ghonkaba braced himself for discouraging words.

"When my father lay on his deathbed," Ja-gonh said, "he obtained a solemn promise from me that to the end of my days I would abide by the treaties that he and my grandfather, Ghonka, forged with the English settlers. It was in the years of their close association with England that the Seneca—and with them, the other nations of our Iroquois League—became great and powerful. I will grant you that the alliance has been of great benefit to England. We have fought beside her in her wars with the French and other enemies in the New World. We have taken her side in the peace conferences that have resulted in treaties with France and Spain and with many Indian nations. But we, too, have obtained many benefits. We have been equipped with modern firearms; we have sent our vegetables and meat to their colonies in return for the produce that they grow. We have obtained many of the white man's benefits, such as blankets and cooking utensils. All this has come to us as a direct result of our association with England."

He took a deep breath, then asked quietly, "Now that grave troubles threaten England, shall the Seneca desert her in her time of need? No, I say!"

"I also say it!" No-da-vo said fiercely. "The Seneca are an honorable nation, and we will not go back on our sworn word."

"My father, my uncle," Ghonkaba replied earnestly, "I can understand how you feel because you fought shoulder to shoulder with the troops of Britain when only the most amicable feelings existed between them and their colonists. But remember that I fought beside Colonel Washington of Virginia and his scouts when the British fled from the troops of France and their Indian allies. My first battles were fought at the side of the Americans, and I cannot forget my astonishment. The Americans think as we think; they fight as we fight.

They are truly our brothers. If they take up arms against England, I shall be strongly tempted to join forces with them."

"You must do what your conscience compels you to do, my son," Ja-gonh said, with an underlying sadness echoing in his voice. "Your mother and I have often discussed your dilemma. As a war chief, as the father of three children, you are capable of making up your own mind. It is my hope that you will not take up arms against your own people, but I cannot and will not hold you to the Seneca against your will."

"If I join the Americans, I will never fight against the Seneca or the other nations of the Iroquois," Ghonkaba said vehemently. "No matter what my feelings might be, I am a Seneca, first and always, and until I die I will be true to the precepts and the beliefs of my nation. This feeling is as natural as the breath I take. I see the world through the eyes of a Seneca warrior."

"It appears to me that we are jumping to conclusions too readily," Ja-gonh said. "We already are speaking of a parting of the ways when no such parting may ever threaten us."

No-da-vo was quick to take up the same theme. "Several moons have passed," he observed, "since we last heard of a worsening of relations between the British and the colonists. We would be wise to send Ghonkaba to Boston as the emissary of the Seneca, so he will be able to see with his own eyes and hear with his own ears what is happening. Then, since he is familiar with the colonies and their wishes, he could return with a detailed report on the situation as it stands."

"Are you willing to volunteer for such a trip, my son?" Ja-gonh asked tentatively.

"I have little to occupy me here during the long winter months that lie ahead," Ghonkaba replied, "other than the education of my children. And this I can leave for others to oversee. I will gladly go to Boston, and when I return, I hope I shall bring enough information to enable my beloved Seneca to chart a safe course through troubled seas."

Toshabe, the wife of Ghonkaba, was a Seneca traditionalist who rigorously followed the unwritten rules of the nation. She brought up her children according to the strictest precepts of Seneca law.

Regally handsome, she sat now in the main room of her house, keeping a sharp watch on her three children as they prepared the evening meal. Her daughter, Ena, a lively and exceptionally pretty girl of thirteen, was preparing a stew of vegetables. She cleaned corn, beans, and squash and put them into a pot with a variety of herbs. After placing them over the fire in the center of the room, she stirred them gently from time to time. As always, she was completely in earnest, absorbed by her task. Of all the children, she was the most conscious of their unique heritage. Named for her great-grandmother, she was determined to live up to her ancestors' high standards.

Renno was busily removing the scales, skin, and bones of the several whitefish he had caught earlier in the day, and Toshabe nodded approvingly as she watched his agile fingers at work. At age eleven, he gave clear evidence of having inherited the physical talents of his father, grandfather, and great-grandfather, and Toshabe never doubted that he would grow up to be a first-rate hunter and warrior.

His younger brother, El-i-chi, appropriately named for the original Renno's brother, was a serious-looking boy of nine summers. He was occupied in pounding a large slab of buffalo meat with a rock, so that it would become more tender. Occasionally he glanced quickly at his mother and then at his brother and sister. He was ready, as Toshabe knew, to abandon his efforts and suggest a game of hide-and-seek in the forest. His mother's presence, however, made it impossible for the children to desert their jobs.

Ghonkaba entered the house, and the effect on the family was immediate. Toshabe rose and was greeted with a warm, meaningful smile. Ena stopped her stew-making long enough to fly to her father's side.

Renno straightened and, with his shoulders back, returned to his task. Ghonkaba moved closer and watched his son's work on the fish. He smiled in silent approval. He used praise sparingly, as was the Seneca tradition.

El-i-chi stopped pounding the buffalo meat and cast a covert glance at Ghonkaba. "My father," he said, "I will make you this wager: if you give me a headstart of but three minutes, I will find a hiding place in the forest without leaving a single trace or clue as to my whereabouts."

Ordinarily Ghonkaba would have accepted the challenge instantly, but he only smiled tolerantly and replied solemnly, "My son, let me remind you of the ways of your ancestors. A boy who ceases work on his chores before being released from them by his mother eats no more food that day. Your appetite is prodigious, so I would regret seeing you denied your supper."

El-i-chi responded by pounding the buffalo meat furiously.

Ghonkaba seated himself opposite Toshabe and began to fill a long pipe. To her, it was evident that he was perturbed, so she said nothing.

"I have been discussing with my father and uncle the plight of the colonists," he said. "We spoke of the anger felt by the Americans because they are not allowed to elect members to the British Parliament, yet Parliament has the right to collect taxes from them on the basis of any law Parliament passes and to expect payment in full."

"Did you reach any conclusions," Toshabe asked,

"about the low opinion the British hold of the American militia?"

"No," he said. "But the British have heard from militia leaders that they feel disgraced because a colonel who commands a full regiment of militia ranks below a mere captain of British Regulars."

He paused to relight his pipe. "My father and uncle also know," Ghonkaba said, "that the American colonists are required by law now to open their doors to troops from England and to permit British Regulars to live under their roofs. It's small wonder that they feel like an occupied nation that lost a war."

Ena looked up from her work. "My father," she asked, "why don't the colonists rebel? What prevents them from taking up arms after saying to the British, 'You are our brothers, not our masters. If you do not treat us fairly, we must go our separate way'?"

Ghonkaba was startled by Ena's perceptive understanding of issues. He took care to answer her in full, to treat her as he had been treated at her age.

"Many Americans do advocate such open rebellion, my daughter," he explained. "But the problem is not an easy one to solve. Those who fail to obey the British are considered traitors to their mother country, just as all Iroquois must obey the edicts of your grandfather or be regarded as traitors to their nation and to the Iroquois League."

With more pressing matters on his mind, he now turned to Toshabe.

"My father and uncle," he told her, "have decided that I should travel to Boston, the center of ferment, in order to learn more about the true state of affairs. Only when our leaders have the necessary information about what is happening in the world of our white brothers can they finally set the course that the nations of the League should take."

Ena interrupted, the seriousness of her expression

masking an elfin smile. "I have a request to make of you, my father," she said. "May Renno and I go with you to Boston?"

Her brother quickly picked up the idea. "It would give us a great opportunity to expand our use of the English language," he almost shouted. "We use it only within the family. Also, we would have a chance to learn more about the ways of the colonists."

Ghonkaba found difficulty in keeping a straight face. "I'm sorry to disappoint you, my children," he said, "but I'm not going to Boston for my own pleasure. I will go as an envoy of the Seneca and the Iroquois. I must travel with all possible speed and reach Boston as soon as I can. Then, when I have fulfilled my duties there, I must rush home."

His children appeared at first to be crushed by his words, but a quick exchange of glances between them suggested that they would try again. Every day they were reminded that they were direct descendants of the great Renno, and they were determined to follow the example their distinguished forebear had set in self-discipline and restraint.

Toshabe took the slab of buffalo meat, dipped it into a mixture of finely pounded cornmeal, oil, and herbs, and then placed it on the grill just over the fire. After telling Ena to begin cooking the fish, she asked her husband, "Where will you stay in Boston?"

"I believe I'll seek lodging with Sam Adams," he said. "Not only is he an old friend who always makes me welcome, but as a prominent journalist, he knows at least as much as anyone else in Boston about current developments. I can rapidly learn much from him. Be sure you make a list of the books, cooking utensils, and other objects that are available only in the communities of the white man that I am to bring home with me."

Toshabe smiled. "I'm already composing such a list in my mind," she said. "When do you go?"

"I shall leave at dawn tomorrow. When the Great Sachem of the Iroquois wishes information, one does not lose time in obtaining it for him."

When the meal was ready, Ghonkaba followed the custom of offering thanks through the manitous to the gods of the Seneca for their food. It was El-i-chi's turn to recite a brief additional prayer, and although he stumbled once, no one offered assistance. It was his responsibility to correct his mistake and finish his prayer. At the end, he added the fervent wish that the manitous would assist his father on the mission to Boston.

Ghonkaba was struck by the significance of his mission. He would not be seeking random information but exact and specific facts and insights that would determine the future for himself, his wife, and their offspring. In fact, if a full-scale war developed, every Indian nation on the continent of North America would be affected.

Ghonkaba lost no time in completing the necessary preparations for his important expedition. Early the next morning, he was on his way. But before he had traveled half a mile from the main camp of the Seneca, he was halted by an unexpected obstacle in his path.

Looming ahead of him on the trail, obviously intent on a confrontation, stood the burly figure of one of his fellow war chiefs, Tredno, who often in the past had seized any occasion to emphasize his feeling of rivalry with him.

Over the years, Ghonkaba had tried to avoid Tredno's company because he could see no point in expending his time and energies in endeavoring to counter the angry, hostile expressions that he seemed always to provoke whenever Tredno saw him.

He was aware that Tredno had had a difficult life, and he easily found it in his heart to extend a helpful hand, but after one or two early efforts had been rebuffed sarcastically, he had given up. Tredno's great difficulty, Ghonkaba realized, resulted from a tragic affair many years earlier—Losee, his father, had been banished from the tribe in disgrace as a result of an offense too horrible to be spoken of. Losee's entire family had suffered for a long time after his disappearance, and in effect the family withered under what the members considered endlessly imposed rejection by the entire town. Only Tredno had withstood the buffeting in any upstanding manner, like a lone pine tree standing in solitude against the cold winds of winter. But in spite of his courage, Tredno's personality had taken on a twisted and misshapen aspect. Instead of developing straight and admirable in his loneliness, the warrior had become insolent, bitter, isolated, and provocative.

Tredno's ideas and attitudes almost invariably went to unreasonable extremes, and Ghonkaba knew that he had expressed an inflexible outlook on the conflict that was rocking the white man's colonies. He had frequently voiced strongly antagonistic feelings toward the American colonists, and Ghonkaba suspected that these feelings might relate somehow to Losee's infraction of Seneca law. Predictably, Tredno was equally irrational in his support of the British. He could be expected to be completely hostile to any Seneca who saw worth in the Americans' cause. Ghonkaba found such fanaticism appalling, especially when it appeared in a Seneca brave.

Even while being aware of all these unhappy ingredients of their relationship, he was amazed to be accosted at this unlikely spot and in such a manner. It was as though Tredno had been lying in wait for him along the trail.

Nonetheless, Ghonkaba raised his left hand as a sign of greeting, which Tredno belatedly returned with no indication of pleasure.

"Is it true," he asked gruffly, without prelude, "as I have heard, that you may favor the cause of the

Americans if they go to war to fight for their independence against the British?"

The question struck a sensitive nerve in Ghonkaba, who found it impossible to answer directly. "I have the greatest admiration, as you know, for the colonists," he said, "especially for the Virginians. They are, after all, my blood relatives through my grandmother, the wife of the great Renno. Also, it was my misfortune to meet King George in London soon after he gained the throne, and I was not impressed by him. However, I am fully aware that we Seneca are bound to the British by a treaty, so I cannot say where I will stand if the colonists declare their independence."

Tredno snorted impatiently. "You speak rubbish with the tongue of a woman," he sneered. "Our obligation to join the British is very clear. As the leaders of the Iroquois League, it is our sacred duty to keep our word. And it is your own family who swore that we would stand beside the British in combat against all foes. Not only that, but it makes great sense. They are powerful beyond measure, and they have many great rifles to advance their cause. So if they must go to war, I shall take up arms on their side—as should all our braves! Remember that on this foolish mission you are undertaking."

At that, Ghonkaba turned aside enough to pass by Tredno and resumed his trot eastward. He was troubled by the necessity of confronting Tredno's unreasoning hostility and irritated by the delay, but he forced himself to dismiss it all from his mind. Still, he knew, such mindless fanaticism would lead to conflicts that would have to be settled on other occasions.

As he sped through the forest, the drums of sentries, first of the Seneca and then of their close allies the Mohawk, gave notice of his presence. After several days, he came to the Massachusetts Colony, but did not pause in Springfield, where he had many friends; instead he hurried on toward Boston. He identified himself through his generous use of war paint, but was not surprised that most colonists seemed to fail to recognize the distinctive Seneca colors.

Two nights before reaching Boston, after traveling all day at the punishing pace customary for a Seneca warrior, Ghonkaba made his camp as usual in the wilderness. This was not easy, as so much of the land in the area was being used for farming by the energetic colonists. He chose a small clearing surrounded by a thick clump of evergreens. After downing his parched corn and jerked beef, he rolled in his blanket and settled down for the night.

Unexpectedly, he began to dream. He found himself standing alone among evergreens. While he examined his surroundings, the trees parted and a warrior's figure came into view. The warrior seemed transparent at first, but he gradually took shape and was revealed to be Ghonkaba's grandfather. But he was not Renno as he had looked during his last days on earth. His body was younger and more vigorous, his strong muscles were evident, and his face was fully fleshed and unlined. Ghonkaba realized that his grandfather had looked like this when he was Ghonkaba's present age.

The warrior bowed low before the awesome figure.

"Stand erect," Renno said, in a voice that was clear and incisive.

Suspended between sleep and awareness, Ghonkaba rejoiced at the vision. He had been longing for a signal of how he should deal with the grave responsibility that he faced, and he hoped his grandfather had returned from the land-beyond-the-great-river in order to direct him into the proper channel of thought and action.

"You did well," Renno told him with a smile, "when you refused permission to the boy you have given my name and to the girl who bears the name of my mother."

"I could not give in to the whims of the children at a time that is so important," Ghonkaba explained.

"It is important," Renno replied, "not only to you and to those who are descended from me, but to the entire Seneca nation."

"I hear the words that you speak, my grandfather," Ghonkaba said.

"Open wide your eyes and your ears and, above all else, your mind, while you visit in Boston," Renno told him. "The conclusions that you draw will have a great bearing on the role the Seneca will play in the world for many years."

"What should I seek in particular?" Ghonkaba asked. "What aspects are of the greatest significance to the Seneca and to our family?"

Renno smiled at him. "You are no fledgling," he said. "You are no young warrior untried in the ways of battle. You have lived for almost forty summers, and you have so distinguished yourself that you have earned your place as a war chief of our people. That in itself speaks of your intelligence and your prowess. You need no instructions. Do what comes naturally to you, and you will prosper in your affairs. Do not allow your personal sympathies to interfere with your judgments. Remember the principles you learned from me and from your good friend and superior Colonel Washington."

Ghonkaba was confused. "Help me, my grandfather," he pleaded. "The more you say to me now, the less I understand."

Renno smiled enigmatically and began to fade from view.

"Don't leave me now, I beg you, my grandfather," Ghonkaba cried. "Help me in my bewilderment to solve my dilemma." He found himself talking to thin air. He was alone again in the small clearing.

Opening his eyes, Ghonkaba looked around speculatively. He was in the identical place of his dream, but he was certainly alone. Whether his grandfather had in truth appeared to him or whether he had imagined the entire incident was a riddle he could not fathom. It was enough that his grandfather had spoken words of wisdom. When he reached Boston, he would abide by Renno's words and would keep his ears, eyes, and mind open. Perhaps he would uncover some clues that would help him to decide what he and his people should do.

Ghonkaba found Boston exhilarating, as he had on his first visit a quarter-century ago. People walked briskly, with a sense of purpose.

As the colony's capital and the largest community in North America, Boston was a busy, bustling city of more than ten thousand persons. Her harbor was crowded with transatlantic ships that carried merchandise to and from England, smaller vessels that engaged in the intercolonial trade of the eastern seaboard, and ships of intermediate size that were responsible for the lucrative trade with the West Indies.

The only iron foundries, clothing mills, and shoe factories in the New World were located here.

The Puritan standard of hard work and sobriety prevailed in Boston, and everyone abided by it, from the physicians, attorneys, and newspapermen, who were America's best, to the academics at Harvard College; and to the businessmen who were building impressive homes on Beacon Hill.

In contrast, sailors of a half-dozen nations, speaking as many languages, filled the saloons and the brothels of the waterfront district. Indians of questionable character, members of small tribes, tried to get by in Boston without actually earning a living. Cardsharps, confidence men, and other petty criminals were attracted to Boston by its size and affluence.

In the main, the residents obeyed their own rules. John Hancock, who lived in one of the great mansions on Beacon Hill, possessed a fortune from smuggling. John Adams, most distinguished of native-born lawyers, arrived at his desk before sunup and was still there long after sundown. His cousin, Sam Adams, was unique among journalists. He had founded the Committees of 'orrespondence, through which citizens of one colony nformed those of the other twelve colonies of developments in their continuing quarrel with Great Britain. vriting under a dozen pseudonyms for newspapers in .oston, New York, Philadelphia, and elsewhere, he ured out endless information and ideas about the colonies' cause from his inexhaustible pen.

Ghonkaba stayed alert for nuances, as his grandfatner had directed in his dream, and they were not difficult to find.

People continued to bustle as they had twenty-five years before, intent on their own business, but he felt a difference—a major difference—in the composition of the public on Boston's streets. Everywhere were "lobsterbacks"—scarlet-uniformed British soldiers— walking in twos and threes. Armed with bayonets and muskets, they had a minimum of friendly contact with the people of Boston, though some of them were being quartered in Bostonians' homes—a source of general vexation. Pedestrians crossed a street rather than brush shoulders with the British troops, who met stares of open hostility everywhere. As Ghonkaba watched, he saw that the troops neither greeted anyone nor were greeted. These soldiers, members of outstanding British regiments, were as isolated as if cast away on a desert island.

Girls seemingly were unaware of the troops' existence; young men glared with hatred and, under their breath, called them names; and boys shouted at them abusively. Most adults treated them with faint but distinct contempt.

Equally important, he found the usual high spirits

of the colonists lacking. People seemed surly and withdrawn. Their silence and churlishness contrasted with the openhearted spirit of good cheer of the past. ritish officers in tunics of scarlet and gold, with high-owned beaver shakos towering above their heads, raveled in groups of threes, and all seemed to go out of heir way to offer amiable greetings to the colonists. These salutations were generally ignored. No snub, honkaba decided, was as harsh as that issued by a ostonian. As he continued on his journey, he realized .at the British troops were taking care to avoid him. Knowing nothing of his identifying war paint, they wanted to avoid trouble.

At last he arrived at the large gray-shingled house of Sam Adams on Purchase Street. His knock on the door was answered by a small boy, who bellowed for "Papa," and Ghonkaba promptly found himself surrounded by a small army of shouting children, barking dogs, and exuberant cats.

Adams, looking fit in his shirt-sleeves, though he tended to bulge at the seams, soon rescued him.

Mrs. Adams greeted him with great warmth, informing them that noon dinner soon would be ready, and then hurried off to the kitchen.

Moving a pile of papers and books from a chair in the study so that Ghonkaba would have a place to sit, Adams asked jovially, "What brings you to Boston?"

As Ghonkaba explained his mission, Adams listened carefully, his eyes shining. He pointed to a stack of documents on his desk that appeared to be letters not yet dispatched.

"You have arrived at the very best of times, Ghonkaba," Adams said enthusiastically, rubbing his hands together. "You've arrived at a time to watch history in the making. Do you have any engagements planned for this evening?"

"No, none," Ghonkaba said. "I'm entirely in your hands."

"I suggest that you spend a couple of hours with some good friends of mine. I won't be able to be with you myself, because it is necessary that I be seen elsewhere in Boston this evening. I'm always under suspicion whenever there's any demonstration, so tonight—of all nights—I've got to grit my teeth and absent myself to attend a soiree arranged coincidentally for tonight by cousin Abigail. It's my only way of staying out of real trouble!"

Ghonkaba had no idea what Adams meant, but decided to refrain from asking questions unnecessarily. He judged that he would be shown, step by step, what Adams had in mind.

Dinner at the Adamses' table was an extraordinary experience. Ghonkaba found himself surrounded by children, and he had no idea which were Adams's and which were the sons and daughters of friends. The table talk was boisterous and candid, with all the young people expressing their dislike of the redcoats and of King George III.

After the meal, Sam Adams returned to his study with his guest and again busied himself with writing page after page of foolscap. "I'm sorry," he said to Ghonkaba, "but it's essential that I attend to these writing chores immediately."

Given a copy of *The Massachusetts Spy* to read, Ghonkaba waded through it. He read letters to the editor bitterly attacking the British as foreign occupiers of American soil, together with urgent proposals that Americans band together and proclaim their independence. At first, Ghonkaba was somewhat surprised at the unanimity of the views. But on reflection, he finally realized that Sam Adams was up to his old tricks. Writing under numerous pseudonyms, he was responsible for the letters. His one-man campaign against the

British was being carried out with great cunning and skill.

A light tap sounded at the back door, and Adams hastened to answer the summons. Waiting in the study, Ghonkaba could hear him conversing in low tones with another man. When Adams led the man into the study, Ghonkaba was astonished to see a colonist dressed as an Indian, complete with streaks of war paint on his face.

Adams quickly reassured this new arrival that Ghonkaba was an old friend who could be trusted.

The visitor, who was not identified by Adams, spoke to Ghonkaba. "Seneca," he said, "you've come to Boston at the most opportune of all times. Can I persuade you to take part in an adventure that I think I can guarantee will cause you no injury?"

"If you'll accompany him," Sam Adams added, "I'm sure you'll gain a far better understanding of our position, what we stand for, and how we intend to go about achieving our goals."

Ghonkaba felt a surge of recklessness. "Lead on," he said. "I'll follow you."

"You'd better take him back to your place for the night, Josiah," Adams suggested. "I'm certain this house will be carefully watched later."

"There's no doubt of it, Sam," the visitor replied. "Never fear, we'll take no chances."

Adams went to a closet and from a hiding place produced a short, double-edged ax, which he handed to Ghonkaba. "This," he said, "is the closest we could come to an Indian hatchet and yet have a practical tool for the work that needs to be done tonight. Guard it well." After shaking hands with the pair in turn, he escorted them to the side door and silently let them out through the garden entrance.

Treading as silently as in the wilderness, Ghonkaba followed the stranger through numerous back streets and alleyways. He realized the man was deliberately avoiding streets where people would be abroad and they would be noticed. When they reached Hutchinson Street, near the waterfront, Josiah's efforts to maintain absolute quiet seemed more intense.

At last they arrived at a roofed building on the waterfront and slipped inside. There Josiah finally spoke.

"Are you familiar," he asked, "with the situation regarding tea?"

Ghonkaba shook his head. "I have just today arrived from the land of the Seneca," he said, "and I know very little about recent developments here."

"Great quantities of tea are used in the colonies," Josiah explained, "and all of it, of course, is imported from India and China by way of Great Britain. The House of Commons has imposed a tax on tea, but every colony, inspired by the stand that Sam has taken, has flatly refused to pay it. Consequently, ships carrying cargoes of tea were being turned away and sent back to England. But the tax collectors are shrewd. They will not accept the refusal of the people to buy tea, and they insist that until the tax is paid, the cargoes will remain loaded on the vessels that brought them here. These ships are clogging our harbors and interfering with our trade."

Josiah laughed humorlessly. "You Seneca have a saying, I believe, that goes something like this: there is more than one way to skin a polecat."

"That is not our precise saying," Ghonkaba told him, "but it is close enough."

The man chuckled again. "We're about to participate in a verification of that saying." He fell silent for a moment and then resumed in a lower voice. "It is ironic that we chose disguises as Indians and that you, a true Indian, will be with us. We intend to keep the identity of everyone who participates in tonight's venture a permanent secret. The British would send us all to

22

rot in prison forever if they found out anything about us, and we are determined to prevent that."

Before Ghonkaba could question him, the door of the wharf building creaked open a few inches, and two more men disguised as Indians slipped inside.

Both men showed surprise at the presence of the Seneca. Josiah explained the situation to them in a low tone, and they smiled in silent satisfaction.

This scene was repeated again and again as more than twenty men gathered in the dimness.

Utilizing his extraordinary ability to see in the dark, Ghonkaba recognized that all the "Indians" were young, in their twenties and thirties. All were armed with double-edged axes. At last the man called Josiah, who seemed to be the leader, counted heads, and said in a low but clear tone, "We're all here, so I suggest that we be on our way. A final reminder, gentlemen. If trouble unexpectedly develops, scatter. Remember, it will be up to each of us to save himself. We are not to become embroiled in a fight with redcoats or resort to violence against other persons. Let's go." Motioning to Ghonkaba to stay close beside him, he left the wharf structure and headed out into the night, followed by the entire party, four abreast.

They made no attempt to conceal themselves now; rather, the adventurers seemed to be trying to attract attention. Merchant seamen gaped at them and then turned away and went about their business resolutely. They knew instinctively that this party of "Indians" was up to no good, and they wanted to separate themselves from any association with them.

They soon came to Griffin's wharf, where two large, graceful merchant vessels were tied. Spreading out, the men began to head out along the wharf.

Two watchmen, armed with old-fashioned cutlasses, appeared out of the shadows at either side of the wharf. The party did not hesitate. Josiah called softly to his companions and then bolted forward and threw himself headlong at one of the watchmen, bearing the man to the ground in a hard, vicious tackle.

The second sentry was subjected to an identical treatment, and gags were quickly placed in their mouths. Their wrists and ankles were firmly bound with strips of rawhide.

Ghonkaba observed, nevertheless, that care was taken to avoid injuring the watchmen, who were carried to the main decks of the two merchantmen as the party climbed on board. The raiders obviously had timed the action precisely; at this hour the crew members were haunting the taverns of the waterfront area. No one was left on board.

The organization was superb; every man seemed to understand what he was to do. About half of each company went below and began to pass large, square wooden boxes up from the holds, through the hatches, and onto the open decks. Their comrades split the boxes with their hatchets and then threw the broken boxes overboard into the harbor.

As Ghonkaba watched in fascination, uncertain as to his proper role, box after box was heaved over the rail. "Give us a helping hand, will you?" a man working near him growled. "We need all the help we can get!"

Ghonkaba immediately came to life and, seizing a wooden box, split it with a single, sharp blow of his ax.

So the British tax collectors are refusing to return the cargo untouched to England until the tax on tea is paid, are they? he said to himself. *Well, every fish, clam, and eel in Boston harbor will soon be drunk on tea!*

The intruders were thorough, and practice improved their efficiency. The entire surface of the harbor soon seemed to be filled with broken boxes of tea floating aimlessly on the evening tide, each passing second spoiling the contents of the boxes.

The men who had descended to the holds of the vessels reappeared on deck, their expressions grim but satisfied. They had completed their task, and the entire group lost no time in going ashore. As a final gesture, they loosened the bonds of the two watchmen, knowing that the men would soon free themselves. Then, hurry-g ashore, the "Indians" promptly scattered, heading in all directions for their own homes.

Ghonkaba accompanied Josiah, and keeping their conversation to a minimum, they hurriedly left the waterfront and raced across Boston to a small house, where they left one ax in a partially split log in the yard and took the other into the house with them. There they smeared the ax with mud and tossed it into a bin with several other large tools. Josiah washed off his war paint and disposed of the clothing he had been wearing. Then, dressed again in his own attire, he sat down with Ghonkaba to a meal of cold mussel pie and mugs of small beer.

"We put in a good evening's work," Josiah said, "and best of all, we had no embroilments with the authorities. Sam will be very pleased."

"Did he plan the raid?" Ghonkaba asked.

His companion looked him straight in the eye but did not directly reply. "Since you haven't been near Boston of late, I think you'll be surprised by the reper-cussions tomorrow," was the only answer that Josiah gave him.

They sat up late, and before the evening was over they had emptied the larder of jellied beef, Indian pudding, and other delicacies. Finally they went to bed, with Ghonkaba in a small guest room, which boasted featherbed and thick quilts. The quilts provided warmth that he relished in the December cold, the room was very dark, and he slept surprisingly late the following morning. He washed in a bucket of icy water drawn fresh from the spring. When he joined his host for a breakfast of broiled scrod and chicken's eggs in the kitchen, he saw the weekly edition of *The Massachusetts Spy* on the table. It related in full the story of the previous night's "Indian raid," and the incident was hailed as a victory of major significance for the American colonial forces that were now referring to themselves as patriots.

"The facts are all accurate," Ghonkaba said as he read the account. "But it surprises me that an account could be printed so soon. How is it possible for such details to appear in the press so quickly?"

Josiah smiled slyly. "You may recall," he said, "that Sam was rather busy writing yesterday afternoon. If I know him, he dropped the article off at the printing plant last night."

What most impressed Ghonkaba about the incident was the superb organization. Josiah told him that every detail had gone off precisely as planned, with clocklike efficiency and nothing left to chance.

In the afternoon, as he strolled alone back to Sam Adams's house, he noticed hastily printed notices fastened to large trees. They offered substantial sums for information leading to the arrest of the participants in the raid.

He felt certain, however, that no one would reveal his identity or that of his companions of the previous evening. Their secret was safely locked in the minds of the American patriots, a newly formed group whose size and influence could only be guessed at.

When Ghonkaba arrived at the Adamses' household, he found the usual beehive of activity. Two of the oldest Adams children were making handwritten copies of inflammatory letters about the Boston Tea Party, as Sam Adams was referring to the affair. The letters were to be dispatched to the Committees of Correspondence of sister colonies. Incredible though it seemed, Adams was building the incident he had invented into a major demonstration of intercolonial defiance of the Crown's authority to impose taxes on the colonies.

Watching Adams at work and listening to the varying tone of the letters he sent to the leaders of each colony together with impassioned accounts of the Tea Party, Ghonkaba realized that a master propagandist was at work. If Adams had his way, the American people soon would declare their freedom and strike off the shackles of colonization.

Adams undoubtedly was successful in drumming up public sympathy from Maine to Georgia in favor of independence. Whether he was right or wrong in these efforts was another question, however, and it was this question that Ghonkaba had not yet settled to his own satisfaction.

In obvious high spirits, Sam Adams had a few final words to say about the previous night's incident. "No matter what may come about," he cautioned, "tell nobody of your having taken part in certain events on the waterfront. And for your own sake, don't try to divine the identities of your comrades. Each of them has received this same warning, and the less that's said about the affair, the better. The British will be forced to punish the entire colony rather than single out a few individuals. I'm sure their high command is aware of your identity and your presence here as a guest. We'll let them speculate on the reason. For our purposes, you are paying a social call on me. And now we'll confuse them still more by walking over to South Queen Street, to the house of my cousin John. An old friend of yours is waiting there to greet you. Just remember, say nothing there or elsewhere about your activities of last evening."

A short time later, the pair made their way on foot to the house that John Adams and his wife, Abigail, had rented near the courthouse. They still owned a house in

Braintree, and they used the Boston dwelling principally as a place of business.

John Adams, who always dressed in black, as befitted his reputation as a leading colonial lawyer, was tall and spare. He greeted Ghonkaba with great cordiality.

"I suppose you know, Cousin John, that your house is being watched by the redcoats," Sam said. "They're recording the identity of every visitor."

"They're free to identify everyone who comes to this house," John Adams replied with a smile. "They'll see many more loyalists and Tories than fire-eating radicals like you, Cousin Sam. For that matter, I'll be delighted to show them all my correspondence, as well, including a lively debate by letter that I'm conducting with Doctor Franklin of Philadelphia on the philosophical nature of freedom. If any redcoat understands it, he's welcome to call me a traitor."

All three were chuckling as they entered the drawing room, where an imposing-looking couple was seated. The woman was beautifully gowned, and the man wore the scarlet and gold uniform of a general in the British Army. Ghonkaba was so startled that he fell into a silence from which it was difficult to recover.

"Lady Whiting, Brigadier Sir Townsend Whiting," John Adams was saying, "may I present my cousin, Samuel Adams, and our mutual friend, Ghonkaba, of the Seneca nation."

Sam Adams continued to smile. "I knew Lady Whiting very well indeed when she was plain Beth Strong, the daughter of the commander of our militia. As for the brigadier, I knew him well, too, before he reached such exalted rank."

Ghonkaba said nothing as he bowed over Beth's hand. It was strange, he thought, that he should feel nothing about a woman with whom he had once been in love and whom he had hoped to marry. As for the brigadier, with whom he exchanged a firm handclasp, he had overcome his feelings of enmity when they were comrades-in-arms during the battle for Quebec.

Abigail Adams entered the room, pushing a cart that contained small cakes and a large pot of steaming tea.

"How extravagant you are, Abigail," Beth said with a giggle. "I should think that tea would be too precious a commodity to waste on an ordinary social occasion."

Abigail Adams was ready with an appropriate retort. "Not at all, my dear Beth. We have a source of green tea in Holland, and we anticipate no shortage under this roof."

"How long have you been here, Townsend?" Ghonkaba asked cordially.

"We sailed from London seven weeks ago and landed in New York last week," Brigadier Whiting replied. "We spent a few days there and then set out for Boston by stagecoach, arriving here yesterday."

"How do you find conditions in New York?" Sam Adams inquired eagerly.

"The town is quiet," Whiting said. "Very quiet. In fact, the ferment that is so prominent in the air here is almost completely lacking there. In London we were led to believe that all the colonies are teetering on the thin edge of open rebellion, but although that certainly is the case in Boston, we saw nothing of the kind in New York."

"The people of New York," Beth said, "are so intent on making money that they appear to be ignoring politics."

"That's always the case there," Sam Adams observed casually. "Let them be subjected to an occupation by British troops, such as Boston is suffering, and let the Crown's tax collectors crack down on their purses, and you'll find them screaming for independence. We have some very devoted patriots in New York, and I don't for a moment doubt that they'll stand with us when the time is ripe."

Brigadier Whiting laced his fingers together before speaking judiciously. "You expect, then, Mr. Adams, an open confrontation with the mother country?" he asked. "You actively anticipate a decision to employ force of arms?"

Sam Adams replied in the same vein. "As you know, Sir Townsend," he said, "I'm devoting my entire time, my whole being, to furthering the cause of independence. So I naturally expect a showdown. The only question in my mind concerns when it will occur—whether within months or only after several years. I can't answer that question, nor can anyone else."

"Is there any hope for a reconciliation with the Crown?" Beth inquired.

Abigail Adams injected herself into the conversation. "Of course there is," she replied warmly. "There's always the hope of reconciliation, as long as there are reasonable men on both sides of the conflict. Cousin Sam has the reputation of being the biggest hothead in all America, but I think he'll be the first to agree that a reconciliation is not only possible, but quite feasible."

Sam Adams spoke quietly, almost pensively. "Sir Townsend," he said, "I don't know where you stand—whether you support the Crown without question or whether you have some sympathy for the Americans. Let me just say this: if King George and his ministers want a reconciliation and truly seek one, they can have it in a matter of weeks. No patriot is so imbued with the spirit of independence as to want to shed the blood of his fellows and of his English cousins. We have no doubts regarding the horrors of a war that would be fought on our soil or the sacrifices our people would be obliged to make, the suffering they would be forced to undergo. We have spent many years in full and unquestioning support of the Crown. Now we must have a measure of support ourselves. We do not object to paying taxes, but let them be taxes that are levied fairly and let us have a voice about their imposition.

"Give our elected representatives a voice in the laws that are imposed on us," he continued. "Treat us as the partners that we are in the development of this continent, rather than as you would treat the French who fought against you for so many years. Accept our soldiers as the equals of your soldiers. Don't impose the billeting of troops on our people and ignore the burden it places upon us. Meet us halfway in our disputes, and you'll find that we'll come to you in the same spirit. But deal with us cavalierly, and I promise you, we'll rebel and we'll fight to our last drop of blood!"

"Many people in Britain," Townsend Whiting replied, "agree with you totally. I happen to be one of them. My voice, however, is insignificant. William Pitt feels as you've just expressed yourself, and so does Edmund Burke, to name but two leaders of Parliament who have great influence. Unfortunately, they're not now in power, and the king's men have the upper hand."

"And King George," Sam Adams said bitterly, "is determined to punish us."

"I'm sorry to say," Whiting replied, "that the king is a very stubborn, shortsighted man. He runs the risk of losing his most valuable possessions in North America if he doesn't change his tune, but he isn't the type who will bow to pressure. America will become an independent nation before George the Third wakes up to his mistake."

Ghonkaba listened intently. This was the heart of what he had come to Boston to learn.

"Brigadier," John Adams asked smoothly, "in the event that our differences with the Crown can't be resolved and we take a stand in favor of independence, can we count on your support?"

"I find that a very difficult question to resolve," Whiting said. "I'm not only a loyal subject of the Crown—as all of us are—but I'm sworn to protect His Majesty and his interests from all enemies, foreign or domestic. I should be obliged to resign my commission from the army before I took any other steps." Whiting tugged at his gold-encrusted tunic and straightened his shoulders. "Ultimately, I suppose, I would have no real choice. My wife is a native of these shores, and as such, her sympathies lie completely with her compatriots. If the truth of the matter be known, I feel as she does. I have learned to admire America over a period of many years, and I believe in the principles for which she stands. I'd be living a lie if I supported the Crown and led troops into active combat against Americans." Sam Adams looked smugly pleased, but his more diplomatic cousin did not change his somber expression. "For the sake of us all, Brigadier," he said, "I am grateful that you can express the resolve to face up to the difficult choice. It is most heartening. You have my warmest compliments."

Beth looked inquiringly at Ghonkaba. "Where does your nation stand in this matter?" she asked.

Suddenly the entire focus of interest shifted to the Seneca, and everyone awaited his reply.

"I find it impossible to imagine," he said, "that my father will tear up his treaty with the English. The treaty was first made by my great-grandfather, Ghonka, with King William the Third. It was renewed several times by Renno, my grandfather, and twice more has been given new life by my father. The people of the Seneca do not give their word lightly, and they are bound by the strictest demands of honor to abide by their decisions."

Sam Adams could not restrain a sharp comment. "They would keep their treaty even at the cost of the freedoms that they and we cherish?" he demanded.

"The leaders of my people," Ghonkaba explained patiently, "do not regard it as a fact that they will lose their liberties if they adhere to their treaty with the British. My father gave a solemn promise to his father on his deathbed that he would honor the treaty with Britain as long as he lived, and he is honor-bound to keep that commitment. I see no way that he can be released from his pledge. He regards it as sacred according to the way in which we worship our gods."

"Then we can expect," Sam Adams said bitterly, "to meet you in violent combat as an enemy."

Smiling slightly, Ghonkaba shook his head. "Not so fast, my friend," he replied. "It is true that I have enduring obligations to the Seneca nation, and through them, to the tribes of the Iroquois League. But my primary obligation is to my wife, my sons, my daughter, and myself. I wait patiently for a sign from the gods to tell me what I am to do."

Beth was greatly impressed that he would even consider walking a separate path from his nation. She knew from her many discussions with him in years past that during the decades of their treaty with the English, the Seneca, like the other nations of the Iroquois League, had prospered enormously. They had strengthened their hold on their own territories, they were physically far stronger and more capable than ever, and they were in an excellent position to do exactly as they pleased.

"In the history of my people," Ghonkaba said painfully, "no one—no warrior—especially one who comes from a family of rulers and is expected himself to be elected one day to a position of high leadership, has ever broken his word to the nation. But never have the Seneca faced such a terrible, cruel dilemma." With these words, Ghonkaba paused, recalling the enigmatic message of Renno in the dream. "With the passing of time, all will become clear to me, all will become clear to the gods of my people. They will then notify the manitous what I am to do, and the manitous will direct my feet onto the right path."

As he looked around the room at his good friends, he was struck by the thought that no one knew when they would meet again or what the circumstances of such a meeting would be.

Chapter II

The problem of allegiance continued to hang like a dark, heavy cloud over the Seneca and the other nations of the Iroquois League through the next year and the winter that followed. But no decision was reached, and the Indians knew only that the American colonists and the British continued to quarrel bitterly.

Until the question was resolved by the colonies and their mother country, the Iroquois nations had no decision to make. They minded their own business, made weapons, gathered in their food, and devoted themselves to day-to-day matters.

Ghonkaba refrained from trying to resolve the problem in his mind. Because he had given the problem to the manitous, he was content. Instead, he devoted himself to the rigorous education of his children.

Growing to adulthood was a long, arduous process in the land of the Seneca, particularly for a boy. At the age of seven summers, sons were taken from their families and were taught the rudiments of hunting and fishing, and especially the use of weapons. Traditionally, they learned to handle bows and arrows, tomahawks, and throwing knives. Now they also were taught the principles of using firearms. Then, when they reached their ninth summer, their education began in earnest as the mysteries of the wilderness were unfolded for them.

They learned to regard the wilderness as benign and friendly to those who understood it. They learned which herbs and roots could be eaten and which to avoid. They were taught how to track humans and animals and how to prevent anyone from tracking them. They were taught the art of blending in with their surroundings and the art of traveling without leaving a trail. Above all, they learned the basic elements of the "Seneca trot," the jogging pace that any warrior of the tribe could maintain for many hours at a time when necessary.

All this and more was impressed into the minds of youngsters by senior warriors, who showed the boys no leniency, played no favorites, and forced them to work hard every day.

The sons of Ghonkaba were more fortunate than they knew. Their instructor was none other than their father, a war chief of the nation, who had learned his own wilderness lore firsthand from the great Renno. Their lessons were priceless, moments to be savored and treasured and lived again and again.

Leaving their weapons training and their running lessons to others, Ghonkaba specialized in teaching the tricks of getting along in the wilderness that he had acquired over the years.

He taught his sons to identify plants whose roots were edible, to note the proximity of a body of water when they saw moss gathered, to learn the difference in topography when approaching a salt lick—which invariably meant that a patient warrior would find deer and other game coming there to feed.

Young Renno, conscious of the burden he bore because of his name, was quick to learn and forgot nothing. El-i-chi, his brother, was far less serious. He saw humor in virtually everything, and his own sense of pleasure was irrepressible.

Ghonkaba spent his mornings helping the adult warriors learn the art of handling firearms. His afternoons, when not devoted to hunting deer or larger game, were spent with his sons. They walked to a small, nearby clearing in the forest that traditionally was used by the Great Sachem and his sons.

Here Ghonkaba drove home his lessons. He was strict in his demand for undivided attention. A boy who allowed his mind to wander and failed to devote his whole being to the day's lesson was punished with several hard strokes of a birch switch. Consequently, both Renno and El-i-chi were apt pupils.

An air of masculine mystery surrounded these lessons. Ghonkaba and his sons never mentioned them in the presence of his wife and daughter.

But Toshabe was privy to a secret about which her husband and sons knew nothing. Ena had begged her mother for the privilege of eavesdropping on the instructions that her father gave the boys. Thinking the request was just a passing fancy, Toshabe had consented. But to her surprise Ena persisted in following the lessons closely, never missing one.

Every day that Ghonkaba and the boys went off to the clearing in the forest, Ena gave them a generous head start and then followed at a safe distance. She crept close enough to hear every word that her father spoke and to watch him as he illustrated his instructions.

Thus it happened that Ena, as well as her brothers, was the beneficiary of Ghonkaba's teaching. Toshabe kept her daughter's secret well. She knew how much Ena enjoyed the lessons, and she knew that the instructions Ena received were well learned. She made no objection to this private learning because she could see no harm in it, though she could imagine no practical use for it.

Then, unexpectedly, one day late in the autumn of 1774, Ena's secret was partially revealed. The afternoon began like any other. Ena followed her father and brothers to the clearing; then, aware that most trees had lost their foliage, she lay down in the underbrush and peered through an opening. Intent on her father's words, she failed to hear the soft crackle of footsteps behind her or to realize that someone was staring down at her in amazement.

Ena gradually became aware that someone was only a few feet behind her. She glanced up, saw a sturdy warrior, and was horrified when he opened his mouth to speak. With a desperate expression in her eyes, she put a finger to her lips, begging him to keep silent.

Intrigued by what he saw, the warrior gestured to show that he wanted her to rise and follow him. He led her to a place in the forest out of earshot of Ghonkaba. She recognized him as Ranoga, a senior warrior of the Seneca, an impressively built man who obviously was in the best of physical condition despite his age.

"Now," the warrior demanded, "perhaps you'll be good enough to explain."

"I was . . . attending a class . . . that my father is giving," Ena stammered. "He was teaching my brothers forest lore—and I was taking part in it."

"I find it very curious," the warrior said, "that you would attend a class by hiding in the dead leaves outside a clearing."

Ena realized that she must confess the secret she had successfully kept for so many months. "I have not neglected my lessons in how to become a good Seneca squaw," she told him defiantly. "I have learned to plant seeds and to grow crops. I can pound grain, catch fish, butcher meat, and cook meals. I know how to cure the skins of animals and how to make clothing of them. I have learned all that a girl of fourteen summers needs to know."

Ranoga held up a large hand. "Enough, child," he said kindly, with a small smile playing across his plain features. His generally stern appearance was softened by a warm expression about his dark eyes. "I accept your word that you have not neglected your duties. But you have not yet told me why you wish to uncover the secrets of the forest that are known to warriors."

Ena looked at him, her eyes blazing. "The forest," she declared firmly, "belongs to all of us. Women as well as men of the Seneca make their homes in the wilderness, obtain food and clothing and shelter from it, and learn to use it as a protection against adversity. Why, then, should braves alone understand its mysteries?"

The warrior had never thought in such terms and was forced to concede that what she said made sense.

"I have heard my mother say," Ena went on, "that in the lands of many lesser nations girls are taught the same secrets of the forests that the boys learn.

"Only in the lands of the mighty Iroquois," she went on, "is such information reserved for braves. That is wrong. When I was very small I determined that I would break the pattern of my people, and now that I am approaching adulthood, I am taking advantage of my situation to learn things that were forbidden."

"Your father, of course, is ignorant of all this," Ranoga said.

"That is true," Ena replied, "but my mother knows, and she approves. If you tell my father, it will spoil everything. He will not permit me to violate the traditions of our people, and I shall be lost in ignorance, as are the other squaws of the Seneca."

Her appeal was so persuasive that the warrior could not help but sympathize with her.

"Will you be kind and keep my secret?" she asked.

The warrior was smitten by a sense of adventure. In spite of the ferment in the colonies to the east, life had been dull for several years. Bold gestures appealed to him, as to all Seneca. On the spur of the moment he decided he would help the child. "I can do more than keep quiet about your activities," he said. "I think I can be of help to you."

"How?" Ena asked.

"You have heard much from your father about tracking in the forest, I am sure. You've heard him speak at great length about how to avoid leaving tracks and how to find tracks left by animals and by humans. It seems to me that you have gleaned only the principles involved. You lack actual practice in tracking and in being tracked."

"That is true," Ena said. "When my father assigns such roles to my brothers, I cannot participate. I know only the theory of tracking."

"You shall have ample opportunity to learn by doing," the warrior told her. "Tell me the principles you have learned, and you and I will put them into practice. First you will learn to track me while I evade you, and then I will try to track you while you avoid being caught."

Ecstatic, Ena clapped her hands in sheer glee.

"We shall see," Ranoga said, "how much you can absorb. I charge you with this: be sure you tell your mother that I am participating with you. But do not reveal it to your father, because I do not want the braves in the family of the Great Sachem to frown on my efforts."

To the surprise of Ena, Ranoga kept his word and took her into the forest frequently to practice.

As the warrior explained one day to Toshabe, "It is a rare event to find such great ambition in a Seneca squaw. I would be remiss if I failed to encourage her and to help her achieve her goals."

"Can you see any harm that my daughter will suffer as a consequence of what she is learning from you, Ranoga?" Toshabe asked.

The warrior's smile was open and candid. "I can imagine none," he said. "All that she is learning will better prepare her for life in the wilderness. She may never require what she learns but at least she will know she possesses knowledge equal to that of any brave, and this will give her great satisfaction."

"You well understand the spirit of the child," Toshabe said. "On her behalf, I must thank you."

"I seek no thanks," the warrior said. "The proficiency that she acquires is ample reward. I know now how an uncle feels when his nephews and nieces make progress under his direction. I feel that Ena has become my own niece."

In working regularly with the child, Ranoga was amazed by her progress. Not only was she quick to grasp each principle, but she was easily able to translate principles into specific action.

"I've never seen anyone who learns as rapidly," the warrior reported to Toshabe. "She appears to have a natural instinct for life in the forest."

Ena first engaged in simple exercises in avoiding detection. After each such session, Ranoga met with her and pointed out her errors. She never made a mistake twice and became so expert at hiding in the wilderness that the warrior admitted that he had met his match.

She proved equally proficient at tracking him in the forest, in spite of his increasingly complex attempts to evade her. Stories were still told about the tracking expertise of Ghonka, her great-grandfather, and it appeared that Ena would be able to help carry on the family tradition.

She had natural talents that senior warriors of the Seneca found exceptionally difficult to teach. She could immediately determine the direction in which someone she was tracking had passed through the wilderness by noting the particular way in which grass and tiny plants were bent. Instinctively, she knew how to conceal herself under water, even in an icy river, by submerging herself and breathing through a hollow reed. Such simple but effective feats were second nature to her. She was developing complete familiarity with the mysteries of the wilderness.

Only in her attempts to master the Seneca trot did she falter somewhat. Even so, she persisted in making every effort to develop both the stamina and the technique to become a runner with the steadiness and speed, as well as the grace, that were hallmarks of Seneca warriors. Her persistence was touching to Ranoga, who greatly valued endeavor of such a dogged nature. But one afternoon her insistence on trying to keep pace with him almost proved to be her undoing. Running almost beside him at first, she began falling farther back as the pace went on and on; with a burst of speed requiring untold amounts of energy she caught up with him twice despite feet that were becoming painful, legs that ached, and a sharp, sickening sensation in her side. At last, Ranoga looked back and saw that she was stumbling—still without complaint—nearly a hundred yards behind him. She was so evidently approaching complete fatigue that he hastened back to her. Seeing her bleeding feet even as she attempted to run on, almost staggering as she did so, he caught her and held her upright within his strong embrace for a moment before gently easing her to a seat on a large rock. "Rest now," he instructed with a harshness that he did not feel at all. "After you've caught your breath we'll bathe those feet in the brook that's just over the rise. And let's have no more foolishness about trying to accomplish the impossible.

"You are already the equal of most warriors in your knowledge of the forest," he pointed out. "Be content with what you know. In trying to best the braves, you are wasting your substance and your time. Be glad that you have achieved so much and know that when you decide to reveal your abilities to your father, he will take great pride in you."

Early in the next spring, Ranoga surprised Ena with a gift. He made a special pair of moccasins suited for her small, narrow feet, and he told her, "Now you can cover at great speed the distances that are expected of a Seneca scout."

Overwhelmed, Ena tried, but in vain, to work up her courage to reveal to her father the unsuspected talents she had acquired.

In late April, a runner of the small Massachusetts tribe reported to a sentry of the Mohawk, who in turn sent along word to the Seneca, that an extraordinary sequence of incidents had taken place in two little towns near Boston. There, troops of the British Regular Army and the Massachusetts Militia had exchanged rifle fire in an active skirmish.

Ghonkaba immediately set out to learn every detail of the incident and then quickly reported to his father and uncle.

"The fight may have started by accident and easily could have been ignored by both sides," he told them.

"This is exactly what Sam Adams has been awaiting, and obviously he had no intention of losing his great opportunity to score at the expense of the Crown. From Boston all the way to Georgia, I understand, newspapers are trumpeting the event. Patriots have been stirring up sentiment everywhere, and leaders from all thirteen colonies have been called to a meeting in Philadelphia of what they are calling the First Continental Congress. I'm sure this is the beginning of the end."

"What makes you so positive?" Ja-gonh asked.

"The leaders of the Massachusetts delegation are Sam Adams and John Hancock, the shipowner. If I know Sam, he won't be satisfied unless the Congress formally breaks relations with Great Britain and declares war."

No-da-vo stared at his nephew, his dark eyes piercing. "You think," he asked, "that relations have actually deteriorated that much?"

"I can imagine no other reason," Ghonkaba said somberly, "for the summoning of representatives from all the colonies. Sam and the other patriot leaders have been planning their moves for a long time, and the skirmish appears to suit their needs perfectly. I'd be astonished if this isn't used as the break that the patriots have been seeking."

"Our position was determined long ago," Ja-gonh said. "I see no need to summon the leaders of the Iroquois to a council meeting until relations between Britain and her colonies are actually ruptured."

No-da-vo agreed with him, but turned next to Ghonkaba. "What about you? How does this affect your thinking?"

"I don't know," Ghonkaba replied, sounding miserable. "Now that I know this news about Lexington and Concord, I shall ask the manitous to show me the sign I've been awaiting for so long. They have yet to heed my request of many moons ago. Until they do, I'm immobilized and am unwilling to make any decision."

Wrestling with his seemingly insoluble problem, Ghonkaba frequently sought the solitude of the deep forest. There he could be alone with his thoughts and suffer no distractions as he weighed the pros and cons of the positions that he might take.

During one such journey an incident occurred that was to affect his outlook considerably, causing him to reflect on the harm that can be needlessly inflicted on innocent people through hasty judgments and reactions based on personal prejudice.

Having caught the scent of a campfire in the distance, he cautiously approached it. Through the underbrush, he saw Tredno at one side of the fire, but the rest of the scene chilled Ghonkaba's blood. Supine and helpless on the ground beside the burly war chief was a white man in the uniform of an American militiaman, with wrists and ankles bound. His shoes and stockings had been torn from his feet. Tredno, preparing to torture him by applying a small burning brand to the soles of his feet, was so busy that he failed to hear Ghonkaba's approach.

Ghonkaba raised his voice. "What goes on here?"

Tredno looked up and sneered. "I caught this spy for the colonists," he said, "and I'm forcing him to reveal what he knows. I will then report it to the commandant of the British garrison nearest to us."

Ghonkaba gestured forcefully. "Do nothing more for a moment," he ordered. He looked down at the helpless soldier.

"Who are you," he asked in English, "and what is your business in the land of the Seneca?"

The soldier's eyes widened in surprise when he heard himself being addressed in his own tongue. "I have nothing to hide," he said. "I'm a courier in the

45

Massachusetts Militia, and I am to deliver a letter to the American militia commander stationed in the land of the Mohawk near Albany. I mistakenly traveled too far to the west. This madman seized me and, as you can see, is torturing me. If you're going to kill me, do it, but don't play your vile Indian games on me."

Turning back to Tredno, Ghonkaba reverted to the tongue of the Seneca. "By what right," he demanded, "do you subject this man to torture?" He knew what the stolid, bitter war chief's answer would be.

Tredno bared his teeth. "In time of war," he said, "any action is permitted against the enemy."

"I did not know," Ghonkaba answered, "that the Seneca and the other nations of the Iroquois League were at war with the Americans. The Council has not voted on such a matter, and so I call your actions totally unauthorized."

"If we are not already at war with the Americans, we soon shall be," Tredno argued. "It is only a matter of time. They are insisting on breaking relations with the British, and our treaty with Britain is sacred."

"No treaty made by man is sacred," Ghonkaba replied in annoyance. "It must be judged on its own merits in due time. When my ancestors made this treaty with the English, the whole world was threatened by France. We and our fellow nations fought beside the English. In defeating the French, we ended that threat to our freedom and security. But now circumstances are different. The Americans are descended from the English who came to these shores from the Old World. The wilderness has left its mark on them, and they've grown to be much like us. It is difficult, perhaps impossible, to call such people enemies of the Seneca. They have become our friends, and it is the British who are alien to us. It may be that we should take up arms at the side of the Americans if they come to blows with the British."

Tredno laughed unpleasantly. "You are stupid," he said. "The English are very strong. They have many thousands of warriors who carry the most modern and efficient of weapons. They have ships that have enormous guns with tremendous destructive power. Any who oppose them in war will perish."

"That is not necessarily true," Ghonkaba said heatedly. "The English have their base many days' journey from here across the Great Sea. The Americans are our neighbors and live side by side with us. They outnumber us greatly, and if we become their enemies we well may regret it."

Wearied by the fruitless argument, he turned and slashed the bonds on the militiaman's wrists and ankles. Startled by the unexpected deliverance, the man sat up at once, rubbing his ankles in order to restore circulation to them.

Furious, Tredno reached for the knife he carried in his belt.

Anticipating just such a move, Ghonkaba turned to him. Still gripping his own knife, he made it plain that he would strike at the first hostile move.

Tredno released his grip, but his long look of sheer hatred revealed an enmity strongly suggesting that blood would have to flow before their feud could be settled.

The military sentries stationed at the gates of Whitehall Palace on Pall Mall in London were bored. Their duties were principally ceremonial, rather than practical, and only rarely were they called upon to deal with intruders or with others unwelcome in the king's mansion.

They were well acquainted with everyone who called regularly at the palace, recognizing at a glance the members of the Tories and Whigs in the House of Commons. They knew, too, most of the country's military and naval officers, the leading aristocrats, and other supporters of the Crown.

The sentries saluted each visitor, frequently concealing yawns behind stiff faces. This morning, however, was different. The lone visitor, resplendent in the scarlet and gold uniform of a full general, arrived on a sleek gelding. Although his high rank entitled him to an escort of a full troop of cavalry from the Royal Household Guards, not a single aide-de-camp accompanied him.

The sergeant of the guard, instantly alert, bawled an order. The troops of the guard detail sprang to rigid attention and stood motionless.

General Lord Jeffrey Amherst, whose exploits against the French in America had won him his exalted rank and his place in the peerage, dismounted, handed his reins to the sergeant of the guard, and proceeded to inspect the sentries. Other military leaders sometimes went through the motions of making such an inspection, but Lord Jeffrey was always in earnest. He made certain that brass was shined, cross-webbing spotless, and muskets and bayonets cleaned.

Satisfied with the state of the sentries, he entered Whitehall.

An equerry hurried toward him. Lord Jeffrey greeted the man pleasantly but remotely. "Good morning," he said. "His Majesty is expecting me. There's no need for you to come with me. I know the way."

Unexpectedly rebuffed, the equerry fell back.

Amherst's leather-heeled boots echoed on the marble floors as he made his way through a succession of anterooms to a broad staircase that led to the audience chambers on the second floor.

George III had been enduring a difficult morning. He had received news of impending labor difficulties in the city of Sheffield, a decrease in the output of molasses in the Caribbean colony of Jamaica, and a troublesome mutiny in the Royal Navy. Now the monarch, florid-faced and pudgy, was enjoying a respite from his woes. He sat in a thronelike chair at the head of the long table, a linen napkin tucked into his neck to protect his stock and the fabric of his embroidered coat. As he went through a pile of documents—all of which seemed to contain unpleasant news—he sipped a cup of his favorite brew, a thick pea soup, redolent of garlic, onions, and sausages. It was a dish that had been a family favorite for generations.

Frowning when he heard approaching footsteps, he recognized his visitor, and his face became wreathed in a broad smile. "Amherst!" he cried. "Welcome, my dear fellow!" He shook hands with more than his customary vigor.

At the king's request, the general took a chair facing him.

"I trust you enjoyed the fishing in Scotland," George said.

Amherst nodded comfortably. "Yes," he said. "In fact, I've had my cook smoke a particularly large and succulent salmon for Your Majesty's table. I'm having it delivered later today, and I hope you'll accept it with my compliments."

The monarch moistened his lips in anticipation. Smoked salmon was one of the delicacies he relished most. Eager to return the compliment, he reached for the tureen beside him. "Have some soup!"

General Amherst fought back a desire to shudder. Several weeks earlier he had dined at the regimental mess for a regiment of mercenary Hessians. A similar soup had been served, and he had suffered from indigestion for several days. *It's very unfair,* he thought, *for the king to indulge in a non-English food that features both garlic and onions.* "I'm sorry, Your Majesty," he said, "but my doctor has put me on a rather strict diet recently."

George III was not easily thwarted. "Would you

prefer some consommé?" he inquired. "Let me send to the kitchen for some consommé for you."

"Thank you, Your Majesty, but I don't care for any refresnments," the general replied firmly.

Having disposed of his responsibilities as a host, George III ladled himself another cup of pea soup. Sorry to take you from your desk," he said, "but I'm anxious to discuss a matter of great urgency with you."

"I'm at Your Majesty's disposal," Lord Amherst replied simply.

"Were you able to keep abreast of developments in the New World while you were on holiday in Scotland?"

"Not really, Your Majesty, but I read the full report of the regimental commander in Boston on the incident at Lexington, and I must say it was blown up out of all proportion to reality."

"Be damned to the Lexington insurgents," the king muttered. "I was referring to the meeting they call the First Continental Congress.

"They're a company of radicals who claim to represent all the colonists, but there isn't a reputable citizen among them. They've had the colossal nerve to make a series of impudent demands on me, and they've openly resorted to threats. Unless I give in to their outrageous demands, they're going to persist in their rebellious and traitorous ways. They claim they can get along without our protection. Can you imagine anything more outrageous?"

General Amherst wanted to reply that he was sure a terrible misunderstanding must exist between the Crown and His Majesty's subjects in the colonies, but this plainly was not a moment suitable for the expression of such views.

"My good friends in Commons assure me that as this is a matter in which national honor is at stake, they'll have no problem in putting a series of punitive bills through the Parliament. I intend to enforce those new laws by sending the largest army we can muster to merica. Twenty thousand men, thirty thousand, perhaps as many as forty thousand. The Royal Navy will dispatch its most powerful flotillas to America, and Admiral Lord Howe has given me his word that he'll command them in person."

The general whistled softly under his breath. The full strength of the armed forces was going to be used in subduing the rebels.

"The reason I sent for you this morning, Lord Amherst, is to offer you the post of commander in chief n all of my armies that are going to smash the rebels."

"I see," General Amherst replied, and a long silence followed.

King George looked at him expectantly, waiting for his acceptance of the offer.

The pause lengthened until the silence began to grow awkward.

"I appreciate the high honor of Your Majesty's offer," Jeffrey Amherst said, "but with all regrets, I simply cannot accept."

The king stared at him incredulously. The offer of the command of troops in America was a mere formality. He could have issued an order that would have been obeyed. Never had he heard of an officer refusing to accept a high assignment. At the same time, he had to move with care. He knew that the opposition in Parliament to his policies was strong and that the colonies had many supporters there. If it became known that Amherst, the most popular of generals in the entire army, had rejected command of the army in America, more trouble inevitably would result.

"What reputation I possess as a fighting man," General Amherst said, "I owe to the years that I spent in America in combat against the French. My two most renowned victories, that at Fortress Louisburg on Cape

Breton Island and, later, the capture of the capital of
New France in Quebec, were due entirely to the skill
of the intrepid colonial militia regiments. The colonials
not only outfought and outmaneuvered the French, but
they also showed up my own divisions of British
Regulars."

George III was so upset his soup went untouched
and grew cold.

"My American comrades-in-arms," Amherst went
on, "were among the closest friends I formed in all the
years that I spent overseas. Some of those higher-ranking
officers are sure to be senior commanders in the
American militia today. It would be impossible for me to
make war on such close associates and treat them as my
enemies. They are not my enemies, Your Majesty. I
continue to regard them as close colleagues and good
friends." The general spoke without a hint of compromise in his tone.

The king was obliged to think quickly. Amherst's
position meant that he would be forced to rely on lesser
generals, like William Howe and John Burgoyne, to
lead his forces abroad.

In the meantime, he continued to handle Lord
Amherst in the most gingerly manner possible. "I respect your decision, my lord," he said, "and therefore I
must abide by it."

Sir Charles Dundee, special representative of Lord
North, the prime minister, traveled in style. A half-
troop of Royal Horse Cavalry, forty strong and heavily
armed, guarded him on the road and in the wilderness.
He traveled with accoutrements that offered the greatest possible comforts, such as a silk tent with a hardwood floor, the finest of outdoor stoves, and a portable
featherbed. His party included a secretary, his cook,
and his private valet.

Having sailed from London, they arrived a month

later in New York without fanfare. Before their presence was quite realized, they made their way north to Albany and then, accompanied by a single guide, struck out through the land of the Mohawk for the sectors of other members of the Iroquois League.

Sir Charles went straight to the land of the Seneca and there presented Ja-gonh with numerous gifts. From this inauspicious beginning, it became increasingly plain that the emissary knew nothing of the New World and its ways.

"He must take me for a total fool or a complete savage," Ja-gonh said to his wife, Ah-wen-ga, as he showed her the gifts.

She giggled as she went through them. They included two brightly colored blankets, several strands of colored but inexpensive beads, two small hand mirrors, several frying pans and pots, and a small knife, too dull to be used for scaling fish or even for cutting twigs.

"I've already warned the members of the council," he told her with a smile, "not to speak English, much less show their ability to read and write the language, or to reveal that any of us have traveled as far as London. If this fellow chooses to regard us as ignorant savages, the fault is his."

Later that afternoon, the medicine men, elders, and war chiefs who made up the council of the Seneca gathered in their special meeting lodge for a session with Sir Charles.

In appointing Ghonkaba as the translator, Ja-gonh warned him not to admit knowing more English than necessary.

Sir Charles's address was inept and fumbling. He patronized his listeners by referring constantly to George III as their "Great White Father," and he repeatedly reminded them of their treaty with Great Britain. If they abided by the terms of that treaty, Sir Charles promised them, they would receive many gifts from the

Crown. His remarks were so simple, so out of touch with reality, that his listeners soon became restless. While Sir Charles droned on, using terms that had not been employed for decades, his audience engaged in a lively discussion in subdued voices about the demands they could make on the Crown in return for abiding by the treaty.

At last Ghonkaba, at a certain look from his father, cut into the endless diatribe. "Exactly what does the 'Great White Father' of the Seneca propose to offer us in return for our support?" he asked. His father's glance had signaled that Ghonkaba could use his knowledge of English and bargain freely with their guest.

Sir Charles was unprepared for a descent into specific bargaining. But he recovered quickly. "It may be," he said coyly, "that your white father will provide firesticks for your warriors."

"Good," Ghonkaba replied firmly. "Let them be modern, breech-loading muskets of new manufacture, complete with bayonets, and let them be of the type used by the regiment of Coldstream Guards."

The British envoy looked startled.

"We will require two thousand of them for our own warriors, and another eight thousand for our allies in the Iroquois League. We shall also need ample provisions of ammunition and gunpowder for these weapons," he added.

Sir Charles was swept off his feet by the bold demand. Before he could recover, Ghonkaba struck still harder. "If Lord North chooses to reject the Seneca request or to quibble over the numbers involved," he said dryly, "let it be understood that we will accept an identical offer from our good friends and neighbors, the colonists." He was speaking sheer gibberish. The rebels lacked funds to purchase ten thousand new muskets, which would cost far more money than they had in their treasury.

Sir Charles had no idea that he was being subjected to a monumental bluff. He was under strict orders to conclude his negotiations successfully with the nations of the Iroquois League, no matter what the cost. He disliked thinking of the expense involved in purchasing ten thousand muskets. But if that was the price that had to be paid, he had no choice. He swallowed hard. "Very well," he said. "On behalf of His Majesty's government, I accept your terms."

The meeting was soon adjourned, and Sir Charles and his party took their leave. Then Ja-gonh called the council into session again. In his opening words, he praised his son.

"It is not seemly," he said, "to lavish words upon one's own kin, but I would be remiss if I failed to recognize the great contribution that Ghonkaba has made to our cause. Thanks to him, every warrior of our nation will be equipped with a modern musket, as will the braves of our fellow Iroquois nations. We are in Ghonkaba's debt."

"Now," No-da-vo said, taking over, "a new question arises that only the council is capable of solving. We are obligated to enter the war on the side of the British and against the colonies. Do the warriors agree to such action?"

The assemblage became very still as warriors looked at each other, but no one moved, and no one spoke. Then Ranoga raised a hand, asking for recognition, and climbed to his feet. "Where does Ghonkaba stand in this matter?" he asked.

With great reluctance, Ghonkaba replied. "My position," he said, "is not like that of most other Seneca. For one thing, like my father, I am related by blood to American colonists in Virginia and in Massachusetts. For another, I regard all Americans as my blood brothers, since I fought side by side with them in campaigns against the French and against many of our ancient enemies, including the Huron, the Algonquian, and the Erie. I cannot be true to my own beliefs as a Seneca if I turn now on these brothers."

A burly war chief of about his own age lumbered slowly to his feet. "You have decided, then, to enter this war on the side of the Americans?"

Ghonkaba shook his head. "For many moons," he said, "I have awaited a sign from the manitous, who will instruct me on what I am to do. So far they have disappointed me; they have not given me any indication of whether I am to join the Americans in their fight for independence. But this much do I know. Never will I take up arms against my American brothers and make war on them and their families. I will not attack their cities, and I will not raid their farms. At the very least, I will be neutral in this war."

The braves absorbed his remarks in silence. Ja-gonh allowed them to take the lead in the meeting because he wanted to be sure to give each an opportunity to speak his mind.

The burly war chief, still on his feet, looked at his colleagues. "My heart and my mind agree," he said. "I join with Ghonkaba in the stand that he is taking. I will not join the Americans in their cause. But at the same time, I will not join the British and take up arms against those I have long regarded as my brothers."

After a long moment of silence, a rumble of assent welled up in the council chamber. The men who would be called on to do the fighting for the nation clearly felt much as Ghonkaba did.

Ja-gonh bowed to the inevitable. "I heed your voices, and the Seneca will not act contrary to your will. At the same time, however, I promised Renno that I would honor his commitment and that of his father to Great Britain. Thanks to the treaties they made and kept with the British, our nation has prospered and grown strong. Thanks to those treaties, our lands have become secure and we have acquired the reputation of being the fiercest tribe in North America. I cannot rest within myself if I break my word to my late father."

As he paused for breath, he saw that the faces looking up at him were bewildered now, as the braves wondered how he could reconcile his position with the one they had just taken.

"We will enter the war on the side of the British," Ja-gonh said emphatically. "But I shall make it clear to them that we will engage in no battles against the colonists. We will notify the Americans that we are keeping our word to the British and that our land no longer is open to them. We will avoid combat wherever possible, and only if we are forced to make a choice and no longer have any alternative will we join with Great Britain in active pursuit of the war."

The compromise seemed satisfactory to the braves, and the meeting came to an end.

The news of war developments that drifted out to the land of the Seneca seemed to confirm the wisdom of the equivocal stand taken by Ja-gonh. The Seneca were elated when the ten thousand muskets and ammunition were delivered promptly to them and to their Iroquois colleagues. The weapons had been stored in warehouses in New York Town. They were transported up the Hudson River to Albany after Sir Charles Dundee made his agreement, and then they were delivered promptly to the Indians.

Therefore, no matter what the outcome, the Iroquois were equipped with the most modern arms available.

Not long after, word was received of a sensational development in land adjacent to the territory of the Iroquois. Fort Ticonderoga, the western gateway to British Canada, was the most important fort in a large area. A regiment under the command of a self-styled colonel named Ethan Allen, whose reckless militiamen called themselves the "Green Mountain Boys," took the fort's defenders by surprise. The British were stunned by the loss, and Americans hailed the fort's capture.

Soon thereafter another bit of unexpected news emanated from Boston. Brigadier Sir Townsend Whiting of the Royal Army resigned his commission, gave up his knighthood, and proudly accepted a commission as a major general commanding a division in the American Continental Army. The defection of Whiting had far more than military significance; at the very least it indicated that an experienced senior officer of the British armed forces had lost faith in the cause that the redcoats represented.

Whiting's action was difficult for Ghonkaba to comprehend.

He withdrew into a shell and became unusually silent and thoughtful, speaking to virtually no one.

The day after the news was received, Ghonkaba left the breakfast table without a word, and Toshabe watched as he walked toward the Room of the Great Faces. She knew he would be praying for guidance, asking the Great Faces for some sign that would enable him to decide whether or not to follow Townsend Whiting's example.

But apparently the manitous refused to heed his request through the Great Faces, for no sign could be perceived.

Then, Ghonkaba vanished into the forest.

Toshabe knew that he would go to the favored clearing and renew his plea to the manitous. Twice in the past, to his wife's knowledge, he had gone to the clearing and asked the manitous for a favorable sign. On one occasion, he had seen a hawk overhead, the symbol of good fortune to warriors of the house of Ghonka, and on another occasion he had seen a large brown bear. Ja-gonh had been named for a bear who had been

Renno's incessant childhood companion, and Ghonkaba had been certain that the bear he had seen had been sent to him by the manitous as a sign of their favor. Toshabe could only hope that the representatives of the gods smiled on Ghonkaba again and ended his misery. He deserved help in reaching the most important decision of his life.

Night came, but Ghonkaba failed to return home. Ena and her brother Renno conferred in low tones and then went to Toshabe and volunteered to go in search of their father.

"Ghonkaba," she said firmly, concealing a smile, "is able to take care of himself in the wilderness, which is more than I can say for his children. Leave him alone, and all will be well. He will return when he's ready."

He was still missing after breakfast the following morning. Toshabe put up a front of unconcern, but kept inventing errands that took her children from home while she set an example for them and busied herself with chores. Renno and El-i-chi were pleased with the frequent opportunities to be off alone, unsupervised as they tried to sharpen their respective skills.

Ghonkaba materialized that day out of nowhere and stood beside her.

Toshabe took one look at his haggard face and the deep hollows beneath his eyes and knew he had neither slept nor eaten in at least twenty-four hours. But she confined herself to a single, practical remark. "Are you hungry?"

He nodded very casually, implying that food was the least of his concerns.

But Toshabe knew her husband well; she prepared a large breakfast of cornmeal cakes, grilled fish, and deer meat cooked over an open fire.

After devouring all the food in sight, Ghonkaba sat back on his haunches and lit his pipe. "I have exhausted every means of seeking help from the gods that is at my disposal," he told her.

"Perhaps," Toshabe said, "it is the wish of the gods that you make up your own mind in this matter without assistance from them."

"I have pondered that along with many other ideas," Ghonkaba said, "but I cannot see my way clear to acting accordingly. All I know for certain is that I cannot take up arms against the Americans. Whether I can see my way clear to join them in combat, I am not yet certain."

"The time is rapidly approaching when you will be forced to make up your mind," Toshabe answered. "I heard talk only yesterday that the council is considering whether to send an expedition that would raid an American settlement in the Mohawk Valley. Their reasoning seems to be that, having received the rifles that the British promised, some show of action may be required. I wonder, though, if it will ever take place and what kind of 'raid' it might turn out to be."

"I know of the talk of such an expedition and I certainly am aware of the need to make up my mind," he replied. "I have even wondered in my anguish whether it would be proper to ask you to come with me to some far distant part of the land."

Toshabe looked at him unflinchingly. "Wherever you lead," she said, "the children and I will follow. It is our duty to go with you where you please to take us and to make no complaints about our lot."

He met her gaze, knew he was putting her to the supreme test, and felt very proud. He could ask nothing more of a wife than she was giving at this very moment.

Ghonkaba was no more demonstrative than were other men of the Seneca nation, but he covered her hand with his and then tightened his grip.

Toshabe had learned that it was the duty of a

Seneca squaw to conceal and control her emotions at all times. But she could not help choking up, and her eyes filled with tears.

To Ghonkaba, it was surprising that the emotions welling up within him, too, were deep and shook him to the roots of his being. He leaned toward her, his lips brushed hers, and then he straightened as though he had been guilty of a misdemeanor.

"I shall not forget, now or ever, your willingness to sacrifice everything that is important to you in life for the sake of my beliefs," he said softly. "Rest assured that you will be foremost in my mind when I make my decision." He remained at home for the rest of the day and amazed his children by his lightheartedness at meals, when they all gathered to eat. They had not seen him in such high spirits for a very long time.

The family had not yet finished supper that evening when Ja-gonh and Ah-wen-ga entered their dwelling. The interruption by the Great Sachem and his wife caused great consternation. Toshabe hastened to get them plates and to fill them, and Ena made sure her grandparents were seated comfortably around the fire. Even the two boys hurried to make sure that their distinguished grandfather and grandmother would want nothing.

Because a visit from his parents at this time of day was unprecedented, Ghonkaba went to great lengths to appear calm. After rising to greet his father and bow to his mother, he sat again and stripped the meat from the bones of fried chicken that Toshabe had prepared in the style of her husband's relatives in the Colony of Virginia.

Ja-gonh looked very much at ease as he, too, gnawed at a chicken bone.

When his parents had finished eating, Ghonkaba spoke. "Only a great event," he said casually, "could cause my father to leave his house at this hour and to visit the house of his son."

Ja-gonh only smiled.

"It is also true," Ghonkaba went on shrewdly, "that my father is accompanied on his visit by my mother, so that people in the town who see him will think he comes on a family matter. They would have no idea that he carries news of importance."

Ja-gonh chuckled. "My son," he said quietly, "has come to know me and my motives too well for comfort."

Both men continued to sit quietly, each waiting for the other to make an initial break.

Ah-wen-ga and Toshabe knew their husbands sufficiently well that they struck up a lively conversation, into which they drew the children. The men of the family were temporarily but pointedly ignored.

"I grew tired," Ja-gonh said, "of waiting for such up-to-date information as I might glean from occasional travelers from the colonies that lie to our east. I finally determined to send messengers to Boston. I thereupon dispatched two young warriors, both of whom can speak English."

Ghonkaba looked at him complacently.

"Less than a week has passed," Ja-gonh said, "since the British Regulars and the American militia fought a great battle for possession of Boston. They're calling it the Battle of Breed's Hill. The British won through superior use of their artillery, their infantry, and their cavalry. But the Americans astonished their enemies with their poise and came within an inch of winning a great triumph of their own. They lost Boston, which their enemy still possesses, but they have sufficient spirit and desire to have laid siege to the city, and they are claiming it will soon fall."

"So it shall, I'm sure," Ghonkaba commented.

"One reason the adherents of the American cause are optimistic," Ja-gonh said, "is that their troops took the heaviest fire that could be rained on them, but they did not panic. Instead, they held their ground and returned shot for shot."

Ghonkaba felt a surge of pride on behalf of his American friends.

"Another reason," his father went on, "is the presence in their midst of an artilleryman named Colonel Henry Knox."

"I have never heard of him," Ghonkaba said.

"Neither had I, but we have not heard his name for the last time, it appears. He is a Boston bookseller who has studied guns as a hobby for years and speaks to cannon as one would speak to cavalry. He appears to be a genius at handling guns.

"Yet another reason for optimism in the American camp," Ja-gonh went on, "is that the Continental Congress has offered the command of the entire Continental Army to your old comrade-in-arms against the French, Colonel George Washington of Virginia. I understand that he's accepted the designation and has arrived to take charge of the siege of Boston. He's received the rank of major general."

Ghonkaba stared at his father. "Did I understand you correctly," he asked hoarsely, "that Washington has assumed the supreme command of the American field forces?"

Ja-gonh had no chance to reply. Before he could speak, his son rushed on, words gushing out in his enthusiasm.

"Washington," Ghonkaba said eagerly, "is by far the finest soldier I have ever seen. As a commander, he far outstrips British officers who have greater experience and who outrank him. He has won the unstinting loyalty of his subordinates, who will follow him into the jaws of hell and will fight their hearts out for him anywhere, anytime, under any conditions. He fights judiciously and well because he is endowed with an instinct for battle that in my lifetime I have seen in only one other fighting man—in Renno, my grandfather."

The women and children fell silent as Ghonkaba raised his voice exuberantly.

"I no longer have need of a sign from the manitous!" he declared emphatically. "The appointment of Washington as the chief of the Continental Army is more than enough of a sign for me as to what I should do. I shall leave for Boston before dawn tomorrow morning and offer my services to General Washington, telling him to make use of me as he sees fit!"

Toshabe and Ah-wen-ga exchanged quick, inscrutable glances.

Ghonkaba turned to Ja-gonh. "If my decision offends you, my father," he said, "I crave your pardon, and I will be sorry until the end of my days. But I must do as my conscience bids me, and I know now, in my heart, that it is right that I join the cause of the American patriots who fight for liberty!"

Ja-gonh looked at him wearily. "I'm not disappointed, my son," he said with a stern expression. "I have known ever since the issue arose what your ultimate decision would be. And when I heard that George Washington had become the chief of the American armies, I knew beyond all doubt that the die was cast for you. Do what you think best, and I shall not interfere, nor shall our people."

Only Ah-wen-ga, who knew him best, realized that he was exerting all his willpower to keep from weeping.

Chapter III

At first glance the American camp in Cambridge, across the Charles River from Boston, bore little resemblance to a military headquarters. Only here and there were men dressed in the blue and buff uniforms of the Continental Army. Most wore a motley collection of attire, ranging from tricorne hats and homespun linsey-woolsey to frontier trousers and shirts of leather.

Their cannon, too, were oddly assorted. These varied widely, from tiny mortars capable only of firing an iron ball weighing two pounds, to several mammoth cannon that threw heated iron weighing up to fourteen pounds. The artillery was commanded by Colonel Henry Knox, of whom Ghonkaba had heard from his father. General Washington was so pleased with the colonel's abilities that he had recommended him to the Continental Congress for promotion to brigadier general.

Ghonkaba threaded his way through the camp, where men were sitting outside tents and lean-to shelters of all sorts and cooking their noon meal, which appeared to consist in the main of fish recently caught in the Charles River. He had prepared for his initial meeting with George Washington. He was wearing new loincloth and moccasins, his head on either side of his center scalp lock was freshly shaved and oiled, and the green and yellow Seneca war paint on his face and torso was precisely applied.

At last he came to a white two-story house, where several men in varied attire stood sentry duty.

He asked politely to speak to General Washington.

After a considerable wait, a young lieutenant appeared from inside the house. Wearing a full, immaculate uniform of blue and buff, he seemed filled with his own importance. "What can I do for you?" he demanded.

Ghonkaba disliked him on sight. "I know of nothing you can do," he replied in accentless English, "except to tell me where I can find George Washington."

The young officer looked down his nose and sniffed. "The commander in chief," he said, "is far too busy to speak to any stray Indian brave who happens to be in the vicinity."

Ghonkaba, outraged, reacted so swiftly that the sentries had no opportunity to intervene. Grasping the lieutenant by the front of his tunic with one hand, he pressed the point of his exceedingly sharp knife against the officer's throat.

"I find your words insulting and your manner offensive," he said. "I tried to deal politely with you, but politeness apparently doesn't pay with someone like you. Be good enough to tell me instantly now where I can find George Washington, or my knife will sink deep, deep, deep, into your throat." The sentries milled around, unable to shoot at Ghonkaba for fear of hitting the officer.

The frightened young lieutenant, believing that the savage meant every word, began to stammer a reply.

Suddenly, a cultivated voice interrupted the confrontation. "What's the meaning of this disturbance?"

Ghonkaba glanced toward the doorway and flung the lieutenant from him like a rag doll. "Aha!" he cried. "This fool tried to prevent me from seeing you." He stood rigidly, at attention, his left hand and arm stiffly extended in a formal Seneca salute. Then, chortling under his breath, he threw himself forward and embraced General Washington in a ferocious bear hug.

The sentries were so startled they did not know how to react. In the short time they had known Major General Washington, they had found him to be an austere and imposing gentleman who never lost his poise and reserved manner. But he seemed to be pleased by the Indian's greeting. Not only was he being pounded on the back by the Indian, but was pounding the brave on his back, as well.

At last they broke, stood apart, and regarded each other fondly.

"Have you dined as yet today?" Washington asked.

Ghonkaba showed him the leather pouch containing the parched corn on which he had subsisted for almost the whole of his journey.

"Come with me," Washington told him. "The best I can do for you will be some tasteless Charles River fish, some new potatoes picked far too early in the season, and some chewy vegetables, but my cook isn't half bad at making them palatable." Linking his arm through his visitor's, he led him indoors.

The sentries, the young lieutenant who had been manhandled by Ghonkaba, and other officers who had collected exchanged bewildered looks. They had been convinced they understood the new commander in chief's personality, but clearly they had been mistaken. They had seen a side to his nature they hadn't even known existed, and they needed to reassess their judgments.

Washington led the way to the dining room. "I hope," he said, "that you haven't caused a rift with Ja-gonh by coming here."

"No," Ghonkaba said. "My relations with my entire family remain very friendly." He went on to explain that he was responsible for acquiring new rifles for the entire corps of the Iroquois nations, and that all of them, including the Seneca, would be nominally on the side of the British in the war but would strive, whenever possible, to assume a stance of neutrality.

Washington smiled. "I'm relieved to learn this," he said. "It's the first news I've had of the stand the Iroquois are going to take. Frankly, I wasn't looking forward to facing ten thousand of the continent's most competent fighting men."

"They may conduct a few minor raids on frontier settlements," Ghonkaba said, "but I think you'll find that by and large they'll mind their own business if the Americans don't invade their lands and molest their hunting grounds."

"I find that very reassuring," Washington said. When an orderly appeared with a soup tureen, he helped his guest to a plate of vegetable soup and then served himself another portion. His ill-fitting wooden teeth caused him to emit a slight whistling noise as he spooned his soup. "Now," he asked, "tell me about why you came from the land of the Seneca to see me."

"For many months," Ghonkaba told him, "I've been unable to decide whether to join the Americans, join the British as my grandfather wished, or remain neutral.

Your appointment as commander in chief of the American forces decided me. I've come to offer you my services in whatever capacity you choose to use them for the duration of the war."

"You're prepared to serve as a scout?"

"I'm ready this very minute, sir," Ghonkaba replied eagerly. "Just give me an assignment, and consider it accomplished!"

"Not so fast." Washington smiled at him but remained silent while the remains of the soup were cleared away and they were served fish with potatoes and vegetables. "No general," he said, "is competent beyond the knowledge he receives on the disposition of the enemy forces that he faces. I've long been aware of this, so I've been forming a unit of scouts that reports directly to me. It's not attached to any division or other organization and takes its orders exclusively from me. It's a rather informal group, but most of the men in it are veterans who had experience with me in the war against the French and Indians." He concealed a sly smile. "You may remember four men named Muller, Ryan, Ginsberg, and MacDavid."

Ghonkaba broke into a broad smile. It seemed too good to be true that his four close associates in the previous war were again in the personal employ of George Washington.

"You're a more experienced fighting man now than you were in the old days," Washington said. "As a Seneca war chief, you should be particularly valuable to us. Therefore, I'm perfectly willing to grant you a commission as a captain in the Continental Army and to put you in command of a full company of scouts."

"You won't regret this, General!" Ghonkaba assured him.

Washington looked at him dubiously. "You're sure you want to commit yourself this deeply?" he asked. "Our cause is shy of many of the essentials necessary for winning a war. We lack manpower and armaments and supplies. We're also lacking in cash reserves, and the Continental Congress is having a difficult time in raising funds, because the individual colonies are refusing to delegate powers of taxation. You may not always get your wages on time, and even when you're paid, the scrip that you'll be given may not be worth its face value."

"The cause of liberty is worth taking a few risks for," Ghonkaba replied.

Washington looked at him soberly. "How do you propose that your family get along during all this time?"

"My wife has assured me," Ghonkaba said, "that she and the children will follow me wherever I may be sent."

The expression in Washington's blue eyes hardened. "That's a charming, romantic concept, but it's far from practical. Can you imagine how chaotic conditions would become if every man in the Continental Army were followed by his wife and children? I shudder to think of what our camp would become."

Ghonkaba had not thought in such terms and was so embarrassed he could feel the tips of his ears burning.

"In view of our long-standing friendship," Washington said, "I think I can offer a realistic solution. Send your wife and children to my estate in Virginia, at Mount Vernon. Mrs. Washington will be delighted to give them a home as long as the war lasts."

Stunned by the general's generosity, Ghonkaba stammered his thanks.

"Some men in our army," Washington said, "are making many sacrifices for the sake of defending their liberty. But no one is sacrificing what you are offering. You are cutting yourself off from your people and your home, and you and your family are condemned to live out your days among strangers, regardless of the outcome of the war."

"You tell me that you need me, General," Ghonkaba said. "That is enough for me."

Ghonkaba learned that the Continental Congress, meeting in Philadelphia, had appealed to the Crown for reconciliation. But George III, who was impressed only by the militant stand taken by American patriots in the Battle of Breed's Hill, had branded the thirteen American colonies as rebels. He persuaded Parliament to pass a bill that provided for the blockading of all ports in the provinces. So many redcoat units were reluctant to take part in the coming campaigns that large numbers of Hessians were hired as mercenaries, and a recruiting campaign was inaugurated throughout Great Britain for soldiers who were more amenable to the idea of seeing action.

Ghonkaba's reunion with his fellow scouts, with whom he had served in the last of the French and Indian wars, was relatively subdued, but even so they laughed uproariously over past events that held no meaning for anyone other than themselves. In low tones, they spoke about the present and future, often using a verbal shorthand that made what they said virtually incomprehensible to outsiders. They smoked only when Ghonkaba produced his pipe at the end of the meal, and they proceeded to pass it around in the circle as they talked.

All five were approaching middle age and could no longer be regarded as young, but they made up in cunning whatever they might have lost in the way of physical strength and stamina. Their knowledge of the wilderness was encyclopedic, and together they made up a scouting unit that was unique. No other scouts of either army could compare with them.

They raised the question of whether to allow younger men to join their exclusive company, but deferred judgment until Ghonkaba was able to begin his service. Washington had granted him a flexible leave, telling him to take as long as he needed to put his personal affairs in order and to start his family on their way to Virginia. Until he had that accomplished, his four companions decided not to burden him with the question of enlarging their band.

Upon his return to the land of the Seneca, Ghonkaba reported to his family that his latest meeting with General Washington had strengthened his resolve that the family must leave the land of the Seneca for all time.

By taking up arms with foes of their allies, the British, he was deliberately forfeiting his future place as sachem of the Seneca and ultimately as Great Sachem of all the Iroquois. Furthermore, his elder son, Renno, was being deprived of the leadership that ultimately would have fallen onto his shoulders after he came to manhood. Great privation and sorrow were to be the lot of Ghonkaba's family for the foreseeable future.

The overriding question, one that no one could answer, was what would become of Ghonkaba and his family, even if the Americans succeeded in winning their independence. Clearly, having deliberately broken the law of their people, they could not come back to the land of the Seneca. Even though the circumstances were extraordinary and they were leaving with the sympathetic affection of the entire nation, they would not be able to reverse the tides of history and demand sanctuary in the land of their birth.

On the night before their departure, Ghonkaba's family was invited to supper with his parents. Also present was Ja-gonh's sister, Goo-ga-ro-no, and her husband, No-da-vo.

No mention was made of the coming breakup of the family, but it was noticeable that for the occasion Ah-wen-ga had prepared all of her son's favorite dishes. Everyone joined in a forced gaiety at the table, and the adults had to curb the tendency for all to talk at once.

The rule against conversation during meals was completely put aside by a special dispensation of the Grand Sachem.

The Seneca had borrowed the custom of drinking toasts from the American settlers, and after the meal Ja-gonh brought out a large jug containing a mixture of apple juice and fermented cider. Gourds were provided for everyone, including the children.

Ja-gonh offered the first toast. "May the gods protect you and yours from all harm," he said, raising his gourd to his son. "May you prosper in all that you undertake, and may you flourish outside the protecting circle of the Seneca, as you would have flourished had you continued to live within our boundaries."

No-da-vo echoed the sentiments expressed by his brother-in-law, and then it was the turn of Ah-wen-ga.

She looked first at her son, then at each of her three grandchildren. Few people anywhere could match her courage, but despite her resolve not to show emotion her eyes filled with tears. "May the manitous keep watch over you," she said, and suddenly her voice faltered. "And may our paths cross often in the days and years ahead."

"Amen to that," Ja-gonh said, inadvertently revealing his many years of training in the civilization of the white man.

After heartfelt words of good wishes and confident expectations expressed by Goo-ga-ro-no, it was Ghonkaba's turn to reply. "I have destroyed my own future in this land," he said, "and at the same time, I have shattered the futures of my two sons and my daughter. But I must live according to the dictates of my conscience, and I must do what I believe is right for me, for my family, and for my people. I thank you, my father, and you, my mother, for not once trying to dissuade me or to change my mind. You have given me a free hand to do what I know is right. I know of no greater sign of love than that."

Ja-gonh linked arms with his son, took a sip of his cider, and declared solemnly, "To you, Ghonkaba, my son, and to you, Toshabe, my daughter, I make a solemn pledge. I swear to you, in the names of all of the gods who oversee the destinies of the mighty Seneca, that never will a weapon of the Seneca be fired at you, your children, or their children after them."

Ghonkaba was quick to return the compliment. "And I assure you, my father, that neither I, my sons, nor their sons after them, will ever raise a weapon in hostility against the Seneca nation."

Of all the speeches made, the most effective was the very brief statement made by young Ena. "My grandfather and my grandmother," she said, "my great-aunt and my great-uncle." She paused, swallowed, and then blurted, "I love you." Blinking rapidly, she sat down and narrowly avoided bursting into tears. Ghonkaba realized he had never seen his parents looking so old and so vulnerable.

That moment was never forgotten by anyone who was present at the supper.

The rigid, lifelong training to which everyone present had been subjected prevented the party from becoming maudlin. The difficult, delicate moments were bridged, and at last the evening came to an end.

At dawn, the family assembled again to see Ghonkaba's family on their way. As the sun rose over the forest to the east, a startling surprise awaited Ghonkaba. He counted twelve other warriors, two of them war chiefs, and twenty squaws and children who had assembled with their belongings and were awaiting him. Ranoga acted as spokesman.

"Where you go, Ghonkaba, there will we go, also. We have decided to cast our lot with you."

Ghonkaba instinctively turned to his father, and

only after Ja-gonh spoke his assent did he agree to accept the warriors and their families. He had no idea that Ena was elated because Ranoga was going with them.

The party started out, traveling at a much slower pace than if the warriors had been alone.

Ghonkaba, bringing up the rear with Toshabe, turned and saw his parents standing outside the town's gates, watching the departure of those who were bidding farewell to their nation. His left hand shot upward in a Seneca gesture of hail and farewell. His father returned the salute.

Nothing more could be said, nothing was to be gained by prolonging the moment, but Ghonkaba briefly put an arm around Toshabe's shoulders before they trudged forward on their journey to the American encampment in Cambridge.

Because of the presence of women and children, their travel was slow through the wilderness that early spring. They anticipated no problems with enemies, as they were going through the land of the Mohawk before finally coming to the outposts of the American colonies. But Ghonkaba, who assumed overall charge, took no chances. He assigned three warriors to act as a scouting vanguard and three others to protect the party from attack at the rear.

Progress was steady and uneventful. The squaws and even the smallest children were thoroughly familiar with the forest and felt completely at home there.

Ranoga was one of the warriors assigned as an advance scout. Ena asked him to let her accompany him ahead of the expedition. Afraid that he would come in conflict with Ghonkaba, the warrior at first refused, but Ena persisted. He finally gave in, but made sure that Ena returned to the main body before the end of each day, when her father might otherwise become aware of her absence. At Ranoga's insistence, Toshabe was told of her daughter's newest activities and reluctantly was sworn to apprehensive silence.

Ena soon demonstrated that she was endowed with natural talents as a scout. Having inherited the hearing and eyesight of the great Renno, she could hear the slightest movement made by a fox stalking a rabbit in the underbrush and could catch a glimpse of a deer through the foliage.

"The child is a natural in the forest," Ranoga told Toshabe. "With a little experience, she'll be the equal of the best of Seneca scouts."

Toshabe was strongly inclined to tell Ghonkaba about Ena's exploits, but her daughter begged her to continue to remain silent. "My father," she said, "holds the most strict and old-fashioned of Seneca views. He believes that a woman's place in society is limited, and he will refuse to permit such activity on my part. Once he issues such an order, I shall be forced to stop going out every day with the scouts. I do no harm, and I enjoy myself more than I do in anything else."

Toshabe weakened and went along with her daughter's urgent request. She was motivated by the thought that her children were exiles now, cut off from their people and denied the rich heritage that they deserved.

The warriors brought down three deer, which provided the party with ample meat supplies. One day, after a long, arduous march, the women caught a large number of fish in a lake. The next morning, the entire company enjoyed a breakfast of fish broiled over an open fire, together with corn bread made on heated stones.

Ghonkaba was pleased that his family seemed to be suffering no ill effects. They remained cheerful, and their appetites were good. His sons, in particular, ravenously ate all they were given at meals.

One morning, however, Ena was strangely silent

and seemed morose, staring into the small fire and refusing to respond to the jokes of her brothers.

Her mother became concerned and asked what was wrong.

"I had a strange and powerful dream last night," Ena said. "It was so real to me that it did not seem like a dream."

Ghonkaba instantly became alert. He had inherited a trait that one male in each generation of the family had displayed, that of being able to foretell the future by his dreams. He had no idea how he had acquired this talent, and he never knew when a dream would hold meaning for the future, but he believed implicitly in the extraordinary ability, as had his forebears. It was possible that his daughter had inherited the unusual knack. He had never heard of a woman who had such an ability. Nevertheless, Ena's dream was worth exploring.

"What did you dream, Ena?" he asked.

Speaking hesitantly at first, she related how she had dreamt that she and her brothers had gone into a house to sleep. The house, built by white settlers, was made of wood, was painted white, and had the usual glass windows said to be common to such buildings. Speaking with increasing confidence, she told how she had suffered a grave premonition of extreme danger and had awakened her brothers and persuaded them to leave the house with her immediately. No sooner had they vacated it than a great iron ball fell out of the sky and crashed through the roof into the room where the boys had been sleeping.

Renno and El-i-chi listened wide-eyed to their sister's tale.

Ghonkaba questioned her repeatedly in an attempt to learn more, but she could add no details. But neither could he shake her story.

"What is the meaning of my dream?" she asked, her eyes looking enormous.

Ghonkaba replied, choosing his words carefully. "The meaning of a dream is not always immediately clear, even to the one who has had the dream. If you have inherited my gift of being able occasionally to foretell the future through dreams, what you dream will unfold before you in reality one day. But if your dream was meaningless, nothing will happen that you can connect with it in any way, and you should put it out of your mind."

Ena was very disappointed. "I was hoping that my dream had a great significance," she said.

Her father reached out and patted her shoulder. "We will remember your dream for a time, and then we shall see whether you have inherited the gift that I possess. Don't be impatient, and don't dwell on the dream in your memory. Put it aside and let what will happen develop normally, as it will. We may know within a matter of days whether your dream had any meaning."

The following day they left the land of the Mohawk and entered Massachusetts. The presence of farms and villages made it unnecessary to maintain scouts in advance and at the rear, and the entire party now traveled together.

The commander of the frontier militia in Springfield, hearing that a company of Seneca was crossing his territory intending to join General Washington in Cambridge, took proper steps to expedite their travel.

The militia furnished a small cavalry escort, which proved to be a great help on the road. The horsemen not only provided the travelers with accurate guides, but helped them acquire food from farmers.

As they drew nearer to Cambridge, the lieutenant who commanded the cavalry detachment took Ghonkaba aside. "From this point on," he said, "make sure that your entire company stays together at all times. Don't allow anyone to stray or to march apart from the entire group. Bands of redcoats—often accompanied by loyalist sympathizers—are abroad in the countryside. All of them are heading toward the British lines in Boston, where they hope to be reunited with the main army. They treat anyone who isn't on their side as an enemy, and they're utterly ruthless. So it's best to be prepared."

Ghonkaba then issued orders to his followers to stay together on the road at all costs.

Late in the day, when they halted to make their campfires and cook their evening meal in the rolling hill country to the west of Boston, Ghonkaba set up a schedule of sentry duty.

The militia commander approved heartily. "That's good," he said. "Far better than you know. Listen!"

Ghonkaba heard the distant sound of thunder and was mildly surprised, as the sky overhead was clear.

"That is not thunder," the officer said. "That's the sound of artillery that accompanies the redcoats as they try to fight their way through our lines to reach their comrades in Boston. At least they proclaim their presence openly, and we should be grateful to them for that."

The campfires of the Seneca attracted attention at the nearby village of Wellesley, and a delegation soon called on the Indians. The residents explained that several houses were lying vacant, their owners having enlisted in the Continental Army for the duration of the war. The visitors suggested that the women and children in the Seneca party avail themselves of the villagers' hospitality by occupying these dwellings for the night.

Soon thereafter, the assignment of women and children to the dwellings began. Ghonkaba was standing in the middle of the road speaking with one of the war chiefs when his daughter hurried up. The look on Ena's face was intense, her hands trembled, and her grip on his bare arm was so intense that her fingernails dug into his flesh.

"This is it, my father!" she said. "This is the same place I saw in my dream."

Ghonkaba was not impressed. Experience had taught him that often he, too, had seen a place that reminded him of a spot that he had visited in a dream. And then on close examination he had found that his memory had been playing tricks on him and that it was not the identical location at all. He did not take the time to explain this to Ena. Her first experience with a dream could provide the opportunity for her to learn various truths for herself.

Ena later joined her mother and brothers in a small house set back from the road. Ghonkaba spent the night in the open with the other warriors.

He awakened long before dawn, and while he was gathering wood for a fire, Toshabe joined him. She, too, arose early in order to have ample time to prepare the herb tea that she and her husband drank for breakfast every morning.

"I spent a difficult night," she said. "Ena gave me little opportunity to rest."

"What was wrong with her?"

"She was suffering from a bad case of adolescent imagination," Toshabe said. "She kept muttering about her dream. In fact, she was awake before I ever left the building this morning."

Even as she spoke, they saw Ena leading her sleepy brothers out of the house in the dim light. Evidently she had just awakened the boys and was forcing them into the open.

Ghonkaba was tempted to laugh. He of all people could understand how compelling a dream could be, and why Ena felt forced to obey the dictates of what she had imagined in her sleep.

As the three children started to walk toward their

parents, they could hear a soft rumble in the distance, gradually becoming louder. Suddenly, in the early morning light, an iron ball loomed almost overhead, a shot from a redcoat cannon. It crashed through the roof of the house that Ena and the boys had just left.

Ena grew pale. "My dream has been fulfilled," she said. "I saw all this happen before. An iron ball fell from the sky and broke through the roof of the house where Renno and El-i-chi were asleep. This is exactly what I dreamed."

Her dream had come true, Ghonkaba realized, now assured that his daughter had inherited the rare trait. Ena undoubtedly was endowed with a second sight that the gods had given her. But now she would have to learn that she could not summon this vision at will and that it manifested itself only at the will of the gods when they wished to convey a message to mortals whom they favored.

The British Army under the command of Sir William Howe sat in Boston, keeping the lid clamped on the surly, restive city. The redcoats were forced to travel in groups as they went out on patrols, and no officer or enlisted man dared to be seen in public alone.

In the meantime, General Washington, demonstrating a characteristic patience, organized the Continental Army. He drilled his troops incessantly, sharpening their combat skills and teaching them the need for discipline.

While this was going on, Boston was without political leadership. Sam Adams and John Hancock, newly distinguished by the price on their heads, offered by Howe for their capture, were delegates to the Continental Congress in Philadelphia, as was John Adams.

Dispatches from other fronts appeared to be favorable to the American cause. A force under General Richard Montgomery captured Montreal, while another wing under Benedict Arnold laid siege to Quebec. Not until later in the spring was it learned that Arnold's force had been defeated by the cold of Quebec and that, as defense of Montreal was impossible without the capital, Montgomery's army was forced to withdraw.

In March 1776, Washington made his initial move and occupied Dorchester Heights, south of Boston. There, the guns of General Henry Knox dominated the scene, able to bombard the redcoats in the city without mercy. General Howe had faulty intelligence on the Continentals' supplies, and lacking accurate information as to how short they were of ammunition for cannon, he decided to evacuate Boston, with the heavy guns looming high above his position.

Naval transports removed Howe's entire army and sailed off. The entire area had been swept clear of redcoats, and Boston was restored to the young nation.

Washington and his army were greeted as heroes by the deliriously happy citizens of Boston, who were about to taste real independence for the first time.

Across the sea in England, King George, ignoring the strong support for the Americans that was shown by many of his subjects, completely lost his temper and became irrational. "The damned rebels have got to be beaten to their knees and taught a lesson they'll never forget!" he shouted. "Every American who opposes me is a traitor and must be dealt with accordingly! This revolt must be stamped out and ended for all time."

In the midst of the happy turmoil in Boston, the party of Seneca arrived to find the city in American hands. Ghonkaba reported to General Washington, and his Seneca warriors were incorporated into the company of scouts that would report directly to the commander in chief.

Arrangements were made for Toshabe and her children, as well as the families of the other Seneca warriors, to sail for Virginia, where they would be under the care of Mrs. Washington.

At the wharf from which they were to depart, Ghonkaba bade farewell to his family in a manner that befitted a war chief of the Seneca. He clapped each of his sons on the shoulder and told them to remember all they had been taught and to continue to grow wise in the ways of one who made war. Toshabe and Ena were treated far more leniently, but without sentimental farewell. Ghonkaba briefly embraced his daughter, kissed his wife, and then stood with his left arm extended while their ship sailed out of sight. They did not put into words their innermost thoughts. None of them knew when they might meet again or what the circumstances of that reunion might be, but they restrained any temptation to feel sorry for themselves.

They, like the two and a half million colonials who called themselves Americans, were at war now with Great Britain, and no man could predict the outcome.

Once Ghonkaba saw his family on the way to Virginia, he devoted his full time and attention to the very considerable task of transferring Washington's entire army to Long Island, where they hoped to confront the British under Howe in the near future.

As summer approached, a climactic battle became likely, presumably on Long Island. The British, having lost Boston, were determined to seize the strategic port of New York, and Washington was preparing to meet this challenge. Meanwhile, all political ties of the colonies with England were severed when the Continental Congress, sitting in Philadelphia, issued its Declaration of Independence early in July. The thirteen colonies, now calling themselves the United States of America, had launched their new nation.

The individual states granted few powers to the central government and were especially reluctant to give up any rights of taxation. Consequently, the Congress was constantly strapped for money and lacked funds to wage an effective war. In all, the rebels' entire military strength amounted to fewer than one hundred thousand men. The Continental Army and the muster rolls of individual state militias included men who would enlist for only a few months.

The British, meanwhile, were sending regiment after regiment of well-trained, superbly disciplined redcoats and Hessian mercenaries across the Atlantic to crush the insurgents who had dared to challenge the majesty of the most powerful nation in the western world.

In England and elsewhere in Europe, the general expectation was that the Americans would be soundly defeated within months, at most. Only the Americans themselves appeared supremely unaware of the prophecies regarding their future.

By early August, both forces were gathering their strength for the inevitable major battle that would be fought on Long Island. As word of the impending conflict spread, volunteers began to arrive and present themselves to General Washington for assignment. He was grateful for the presence of these recruits, but their lack of military training was a handicap, so he spread them out among units that at least had had some military training.

The Continental Army's company of Seneca scouts, as it was coming to be known, not only was kept busy, but did its job with customary thoroughness. The quartet of seasoned veterans, Muller, Ryan, Ginsberg, and MacDavid, roamed far and wide. It was rumored—without confirmation or denial—that they had masqueraded as redcoats for forty-eight hours in order to gain first-hand information on the size and composition of the British forces.

The British were confident of the outcome of the impending battle, and consequently, General Howe acted contrary to the military traditions prevalent in all armies and took no pains to conceal his troop movements. Entire divisions were transferred to Long Island, as were battalions of supporting artillery, not to mention countless troops of cavalry and expert sappers, bridge builders, and other engineers. Washington's camp understood that the Continental Army would go into battle against the finest units that the British could assemble.

Ghonkaba received almost daily reports from his scouts, and when he had accumulated enough information to provide him a complete picture of what was happening, he went to Washington with his report.

The commander in chief was so busy, however, in the farmhouse that he was using as his temporary headquarters that the Seneca had to wait almost a whole day before he was admitted.

"I must apologize for keeping you waiting all this time," Washington told him. "I'm in the position of a fire warden armed with only one bucket of water, who learns of twenty fires breaking out in as many places within the area under his jurisdiction. If you have any bad news to pass along to me," he continued, waving his visitor to a chair, "let me hear it without delay."

Ghonkaba seated himself in a straight-backed chair on the far side of Washington's desk. "General Howe," he said, "is gathering a major force for what appears to be an attempt to bring the war rapidly to a conclusion. He has tens of thousands of men under his command, and every day more and more are being transferred to Long Island from Manhattan and from the mainland. I gather that some have been stationed in various parts of the colonies, while others have only recently arrived from London. But one thing is true of all of them. They're actually eager for a fight, and their morale is very high. They've been told by their unit commanders that they have nothing to fear from us, and our lack of interference with their troop concentrations seems to bear out such a prophecy. They're not in the least afraid of us, and they look forward eagerly to the coming battle."

"If I had just twenty-five thousand men to spare," Washington said wistfully, "I'd put a real crimp in their expectations. But unfortunately I can't afford to splurge in that way."

"It is not seemly for me to offer you unsought advice, General," Ghonkaba said, "but if the Seneca found themselves in like circumstances in a campaign, they would launch a surprise attack on their foes. By catching the enemy unaware and off guard, they would inflict great casualties before the main battle ever began."

"That's precisely what I meant when I told you that I lacked trained manpower," Washington replied. "Suppose I sent twenty-five thousand men into an assault on the British before they're prepared. My troops could inflict a heavy defeat on perhaps fifty thousand men, or even seventy-five thousand, let's say. They lack the experience, however, to disappear into the wilderness, as the warriors of the Seneca would do. They know so little of military affairs that they advance the way they retreat—clumsily and with great difficulty. It would be asking for too much to expect them to know the way into the wilderness. The remnants of the redcoats they trapped would be able to follow them with ease and inflict great damage on them. Then, by the time they had reorganized and were ready to do serious battle, the enemy would have been reinforced and our tired legions would face another seventy-five thousand or more men. The odds against them are so great that I don't dare disrupt the enemy by launching any prebattle attack!"

Ghonkaba gained an understanding of Washington's dilemma that would stay with him throughout the years of the American Revolution. Above all, he was able to grasp the commander in chief's reason for meeting the

British in direct open combat when he knew that his forces were badly outnumbered and undoubtedly would be outfought. The Continental Army and militia had to learn to stand and give better than they received if they hoped to win battles. They could train for countless hours, but only actual combat would give them the experience they so desperately needed. They had to be tested and tried repeatedly in the crucible of actual warfare if they were to be effective and do their part in achieving victory. In the interim, Washington had to reconcile himself to the prospect that he would lose battles and be forced to retreat again and again.

By the middle of August, the daily reports from Ghonkaba's scouts indicated the increasing hopelessness of the American position. It was the Seneca's painful duty to report to the commander in chief that the redcoats and their mercenary Hessian allies now outnumbered the American forces by four to one. Before the month was out, Howe made his long-expected move, and the British launched their full-scale attack. The Battle of Long Island was under way.

Chapter IV

From the outset, the odds in the Battle of Long Island favored the British. Not only did the forces commanded by General Howe overwhelmingly outnumber their foes, but they had the added advantage of full support from a powerful British naval squadron commanded by Admiral Lord Richard Howe, the general's brother. The twelve-inch and fourteen-inch cannon of the larger warships inaugurated the combat by hurling heated iron balls into the ranks of the foe. This was followed by a cavalry assault, and then came wave after wave of redcoat infantry marching in the hollow squares that were renowned in the annals of European warfare.

Never had the American defenders encountered such an enemy. To the astonishment of Ghonkaba and his scouts, the redcoats made no attempt to conceal themselves, openly displaying their intentions as they swept forward.

Some American units fought valiantly. The cannon of General Knox fired so many volleys the overheated guns burst at the seams or, in some instances, exploded, killing their crews.

The relatively few seasoned American foot soldiers dug in grimly and repelled the worst that the British threw at them, then waited for more, daring the enemy to continue its attack.

The greater part of the patriot army was enduring armed combat for the first time and was far less fortunate. Bewildered by the cavalry assaults, the lines wavered under the attack of British heavy infantry, and broke when the light infantry advanced, with bayonets gleaming. Repeatedly the American lines collapsed.

The British displayed contempt for their opponents. Regimental buglers played hunting calls, and the redcoats made a game of the occasion, swarming forward and shooting at will at their stumbling, frightened, paralyzed foes.

The senior American commanders could do nothing to halt the debacle. They stormed and threatened, using the flats of their swords in vain attempts to force their lines to hold steady. But nothing they did was effective. Again and again the ranks of the untried Americans broke and disintegrated as men tried to scramble to safety, forgetting to maintain order.

In this phase of the battle, Ghonkaba and his men took on a responsibility other than scouting. It was their harrowing duty to help provide a rear guard to enable the Continentals and American militiamen to escape certain annihilation. They formed a ragged line in the woods, firing arrows and muskets in a desperate attempt to slow the British advance. Ghonkaba saw valorous work performed by many of his men. Nearest to him throughout the action was Ranoga, as stalwart and unyielding as ever.

Their stubborn stand enabled Americans by the hundred to retreat in order to fight again some other day. In the face of enormous odds, they held their ground.

Ghonkaba, as always, set an example for the men under his command. Concealed in underbrush, he swiftly sent a quiverful of arrows into the oncoming redcoats. Whenever he could, he picked up his rifle, reloaded, and sent a shot into the midst of the enemy ranks. As the result of his fire, the bodies of numerous British officers and soldiers were strewn about the field. He refused to yield one foot of territory. Ultimately, the commander of the British regiment opposite Ghonkaba's unit had to call for help.

When an arrow landed in a tree he was using as a partial shield, Ghonkaba was amazed. He raised himself to one knee and peered toward the enemy line.

In that moment, time stood still. Facing him across the void was his fellow Seneca and bitter enemy, Tredno.

Recognizing him at the same instant, Tredno shot another arrow toward his enemy. Shaken by the unexpected encounter, however, he sent his shot wide of its mark. Later, Ghonkaba thought that he probably could have killed his foe then and there, but he never knew for certain. Unable to force himself to fire at a fellow Seneca, even though they fought on opposing sides, he lowered his rifle briefly, and the opportunity passed. He realized momentarily that he was still haunted by Tredno's hatred and personal enmity.

Any chance of renewing the encounter was soon lost. When the British redoubled their attempts to gain the American position, the American brigadier commanding the sector finally had to order Ghonkaba's scouts to withdraw.

The American debacle was growing worse, and the retreat turned into a complete catastrophe.

Washington, who had feared precisely such an outcome, managed to retain his calm, even though his army was collapsing on all sides. He formed a semblance of a rear guard with his seasoned troops and quietly withdrew the others, pulling the remnants of organization together. He calmed the hysterical and loaded them into boats, to be transferred from Long Island to the forests in the upper reaches of Manhattan Island.

In total defeat, Washington proved a master tactician, extricating thousands of beaten men from the destruction that threatened to engulf them. Having tasted such ignominy, he thought, would make better soldiers of the survivors.

The company of Seneca scouts played a major role in the retreat. First, the Indians and their white colleagues fanned out through the deep woods of upper Manhattan to make certain that no redcoats were lying in wait there. Once they had determined that the way was clear, they formed a rear guard to hold back the British units that they assumed would follow the Americans.

Howe failed, however, to strike the decisive blow that would have ended the American Revolution and would have ensured victory for Great Britain. His political foes later charged that he was motivated by his not-so-secret sympathy with the aims of the American rebels and his approval of their cause.

Whatever his reasons, he did not pursue and annihilate his foes. All through the late afternoon and the night that followed, weary boatmen ferried the exhausted American troops. They now were able to rest and, to some extent, reorganize. Entire regiments had been utterly destroyed, but the survivors were forming new units.

The scouts continued to report no sign of a redcoat pursuit. The American commanders thus were able to bind up their wounds and restore a measure of order.

Washington, displaying his customary cool disregard for his personal safety, spoke to virtually every survivor of the battle. By the time he was done, he had so inspired the men by his example that their pride in themselves and in their army, though crushed and virtually destroyed, was restored.

The following day, the British finally stirred and showed signs of being ready to follow their defeated foes and to deliver a final, devastating blow. As Howe's forces occupied New York City and prepared to march north, Washington again calmly extricated his remaining force from a possible trap by escaping across the Hudson River into New Jersey. Some doubters claimed that his force had been reduced to no more than ten thousand men. Others believed as many as twenty thousand were still in the ranks. In any event, Washington and his senior commanders realized that the troops who now followed the commander in chief were patriots whose resolve could not be shaken. They were determined to carry on the war, no matter how much they suffered or how long it took to achieve victory. This was the unyielding hard corps on which the future of all Americans depended.

The company of scouts, which had performed well, was intact. The burly Sergeant MacDavid spoke for the unit when he said, "Damn my soul, but we've taken the very worst the British could throw at us, and we're still here, we're still intact, and we're still free. I hope Billy Howe has the sense to notify King George that Americans have just begun to fight!"

Now Washington began a long, tortured march southward through New Jersey.

Pursuing, the British on several occasions attacked the retreating Continentals. But the Americans were quick to learn the art of war. Their weary rear guard fought well, holding the enemy at bay, while the main body slipped away. The British came to regard Washington as a magician they could not pin down. All through the autumn months the morale of the retreating Americans continued to improve.

Ghonkaba's scouts performed ably. They made their way through the evergreens that lined the eastern bank of the Delaware, and only when they sent back assurance that no redcoats were gathered there, did the bulk of the army follow. Whenever they encountered a farm, Washington was notified, and his staff promptly came forward and negotiated with the farmer. When possible, the proprietors of farms were persuaded to contribute quantities of food to the American cause. When necessary, they were paid in the dwindling reserves of available cash, and only on rare occasion was it necessary for the staff to seize the property of a Loyalist sympathizer.

As the Continentals drew closer to Philadelphia, the Congress, still meeting there, was reduced to senseless bickering.

At last, Washington withdrew across the Delaware into Pennsylvania, and there he finally came to a halt. His troops, no longer a mere armed rabble, took stock of themselves and of their situation and began to plan for their rehabilitation as fighting men.

The British, following on the heels of the Americans, established their principal forward base at Trenton on the Delaware.

Summoning Ghonkaba to the farmhouse where he had established his headquarters, Washington spoke frankly. "I'll want your scouts to exercise special precautions in the weeks ahead," he said. "Our situation now is especially precarious. I'll grant you that Billy Howe has occupied an exposed position at Trenton, but he has little, if anything, to fear from us in the way of retaliatory strokes. Our Continentals are the only force that stands between him and Philadelphia, which he's certain to regard as a great prize. If he should attack in strength, we'd get the very dubious help of a great many volunteers from the city, but I've had my fill of untrained volunteer troops, who aren't worth the muskets that they're certain to throw aside when they run at the first sign of trouble. I fully anticipate that Howe will make several sorties in strength in order to test our defenses. Our Continentals are developing into first-rate soldiers, but I tell you—in the strictest confidence—that there are too few of them to be truly effective against the redcoats if the enemy decides to attack with his full force. I can put some six to seven thousand infantrymen in the field now, but if Howe concentrates his forces, we'll be facing at least twenty thousand redcoats and Hessians."

As Washington had pointed out repeatedly, Ghonkaba thought, the Americans faced a precarious situation at best.

"At all costs," the commander in chief went on, "we must avoid a direct confrontation between our total force and Howe's. The results would be catastrophic for us and would likely end our existence as a cohesive fighting force. What we must try to do is to strike peripheral blows at the enemy and chip away at their strength. We have no alternative at present. Only if we win some important battles will our people become encouraged enough that the states will meet the quotas for the new troops that the army needs."

Ghonkaba marveled at the general's attitude. Washington stood on the brink of disaster facing a devastating defeat that would destroy his army. Yet he thought and spoke in terms of the victory that he seemed to feel certain would be his. Like his footsore Continental

Army, he refused to acknowledge the possibility that he might be defeated.

"Corn and beans—the kind that you Americans call broad beans—go very well together," Toshabe was saying. "Put the beans on a low boil in a small amount of water for a quarter of an hour, and then add corn cut off the cob. Just remember that the corn requires very little cooking in order to be done."

Toshabe stirred the contents of the big kettle vigorously and stepped back from the oversized stove in the airy kitchen outbuilding attached to the mansion called Mount Vernon.

Martha Washington, handsome and patrician, listened and watched the Indian woman intently. She was astonished to realize how much she had learned from Toshabe in the weeks that Ghonkaba's family had been guests at Mount Vernon. Not only was Toshabe thoroughly familiar with Iroquois and Erie cooking, but she knew dozens of household tricks that had been Indian secrets for hundreds of years. Mrs. Washington was discovering that she had much to learn from this talented woman.

All the Indian women and children who had come to Virginia were housed on the Washington estate. But Mrs. Washington saw only Toshabe and her children regularly, as they were the only members of the party who were fluent in English and could readily communicate with her.

Toshabe tasted a few kernels of corn and two or three beans with a big wooden ladle. "When the vegetables become tender," she said, "you know they are done. Never let them sit in the water. Drain them well, pour on a small quantity of melted butter, and sprinkle a little rocksalt. That's all they need to be ready to eat. They're a useful dish, as the Iroquois discovered long ago, because they're quite filling, and even the most ferocious warrior is no longer hungry after he has eaten a portion. They can be substituted for potatoes at supper, too."

Martha Washington tasted the finished dish and found it delicious. "How do you happen to know so much about cooking, Toshabe?" she asked.

"When I was a young girl in the land of the Erie," Toshabe said, "I learned all that my mother and my aunts could teach me about cooking. Then when I became a Seneca, I was fortunate to be taught by the mother of my husband, who is recognized by the Seneca as a great cook. So I learned the best of all possible ways, from the best of all possible teachers."

Mrs. Washington was curious. "What has become of your mother-in-law?"

"She still lives in the land of the Seneca, where she ranks first among all squaws because her husband, the father of my husband, is the Great Sachem of all the peoples of the Iroquois nations. He follows in the steps of his father and his grandfather before him." She paused for a moment, and a cloud seemed to pass across her face. "That was to have been the destiny also of Ghonkaba, but he chose, instead, to follow General Washington down the path of liberty."

Mrs. Washington was amazed by the ease with which such people accepted great hardship and the loss of everything they held dear. "Suppose that we are defeated and lose the war? What then?"

Toshabe smiled. "We shall not lose the war," she said. "My husband, who was a mighty war chief of the Seneca, said so!"

Martha Washington raised an eyebrow. "And you believe him?"

"Of course! He fought beside General Washington in the war against the French and Indians long ago, and he swears no finer leader of warriors exists anywhere on earth."

Her sincerity was infectious, and Martha Washington smiled at her. "I happen to agree completely with the views of your husband. Come along. The beef pie that the cook has been preparing must be ready by now, and the corn and beans will grow cold unless we eat soon. Besides, we must break the news to your children that we are going north to the outskirts of Philadelphia in the immediate future, and we're going to join our husbands there. The youngsters will have ample cause for good cheer tonight!"

The company of scouts was stretched thin, almost to the breaking point, as the Seneca and the white frontiersmen deployed behind the cover of trees facing the bend in the fast-flowing Delaware River, just above Trenton. So far, the redcoats had made no move, but the company of scouts continued to keep the New Jersey shore under close observation. If General Washington was right—and Ghonkaba assumed that he was—they could anticipate action by the British at almost any moment.

Each member of the unit was stationed within conversational range of his closest neighbor on either side. It was possible for a man to call out in low tones and be heard by the men adjacent to him on his left and right.

Ghonkaba anchored the line, and next to him was stationed Sergeant Ginsberg, perhaps the unit's most accomplished horseman, whose stallion was tethered in the deep pines only a short distance to the rear. He could be dispatched to General Washington's headquarters with news of any consequence.

For eleven days and nights in late November the scouts remained on sentry duty. They were not relieved because they—alone of all men in the Continental Army—were capable of performing this function as well as was necessary.

The company subsisted exclusively on emergency Indian fare of jerked meat and parched corn. Fires were never lighted for fear of giving away their position to an enemy who might be lurking in the underbrush on the opposite shore.

The weather was cold and damp, and for three days snow flurries added to the sentries' discomfort. But as Sergeant Ryan remarked succinctly, "We've known worse."

No man ventured more than several feet from his assigned position, and in spite of the unrelieved tension, the unit was prepared to wait indefinitely for something to develop. The idea of being relieved of the onerous assignment hardly entered their minds.

Then, at dusk one evening, word traveled down the line to Ghonkaba that a fleet of longboats, similar to those used to bring crews of large British Navy ships ashore, was gathering in a small cove down the river. He went to investigate, and in the half light he could make out at least a dozen such craft being moved into the rushes at the side of the river. Each boat could carry a rowing crew of about six and approximately twenty armed passengers. Using those figures, Ghonkaba estimated that an enemy force of two or three hundred infantrymen was being sent across the Delaware. As Washington had said, Howe intended to make a sortie in strength in order to disrupt the enemy.

Hastily summoning Ginsberg, Ghonkaba instructed him on what to report to the army headquarters.

"Do you want any help from Washington?" the hard-bitten Ginsberg wanted to know.

Ghonkaba forced a smile. "Oh, I'd like help, just as I'm sure General Washington would be glad to provide me with some, if he had the manpower available."

"Hell," Ginsberg said as he spat a stream of tobacco juice into the underbrush. "Washington sure ought to be able to spare a battalion for a day or two so we can meet this attack of two or three hundred men on equal terms."

"That's where you're wrong," Ghonkaba said. "The British expect that, and we'd be playing right into their hands. If Washington supplies a battalion to meet this threat and another battalion to meet that threat, his entire army will be worn down before you know it. We're too badly outnumbered by the enemy as it is, and we have no units to spare."

Ginsberg started to mount his horse, but suddenly turned back. "You mean to say that you're going to meet the attack of hundreds of men with only the scout company?"

Ghonkaba smiled easily, and his chuckle was natural. "I don't see why not," he said. "Sure, I will admit we'll be outnumbered by four or maybe even five to one, but every other advantage lies on our side!"

Ghonkaba hastily summoned his entire unit to an emergency meeting, and the men gathered near his position while two or three on the periphery continued to keep watch on the movements of the enemy across the river. "We're going to withstand the impact of an enemy attack by ourselves," he said. "I'm not asking General Washington for any help, and I expect none from him or from any of his divisions."

A murmur ran through the unit, but no one actually objected.

"Hey, Captain," Sergeant Ryan called softly from his position. "It appears like the enemy is sure as shootin' fixin' up to cross the river. They got them boats fillin' up with redcoats."

"Good!" Ghonkaba said. "Let them be filled. When they cross the river, I want no firearms used against them. We'll confine ourselves to bows and arrows for the first few boatloads, and only after we dispose of those men will we take up rifles."

The men chuckled. They understood his strategy

and approved it; only that was needed. As was true of other units of the Continental Army, before action was taken a commander explained his intentions to his unit. Understanding what was expected of them and why, they were able to carry out their assignments with far greater ease and precision.

Before the British began their move, a commotion broke out in the deep woods behind the scouts' position, and Ghonkaba hurried to the rear see what was amiss. To his surprise, he saw three small mortars being hauled to the place by horses, and then being positioned by gun crews of three men to a cannon. Looming in the background was the bulk of General Henry Knox, whose huge body quivered when he laughed. "I understand," he said with a deep laugh, "that you're expecting some company from across the river, Captain. Maybe I can help you give them a proper greeting."

"Yes, you can, General," Ghonkaba said gratefully, and swiftly outlined the strategy he had devised.

Knox approved it and explained the situation to his gun crews. "You give me the signal," he told Ghonkaba, "when you want my boys to open fire with their mortars."

Feeling far more confident now, Ghonkaba deployed his scouts, positioning them ten to fifteen feet apart, and four or five deep from the front rank, which was stationed near the river bank. Night was falling, but his eyesight remained perfect, and he could see the moves on the far side of the river clearly, bolstering his belief that the redcoats were planning on concentrating their attack on a single point. He posted his unit in depth behind what he surmised was that point.

After a time, the first boat pushed out into the water from the New Jersey shore. The current was swift, the river having been swollen by heavy autumn rains, and the oarsmen had to struggle in order to reach the western shore. As the long craft headed up toward the bank and two men leaped out to drag it higher,

Ghonkaba silently strung an arrow into his bow. All of his Seneca were doing the same, even though he had issued no order.

The redcoats began to disembark, and Ghonkaba took careful aim at the chest of a lieutenant who was starting to step across the side of the boat onto the shore. He released his arrow. It made a slight singing sound as it sped toward its target, then buried itself deep in the Englishman's chest. The lieutenant crumpled to the ground without a sound.

At the same time, half a dozen other redcoats fell, and another, wounded but still living, uttered a piercing scream that seemed to shatter the silence and sent chills of gooseflesh chasing up the spines of everyone within earshot.

A second longboat pulled up on shore, and the scouts repeated their attack. Arrows again were notched into bows and were fired, and again most of the shots found their targets. All of the redcoats who had escaped death when the first arrows struck still were conspicuous targets, and many were brought down swiftly. Making a rapid appraisal of the situation as a third longboat headed toward the shore, Ghonkaba realized he had gained an initial advantage. Now it was up to him and his scouts to keep it.

As the next boatload came ashore, the scouts employed their bows for the third time. Ghonkaba estimated that the enemy now had lost fifty to sixty men in killed and wounded. Still, because it was almost completely dark, the rest of the British had no idea of their comrades' fate. Now was the time to thoroughly confound the enemy. Rifles clicked as the entire company of scouts took up their firearms and prepared to use them.

Ghonkaba picked up a rock and threw it so that it landed at General Knox's feet in a prearranged signal.

Knox ordered his gun crews to prepare to touch off the cannon.

With his extraordinary eyesight, Ghonkaba was able to note that the remaining boats of the invaders were in the water, all heading toward the western shore. The crack of his rifle was the signal that both the scouts and Knox's artillerymen awaited. The Seneca and frontiersmen pulled their triggers almost as one man. At the same moment, the fuses of the mortars were lighted. The little cannon made an uncommonly loud noise as they boomed, and their spheres soared high into the air and dropped in the midst of the approaching boats as the rifle shots of the scouts cut through the air.

The redcoats were squeezed into the longboats, with no place to hide or room to maneuver. They were stunned by the eruption of both infantry and artillery fire and had to wait until they came ashore in order to respond to the enemy fire. By that time, the scouts—all of them expert shots—had fired at least two rounds and were reloading to fire a third.

Knox's enthusiastic mortarmen were looping their shots high into the air and bringing their heavy iron spheres crashing down in the midst of the bewildered redcoats.

The British neither panicked nor fled. Under the blistering fire, they did not lose their heads. In spite of the great casualties, they managed to form into cohesive ranks and began to return the Continentals' fire.

Ghonkaba, directing the steady fire of his scouts, had to admire the stubborn courage and tenacity of the enemy. Ordering his troops to fire at will, he loaded his own rifle, fired, loaded again, and fired once more, soon losing count of his shots.

The redcoats were taking a severe drubbing from the artillery, too, and though they tried to hold their own, they had no chance. They outmanned the defenders, but the Continentals' tactics gave their enemies no chance to regroup and to use their superior numbers to their advantage. Slowly they were driven back to their boats, and under the most trying circumstances they were able to drag the bodies of their dead and wounded into the craft with them.

When they put off again in the dark for the New Jersey shore, the rifle shots and the mortar fire of the Continentals followed them until their longboats had had time to disappear into the rushes on the Jersey side.

The skirmish ended in a rousing victory for the Continentals, with the credit shared equally by Ghonkaba's scouts and Henry Knox's versatile artillerymen.

Chapter V

Martha Washington was constantly surprised by the behavior of the three children of Ghonkaba and Toshabe. Only when she studied them carefully could she see signs of their white ancestry in their faces, their hair, and their skins. To a casual observer, they looked like the Indians that they were. But their conduct was paradoxical.

They spoke an easy, colloquial English, complete with American accents. They were completely at home at a civilized table, and their manners were unassailable. They appeared to be familiar with knives, forks, and

104

spoons. They could read and write English, she discovered, and they had no difficulty with problems ranging from the handling of the new currency to the use of carpenters' and stonemasons' tools.

They were unique, she decided. They were true Seneca in all things and at all times, yet simultaneously they were as much Americans as if they had been born and bred in Virginia.

As she supervised the packing of her clothing boxes prior to leaving for quarters near Philadelphia, the general's wife realized how glad she was that the children and their mother would be accompanying her. She knew that the general was fond of Ghonkaba and relied on his expertise as a scout. The versatility of the Seneca's daughter and sons would be interesting to him.

An urgent tap sounded at the door, interrupting her reverie.

She was surprised to find Ena standing on the threshold, a look of grim seriousness on her face.

"If you please, Mrs. Washington," Ena said, "you'd better come at once. One of the field hands has been seriously hurt."

Martha Washington gathered her voluminous skirts and followed Ena down the corridor to the stairs leading toward the tobacco fields behind the cluster of buildings. As they walked rapidly, Ena explained the situation. She and her brothers had been playing a game of hide-and-seek in the fields when they had run across the unconscious body of one of the field hands. His machete had slipped while he had been cutting tobacco plants, and he had cut open his thigh. He had bled profusely. Ena had run to her mother, and Toshabe had sent her to fetch Mrs. Washington.

By the time they arrived at the scene, Toshabe had the situation temporarily under control, while several field hands and their wives were gathered in the background. Their frightened faces attested to the seriousness of the situation. Martha Washington saw at a glance that Toshabe had bound the leg above the cut to stop the flow of blood. But the man had not regained consciousness, and he appeared to be in grave danger.

Toshabe sat on the ground with the victim's head in her lap, trying to make him comfortable. When she saw her daughter, she called to her in the Seneca tongue, and Ena obediently darted off on another errand.

Seeing Martha Washington's blank expression, Toshabe hastened to explain, "I have sent my sons and daughter," she said, "to fetch some of what we call the 'red plants.' Perhaps they are what you call sassafras plants in Virginia. These we will boil quickly and dip cloths into the juice to make poultices to apply to the leg."

Mrs. Washington was surprised. "Will poultices of boiled sassafras really stop the bleeding?" she asked. "It sounds like such a simple remedy."

A hint of a smile touched the corners of Toshabe's lips. "We will see," she answered in a matter-of-fact voice.

Taking charge, she directed the assembled field hands to make a fire, bring an iron pot, put about two gallons of water into it, and then set it on the fire. By the time the task was completed, Ena and her brothers had appeared with armloads of sassafras plants, roots and all. At Toshabe's direction, these were dumped into the water, and one of the field hands was sent for strips of cotton cloth to be used as poultices.

The brew began to boil. The steam that arose from it was acrid, astringent. Toshabe ordered the strips of cloth to be thrown into the pot, as well. The entire brew boiled for ten minutes, while Toshabe sat calmly. She acted as though there were no hurry, no emergency to be dealt with.

Renno was sent to the kitchen for metal tongs, to

remove strips of cloth from the kettle's boiling contents. They were allowed to cool, but while still dripping they were draped over the wound. The unconscious man stirred and moaned.

Next came the one delicate step in the operation. Directing one of the women to take her place and hold the victim's head, Toshabe gradually released the crude tourniquet that she had applied above the cut. The pressure was released very gradually, a half-turn of the tourniquet at a time.

Martha Washington was concerned when she saw the cloths turning pink and realized that the victim was again bleeding.

But Toshabe seemed unconcerned. "It always happens," she said, "that a little blood flows when the pressure of the tie is removed. But there will not be heavy bleeding, of that much I am certain."

Eventually, to Mrs. Washington's amazement, the tourniquet was completely removed. When the cloths had lost some of their liquid, they were removed, one by one, and replaced with other cloths taken from the pot, which continued to boil. The used cloths were thrown into the pot and again became saturated.

This process was repeated for an hour. The cloths no longer turned pink. The worst appeared to be past.

Toshabe directed the field hands to make a crude pallet and carefully transfer the man to it. Then she said, "Take him to his house and place him with great care in his bed. Make sure that wet poultices cover every inch of his wound. Soon he will awaken and will ask for food. Give him as much nourishing broth as he wants, but do not allow him to eat solid food until tomorrow."

"What is left for the doctor to do?" Mrs. Washington inquired.

Again Toshabe appeared indifferent. "There's no need now for the services of a physician," she said.

"The wound has started to heal, and in a few days' time the man will be well enough to dress and walk about. The crisis is at an end."

Like her children, Ghonkaba's wife was a remarkable human being, Martha Washington reflected.

The scouts' bivouac area was in dense woods, but only a short distance from the white, shingled house occupied by the commander in chief. There the four frontiersmen, conscious that they were older than their comrades-in-arms, lounged around their own campfire, drinking huge mugs of hot coffee. All four held the rank of sergeant major, the highest attainable by an enlisted man. For that reason, at least, the rest of the company did not fraternize with them.

Sergeant Muller was telling one of his interminable stories in a soft monotone, his accent occasionally betraying his German ancestry. Wiry Sergeant Ginsberg and lanky Sergeant MacDavid did him the honor of listening to his tale, not only out of deference to his feelings, but also because of his enormous bulk and easily aroused temper. Only Sergeant Ryan escaped, because he had drifted off into a sound sleep, and his snores accented Muller's story.

They heard quiet footsteps approaching, and Ginsberg and MacDavid exchanged a quick glance of appreciation. Apparently they were to be spared the longest part of Muller's story.

Ghonkaba entered the clearing and waved casually.

They returned his wave, but did not stand. Though he was their commanding officer, they showed him no more respect than they did anyone else.

"I don't suppose," Ghonkaba said, "that you lads did me the favor of saving some supper for me."

Muller pretended surprise. "What? Do you mean to tell us you went to a meeting at General Washington's house and he didn't offer you anything to eat?"

"You know blamed well that we were there for a headquarters conference, not for a meal," Ghonkaba replied dryly. "Fortunately, I fortified myself by stopping off at Henry Knox's headquarters for enough food to keep body and soul together."

Sergeant Ryan stopped snoring and opened one eye. "Have some coffee, Ghonkaba," he muttered.

"That's a first-rate idea," Ghonkaba replied, and was surprised to realize that the other frontiersmen were not responding to the suggestion. He looked questioningly at each of them.

Ginsberg seemed to be unhappy as he reached for the coffee pot, which sat on a hot stone.

MacDavid picked up an empty tin cup behind him, rinsed it in the running water of a brook that flowed directly behind where he was sitting, and then held the cup out for his companion to fill.

Muller sighed dolefully, then glared at Ryan. "Trust an Irishman," he said, "to have a mouth big enough to swallow us all."

Ghonkaba suspected the reason for their unusual reaction, and confirmed it with his first sip of coffee. "Damnation, boys!" he said. "I know you like to make your own rules and insist on breaking everyone else's. But I wish you'd remember that you're in the army and that certain rules must not be disobeyed. You know that you had no right to empty a bottle of rum into your coffee!"

"It tastes a heap better with a little rum in it," MacDavid said mildly.

Ryan was wide awake now. "This here," he said plaintively as he fought for dignity, "ain't no ordinary rum. It's the very best that the British government buys for its sailors and distributes every day at sea to the poor devils who wear the uniform of His Majesty's Navy."

"Where did you get it?" Ghonkaba demanded.

Ginsberg sighed. "It's no use, boys. We can't keep a secret from our old friend."

"I reckon we can't," MacDavid agreed.

Muller's high-pitched giggle was surprising from one with such a thick chest. "We got plenty more where this came from, Ghonkaba," he said. "In fact, we got us a whole barrel behind our tent."

Ghonkaba raised an eyebrow and waited. Long experience had taught him that patience was necessary with the quartet.

Ginsberg cleared his throat. "Sergeant Ryan is blessed—some would say cursed—with the gift of gab. I think he can explain better than anyone else can."

Ryan threw him an aggrieved look, but spoke up. "Whether you like it or not, Ghonkaba," he said, "you're gettin' involved with us in an enterprise that may be over your head. But that can't be helped. It began this afternoon when we were out doing some snoopin' across the river. We ran across a British arms depot in a clearing in the forest, where it occupied a whole log cabin built for holding arms and ammunition.

"And," Ryan added, "we was lucky enough to get our hands on some supply wagons this afternoon, too. Now we have the means to transport the munitions as far as the river's edge."

Ghonkaba looked at him in astonishment. The Continental Army was sorely lacking in both arms and munitions, and the discovery could prove to be worth its weight in solid gold.

"A little garrison was in charge of guarding the cache," Muller added, "and they acted like they resented our nosin' around."

"So we had to take care of them right then and there," Ginsberg said, picking up the recital.

"It was a quick, quiet little scramble," MacDavid said, his tone indicating his satisfaction, "but we had no trouble, and those redcoats won't be resenting anything ever again."

"Ever since we got back here to our side of the Delaware," Ryan said, picking up the narrative, "we been wonderin' how we're going to bring those munitions over here, where General Washington has use for them. We finally got it figured out, so we thought we'd celebrate with some coffee to keep us awake, because we aim to do the deed tonight."

"Tonight?" Ghonkaba asked. "What do you have in mind?"

The frontiersmen grinned at each other, and then Ryan said, "You know how it is, Ghonkaba. Army regulations say 'do this' and 'you can't do that.' "

"The way we figure it," Muller added firmly, "General Washington has need of those rifles and bullets and powder. You might say the Continental Army is sufferin' from a lack of such like. So if we just show up and make the army a present, nobody's going to ask us no embarrassing questions."

"That's right," Ginsberg said. "They'll be so glad we provided 'em with the arms that they'll accept them—no questions asked."

"There was a time," MacDavid said, "when you were like us, Ghonkaba, when you were on equal terms with us. Well, for this purpose, you're no commanding officer; you're on equal terms again. Either you're in all the way with us, or you bow out right this minute, and that'll be the end of the matter. We'll give you the munitions when we get back."

Ghonkaba stared at each of the quartet. "No way on earth are you going to exclude me," he said. "You count me in—right now!" He emphasized his words by taking a large swallow of the rum-flavored coffee.

The quartet accepted his decision calmly, as though they had been confident he would join them.

Two of the Seneca warriors were standing sentry

duty that night, and Muller went to them, explaining that all four sergeants were accompanying the captain on a secret expedition. When they came back later that night, they were to be readmitted without delay through the lines.

Then, after smearing dirt on their faces, hands, and bare forearms in order to reduce their visibility, the raiders started out. Each carried only a large hunting knife.

Hidden in the rushes at the water's edge was a canoe. Ghonkaba recognized it as the handiwork of the Erie, a tribe traditionally an enemy of the Seneca and now an ally of Great Britain.

Muller and MacDavid, long experienced in handling canoes, sat fore and aft, and with the others as passengers, they made their way across the river to the shore of New Jersey. There they again concealed the craft in rushes and went ashore.

Offering no explanation to Ghonkaba, they headed inland. They paused when they came to a towering oak tree, and uncovering a mound of branches, they revealed a pile of redcoat uniforms, into which they quickly changed. Instead of four frontiersmen, they now reasonably resembled four British infantrymen. Three of them were privates, and one, MacDavid, was a corporal.

Ginsberg pushed his helmet of burnished brass onto the back of his head. "I reckon we need to get a uniform for Ghonkaba," he said. "He looks kind of strange without one."

The others grunted agreement.

They started off through the forest in single file, with Ghonkaba bringing up the rear. They told him nothing about their destination, but he knew they were headed in the direction of Trenton, with its major British garrison. Treading softly, they made their way through the wilderness for a quarter of an hour and then slowed their pace and listened carefully.

After a time they halted, hearing sounds suggesting that they were near the meeting place of two British sentries, who were pacing up and down.

They had no need to explain the next move to Ghonkaba, who had engaged in identical maneuvers on countless occasions. Acting as a decoy, Ryan openly approached the spot where the two sentries met. In the meantime, the other three scouts concealed themselves in the underbrush and approached the same place from various angles, keeping themselves concealed.

The silence of the wilderness was broken by the clear voice of a sentry. "Halt! Who goes there?"

Silence prevailed again for a few moments, followed by the thuds and grunts of a fight in progress. Ghonkaba, standing very still, knew precisely what was taking place. The sentries were being immobilized, and the uniform of one was being removed.

Two gasps were followed by unpleasant gurgling noises as the throats of the sentinels were cut.

Sergeant Ginsberg returned carrying a redcoat uniform. He handed it to Ghonkaba. "This is for you. We took care to get one that would fit you tolerably well."

Ghonkaba changed quickly, placing his own buckskin shirt, trousers, and moccasins in the knapsack on his back. In addition to his knife, he now carried a British rifle, complete with bayonet. With the extra ammunition and powder in pouches on his belt, he felt better able to cope with whatever might develop.

Ryan took the lead, and the party, now heading north and east away from Trenton, plunged deeper into New Jersey, increasing the distance between them and the river.

Ghonkaba was content to follow Ryan through the forest. All four of his companions were very much at home in the woods.

After trudging for more than an hour, they came to

a large clearing, which they circled cautiously before they entered it. Ghonkaba noticed a substantial building of logs, the chinks between the logs filled with clay. Beyond the building stood three sturdy, oversized wagons, and in a little corral, half a dozen dray horses were nibbling grass.

The area had remained undisturbed since the frontiersmen had visited it that afternoon. They and Ghonkaba went to work with a vengeance, transferring muskets, bags of gunpowder, and long bars of lead, which soldiers could use to make their bullets.

As they labored, Ghonkaba reflected that nothing would be more valuable to Washington. The Continental Army's need for modern arms and adequate munitions was desperate. A trickle of supplies came in from time to time, as the French provided the Americans with arms, but this aid was surreptitious, and the need of Washington's men far exceeded available supplies.

After an hour, the contents of the log building had been moved to the wagons.

Sergeant Ryan continued to act as the spokesman. "So far," he said, "we're makin' out just fine. But now our real troubles begin. We got to take the weapons down to the shore of the river, past a half-dozen British sentry outposts, and then find some way to get these wagons across the water. There's no way they'd float, and the gunpowder will be ruined if it gets wet."

Without asking for Ghonkaba's help, the frontiersmen looked to him for direction.

"What we need," Ghonkaba told them, "is a very large barge of the sort the British use to move heavy artillery across water. We've caught glimpses of several in the vicinity of Trenton, you'll recall. Only with a barge of that size can we be sure of moving all three wagons at once."

"I reckon," Muller said, a hard edge to his voice, "that we'll have to take one of those barges by force."

Ghonkaba promptly corrected him. "Only if all other ways should fail," he said. 'This is going to be a very difficult and delicate operation.

"It's far too dangerous for us to stop to fight when we're trying to get away with tons of arms and munitions," he went on. "Can you imagine the explosion if all those hundreds of bags of gunpowder ignited at the same time? They and everything within a wide area would be blown sky high."

"Can we rely on guile alone to get away with this quantity of arms and ammunition?" Sergeant MacDavid wondered, gnawing his lower lip.

"It's useless, I believe," Ghonkaba said, "to lay out a plan in advance. We'll have to be prepared for any eventuality. All that we've ever done as scouts has been in preparation for this one night. Be prepared to do anything that's required on a moment's notice, and I know you won't shirk your responsibilities. With luck, and if the manitous of my gods approve, we'll succeed. If we fail, the very worst that can happen will be that we'll lose our lives."

Tarpaulins of heavy burlap covered the big wagons, whose contents were securely tied down. Ghonkaba and MacDavid rode together on the buckboard of the lead wagon, Muller was alone in the second wagon, and bringing up the rear were Ginsberg and Ryan. All carried muskets loaded and primed, ready for instant use.

MacDavid started his team of horses in the direction of the river. "If I've chosen the right road," he said, "we should come out at the river, just north of Trenton. Too many redcoats are stationed in the town for it to be a healthy place for us. We'd be sure to be unmasked. I hope we'll come out on the riverfront, somewhere near the station where those barges are. That's all I can aim for at the moment."

"Of course," Ghonkaba said. "We have nothing precise to go on, and we'll use your best estimates."

They started off at a fair pace, and were able to maintain it for almost an hour. They made an abrupt halt when they saw several sentries on the road directly ahead.

"Halt and identify yourselves!" the sergeant of the guard called, and his men blocked the road, pointing their loaded muskets at the men on the wagons.

"Regimental Supply Company, 27th Infantry," Ghonkaba replied, giving a creditable imitation of a lower-class English accent. "We're carrying a supply of codfish up to brigade headquarters."

"Codfish, is it?" The sergeant roared with laughter. "I'm thankful you're not bringing foodstuffs to my regiment." He laughed again, and was joined not only by his subordinates, but by the raiders, who laughed with equal heartiness as the barrier was removed and they drove on.

"How did you know the 27th Infantry Regiment is stationed here?" MacDavid asked in an undertone. "You were taking a mighty big risk."

"Not at all," Ghonkaba replied, and pointed to the insignia on his tunic. "The poor devil on sentry duty was a member of the 27th."

They drove on at a reduced speed, realizing the need for caution. Occasionally they saw small groups of soldiers walking at the side of the road. At one point, a half-battalion of infantry marching down the road in the opposite direction crowded off to one side to make room for the wagons. Ghonkaba pulled his brass helmet lower, and averted his face so that the enemy could not catch sight of his Indian features. He and MacDavid breathed more easily when they had passed the entire unit. The deception again was successful.

"We should be getting close to the river right

about now," MacDavid muttered. "Keep your eyes peeled for a glimpse of the water."

Suddenly a subaltern, a third lieutenant of infantry, stepped into the road from the underbrush beside it and waved the wagons to a stop. "Identify yourselves," he called. "This is restricted territory."

Ghonkaba repeated the claim that they were a supply unit of the 27th Infantry Regiment.

The lieutenant remained unconvinced. "Show me your identification," he directed, "and your orders granting you the right to approach the waterfront."

MacDavid slowly unbuttoned a tunic pocket and began to fumble inside for nonexistent identification and orders.

In the meantime, Ryan slipped from the seat of the third wagon and, circling to the rear, approached the head of the column. He crept toward the officer, his arm raised, ready to strike.

"Be quick about, will you?" the young officer demanded. "I don't have all night."

Aware of Ryan's approach, Ghonkaba stalled for time. "If you'll just be patient for a few moments, sir," he said, "we have the blasted orders somewhere."

The subaltern peered at him suspiciously and opened his mouth to reply. Before he could speak, Ryan struck and expertly broke his neck. Then he caught hold of the young officer's body as it crumpled.

"Quick," Ghonkaba said, "take his uniform. You're about his height and build. It will be useful to have an officer with us."

MacDavid jumped to the ground, and he and Ryan started the grisly task of stripping the uniform from the dead lieutenant. A few moments later Ryan was dressed in it, and Ghonkaba directed him to change places with MacDavid after concealing the officer's body in the underbrush. Then, with Ryan joining Ghonkaba in the lead wagon, they resumed their drive.

At last Ghonkaba broke the tense silence. "Aha!" he said. "There's the river—no more than fifty yards to our right."

"Do you see the path beside it?" Ryan asked.

Ghonkaba stood, saw a narrower road parallel to the river, and motioned to the other two wagons to follow.

The three wagons transferred to the river road and continued to move forward. In the lead wagon, Ghonkaba took the reins from Ryan, as it would not have been proper for a commissioned officer to be driving a cart with an enlisted man beside him.

Ryan stood and peered ahead. "We appear to be in luck. Maybe. At least two of the oversized barges are tied up at a dock, but the area is swarming with redcoats, and we're going to have to neutralize them."

"We'll move one step at a time," Ghonkaba told him, and signaled to their mates in the other wagons to be especially alert.

As they drew closer to the barges, they saw a squad of British infantry on sentry duty at the waterfront. A sergeant was in command, and fifteen men were stationed to guard the craft.

"Be ready to push through onto the barge," Ghonkaba muttered as the wagons slowed to a halt.

The sergeant approached, and as he did, Ghonkaba slipped down to the ground. Ginsberg, who was riding on the rear wagon, did the same. Together they circled around the wagons to the rear.

The sergeant came to the lead wagon and saluted. "Sir," he said respectfully, "I'm afraid you've lost your way and come to the wrong place. This area is restricted, and no one and no wagons are permitted here."

Ryan began to stall for time. "Are you quite sure of that?" he asked. "I was distinctly given orders to bring my wagons to the dock here."

Ghonkaba and Ginsberg came even with the lead

wagon. Grinning wryly, Ginsberg reached beneath his tunic and produced a small tomahawk, which he handed to the Seneca.

Ghonkaba tested the balance of the weapon and found it to his liking. Then he stared intently at his target, the back of the sergeant's neck. He knew he would have to hit the man between the bottom of his helmet and the top of his fore-and-aft breastplate. At best, he had to strike within a range of no more than six inches.

He took aim with great care, realizing that the success or failure of the entire enterprise depended on the next few seconds. Then he let fly.

The tomahawk soared through the air and hit its mark cleanly, its sharp blade burying itself deep in the neck of the sergeant, who pitched forward onto the ground and lay very still.

"Now," Ghonkaba said tersely. "Go!" Even as he gave the order, he leaped forward, bending low to make himself as small a target as possible. Retrieving the tomahawk, he leaped onto the back of Ryan's lead wagon.

All three wagons clattered safely onto the over-sized barge. No need now to give orders: each frontiersman knew exactly what to do. The drivers made their horses and wagons secure, using the barge rail as a makeshift hitching post. Meanwhile, Ginsberg used his knife to hack at ropes holding the barge against the dock.

Ghonkaba realized that they were leaving to him the virtually impossible task of neutralizing the British squad on shore. Lying flat on his stomach, he looked at the astonished redcoats, who were staring in stunned amazement toward the barge, which was beginning to move out into the swirling waters of the Delaware.

Ghonkaba spotted a corporal in the enemy's ranks.

With the sergeant dead, the corporal had become the noncommissioned officer in command.

Fortunately, the corporal was a slow-thinking, methodical man. He lined up his troops in two rows, ordered those in front to kneel, and those in the second row to stand upright. All were aiming their muskets at the barge.

With all his skill and strength, Ghonkaba threw his tomahawk at the corporal. Again his aim was true, and the weapon caught the man full in the face before he could give the order to open fire. The corporal screamed with anguish as he collapsed.

The soldiers were disciplined troops who responded precisely to orders, but now they had no orders to follow. A few fired a ragged volley at the barge, but they were so disconcerted that their aim was wild, by a wide margin. Most of the soldiers waited in confusion for an order to fire, and by the time they had recovered from their shock and astonishment, the barge was disappearing from sight around a broad bend in the river.

Muller's prodigious strength was needed at the tiller to guide the raft and its precious cargo to safety. He hurried aft, seized the tiller in both hands, and succeeded, after a brief but ferocious struggle, in conquering the strong tide and sending the heavily laden craft toward the Pennsylvania shore.

"All to the good so far, boys," Ghonkaba said as he took off his redcoat tunic and removed his helmet.

The others were quick to follow his example. The night was dark, the moon and stars concealed behind a bank of thick, dark clouds, but the frontiersmen wanted to take no unnecessary risks. If their fellow scouts caught a glimpse of a redcoat uniform, the barge would be peppered with heavy fire.

As the ungainly craft was propelled by the strong current closer and closer to the shore, Ghonkaba raised his voice in a perfect imitation of a white owl. He had confidence that because the owl was common in the land of the Seneca and was unknown in the Pennsylvania hills bordering the river, his fellow Seneca among the scouts would recognize his signal and would caution the scouts to hold their fire.

But apparently no one heard his call. A rifle cracked, and then two more sounded. The scouts were opening fire.

The bullets sang out a short distance overhead, and Ghonkaba tried his owl call again, putting his heart and soul into his cry, in an effort to make it as loud as he could.

The shooting stopped abruptly. Moments later, the raft was swept ashore. Ghonkaba's scouts hauled it to higher ground, then swarmed aboard. Their warm greetings gave way to sober astonishment when they realized the extent of their comrades' coup.

A scout raced off to headquarters with the news, and though Washington was asleep, Major General Nathanael Greene, the duty officer, returned with the scout. General Greene inspected the booty. Ordinarily intense and sober, he smiled broadly. "This is one of the more remarkable feats accomplished in this war. If I weren't seeing the muskets and munitions myself, I wouldn't believe such a story."

Gradually the hubbub subsided. General Greene returned to headquarters after promising to inform the commander in chief early in the morning. He ordered a prompt distribution of the booty to regiments sorely in need of it. A strong guard was posted, and the work horses were led away to artillery headquarters, where General Knox would have good use for them.

"I got me quite a little appetite worked up tonight," Muller growled. "I could eat some ears of roasted corn and a slab of that venison steak left over from supper."

He and his companions, accompanied by Ghonkaba, moved to the sergeants' bivouac area. There they built up their cooking fire, put the venison on it to roast, and wrapped ears of corn in dampened husks, preparatory to thrusting them into the coals.

Ginsberg and MacDavid, who had left without explanation, returned carrying tin cups filled to the brim with a potent-smelling liquid. They distributed the cups to their comrades.

"We worked up a powerful thirst tonight," MacDavid said to Ghonkaba, "and the best liquid for curing our dry throats is the rum we brought back after our first foray today."

Ghonkaba raised his cup in salute to his comrades. "Continental Army rules or no rules," he said, "you have a right to get rid of your thirst any way that's convenient to you."

They drank in an atmosphere of contentment and mutual understanding.

In the forests of New York Colony, Tredno jogged evenly, steadily, in the familiar Seneca trot. The men of his patrol were strung out in single file behind him as they traveled from the land of the Seneca to the frontier town of Schenectady, slightly north and west of Albany.

Actually, Schenectady lay within the jurisdiction of the Mohawk, a nation that should have had the right to conduct the first raid against the settlement. But Tredno was as unmindful of such details as of the fact that he was on what supposedly was only a reconnaissance mission. Lacking authority to raid, he was acting on his own, rather than following his instructions from Ja-gonh. His orders were to maintain a neutral position toward Americans.

Tredno was convinced that Ja-gonh's position of a carefully balanced neutrality was sheer nonsense. He disdainfully regarded as only a weak excuse any argument that the issues were complex and that their solution, therefore, was a complicated one to be handled by the leaders of the nation.

In Tredno's opinion, Ja-gonh was a coward and his attempt to save the lives of Seneca warriors was nothing but a flimsy excuse for weakness.

So far, Seneca of all ages, from the nation's elders to the youngest warriors, seemed to agree with the cautious position taken by Ja-gonh and No-da-vo.

All that would change, however, if Tredno could succeed in arousing the tribe's patriotic fervor. His raids on settlements and other acts that showed the nation's warriors at their skilled and daring best were calculated to produce that change.

As for Ghonkaba, when the time was right, Tredno would seek him out and kill him, preferably in battle. Thus, he would conveniently be rid of the heir to the highest office among the Seneca. Popular pressure then would force Ja-gonh and No-da-vo to retire, surrendering their high offices in disgrace, Tredno reasoned. And there would end the dynasty that had ruled so many years, from Ghonka, through Renno, and now Ja-gonh.

Then, the nation naturally would turn to the war chief who had led them to a restoration of their great glory. Tredno felt positive that, by acclaim, he would become sachem of the Seneca and then Great Sachem of the Iroquois League. Having long awaited his chance, he anticipated that at last his time had come. Let Ja-gonh be unhappy and moan like a woman when he learned of Tredno's raid against Schenectady; he would find it impossible to chastise a war chief who had conducted a brilliant raid on behalf of an ally. After maneuvering with care for a long time, Tredno was sure that the manitous were solidly behind him, supporting his efforts.

Before many moons passed, he would wear Ja-gonh's feathered headdress of Great Sachem. By then, Ghonkaba would be moldering in his grave.

Tredno's step was light as he ran, intent on fulfilling his destiny. Unknown to him, at the same moment far to the south, a sharp and completely unexpected chill seized Ghonkaba as he sat comfortably and happily with his comrades. It quickly passed, but he puzzled over its possible cause and meaning. Was it an omen? From what source? Should he seek to find an interpretation of the strange experience? Before he had finished pondering these questions, fatigue overcame him and he fell asleep.

Chapter VI

Martha Washington, accompanied by a number of women and children, including Toshabe and her three youngsters, arrived at the commander in chief's headquarters outside Philadelphia early one afternoon. There they were met by one of General Washington's aides-de-camp, Lieutenant Colonel Alexander Hamilton. He informed her that the commander in chief was absent on an inspection tour but would be back in time for supper.

Colonel Hamilton, handsome and dashing in spite of his short stature, was a man of much talent and even

125

greater charm. A West Indian by birth, he had given up a promising career in order to join the patriot cause. He was married to the daughter of Major General Philip Schuyler, who commanded the New York Militia, and therefore held a prominent place in the society of that colony. He devoted his full attention to Mrs. Washington, until he saw her safely and comfortably settled into the commanding general's house. Then he turned to the other ladies of the party and chose Toshabe to escort to the small dwelling nearby that she and her children would share with Ghonkaba.

Hamilton preened slightly as he strolled beside Toshabe, and she knew instinctively that he fancied himself as a ladies' man.

"I'm afraid there's very little at headquarters to keep you and your children occupied, ma'am," he said. "The children will be free to visit units in training and to observe drills and target practice, but aside from rolling bandages for the physicians, there's very little planned for you ladies."

"That's perfectly all right," Toshabe replied. "I haven't come here to be entertained."

"Oh?" Colonel Hamilton displayed polite interest. "My own wife is free to join me here if she wishes, but she finds life in the field too rugged and prefers the comforts of home with her parents at Albany."

Toshabe saw no reason to mention that she had known General Schuyler when he paid a visit to the Seneca. "It isn't possible for my children and me to stay with my husband's family," she said. "His father is Great Sachem of the Iroquois, and as such, he's an ally of Great Britain."

Hamilton studied her closely as he unlocked the door of the little house and stood aside to let her enter. Then, moving to the light that came in through a window, he gently caught hold of her chin and held up her face for a few moments before saying, "Surely you're not a native Seneca. You're far too pretty for that."

He apparently meant the remark as a compliment, and that was the spirit in which Toshabe accepted it. "I was born an Erie," she explained briefly.

"Ah! That explains it, then. I could have sworn," Hamilton added, "that you were at least partly of French extraction."

"That's very clever of you, sir," she replied. "My father was of French descent, as it happens. I learned to apply cosmetics in the French manner when I was in Quebec City some years ago, and I've been using that technique ever since."

"Whatever it is," Hamilton assured her, "it's most attractive. You far outshine every other lady in the camp."

"That's very kind of you, Colonel." Toshabe felt uncomfortable under his steady, unblinking scrutiny. "I'm wondering if my children followed us here, as I instructed them to do?"

Alexander Hamilton hurried to the front door, opened it, and saw Ena and the two boys approaching up the winding gravel path.

"Lads," Hamilton told them, "the artillery is practicing quick-loading their guns under the direction of General Knox at the riverside this afternoon, and you're welcome to watch them. As for you, young lady, the knitting circle is meeting this afternoon to make socks for the troops."

"I'd much prefer to watch the artillery practice," Ena declared.

"Then go to the riverfront, by all means," Toshabe told her. "Keep an eye on your brothers and stay out of mischief yourself. I'll expect all of you back before dark."

The youngsters scampered off.

Toshabe turned away into the house and began to inspect the place, room by room.

Because only the essentials of furniture were on hand, the house had a barren look, but Toshabe could not complain. She would be sharing quarters with her husband for the first time since they had left home so many months earlier, and she was grateful for the opportunity to be reunited with him.

She mounted a flight of steep stairs to the second floor landing, aware that Hamilton was close behind.

Through the window of one of the bedchambers, Toshabe had a surprisingly good view of the broad Delaware River as it swept southward.

Suddenly she froze, aware that Hamilton had slipped an adroit hand around her slender waist. She had no desire to alienate an aide-de-camp of General Washington by creating a scene and thus making an enemy of Alexander Hamilton. At the same time, however, she could not encourage him, because he was a womanizer who would go as far as she permitted him.

She made no move and stood very still, her lifelong Indian training coming to her help and making it possible for her to remain immobile.

Hamilton's grasp tightened imperceptibly, and his lips were close to her ear. "You're very lovely, Toshabe," he murmured, "and I know you would be capable of giving great pleasure to one you loved." Some response was necessary, and she tried to reply in a noncommittal way. Extricating herself gracefully from his grasp, she offered him a broad, warm smile. "Thank you, Colonel," she murmured.

Hamilton was too much the gentleman to push too hard or to make a scene. The Indian woman was proving her cleverness by simultaneously cutting him off and encouraging him. He could renew his campaign at some future time; for now he beat a graceful retreat.

Toshabe saw him to the door, where he held her

hand far longer than necessary as he bent over it to kiss it in farewell. The look in his eyes told her all too clearly that she had not seen the last of him. Then, to her relief, he was gone.

The unexpected incident left Toshabe badly shaken. She knew that she and Ghonkaba were living on the charity of General and Mrs. Washington. Even if her husband were paid his wages as a captain in the Continental Army—and he had not received a penny in several months—they could not afford to rent a house for themselves and their children.

It was her misfortune to have attracted the attention of an officer who not only outranked her husband but was close to the commander in chief.

Toshabe realized the easiest course would be to follow the line of least resistance and engage in a discreet affair. She knew Hamilton would take great pains to keep their relationship secret and to protect her so that no one would learn of it. But such a prospect horrified her. She loved Ghonkaba, and for many years had cared for no one else. She was certain of one thing: she never could tolerate the touch of any man other than her husband.

The special committee calling on General Washington was headed by John Hancock, the president of the Continental Congress and the highest-ranking national official. Intense, patriotic, and dignified, he was one of the wealthiest men among those seeking America's independence.

Accompanying him was Sam Adams, the Massachusetts firebrand and master propagandist who had whipped the people into a frenzy until they clamored for independence. Still a rebel, he had ruled out compromise of any kind with the Crown and was determined to pursue independence with the singleminded fervor of one who was wholeheartedly devoted to its cause.

Accompanying this seasoned pair was Washington's fellow Virginian, young, redheaded Thomas Jefferson, author of the Declaration of Independence. A scholar and inventor, as well as a philosopher and gentleman farmer, Jefferson was displaying a surprising skill for politics.

Mrs. Washington, aided by Toshabe, served the visitors with green tea imported from Holland and biscuits artfully toasted to conceal their staleness. Then the women withdrew and left General Washington alone with the committee.

John Hancock cleared his throat, sipped his tea, and exchanged quick glances with his colleagues. "I gather you aren't particularly surprised by our request to have this meeting with you, General," he said with spurious easiness.

Washington's smile was natural. "I'm always glad to see representatives of the Continental Congress, gentlemen," he replied. "I never allow myself to forget that I received my appointment from the Congress, and consequently, I'm your servant."

Everyone present knew he was guilty of a gracious exaggeration. The citizens of every state looked up to Washington as the leader of an independent armed force, conveniently forgetting that he owed his position to the bickering Continental Congress.

"We've been meeting in secret for the past week and more," Hancock said, "behind locked doors, and so far, at least, no news on our deliberations has leaked out. We thought it only fair to tell you the results of our meetings."

"Meeting in secret sessions, is it?" Washington asked pleasantly. "That sounds forbidding."

"It's worse than that," Sam Adams blurted. "It's damn near catastrophic."

Young Jefferson's gloomy look confirmed the analysis.

"The funds of the Congress are virtually exhausted,"

Hancock said. "I've given to the best of my ability, and so have several others, but we just can't raise enough money. The states are so jealous of their rights they won't grant us the privilege of taxing the public. And they refuse to raise money themselves, because they fear throwing good money after bad."

"The treasury is severely in arrears," Jefferson added. "The money issued to the Continental Army isn't worth the paper it's printed on. Any government needs solid, popular support to survive and flourish, and so far that support is lacking. The Continental Congress could disband tomorrow, and I honestly believe that no one would give a damn."

"We realize, General, that your need for troops is urgent. I believe you have only ten thousand men at arms under your command at present—"

"Pardon me, Mr. Adams," Washington interrupted politely, "but the number has fallen far below ten thousand. Some enlistments have expired, and those men have simply gone home. Others have deserted. It's only fair to estimate that the Continental Army numbers no more than seven thousand effective troops. That figure is highly confidential, of course. If Howe knew it, he would attack immediately with full strength. We'd cease to exist as a cohesive fighting force."

"It's even worse than we thought, then," Hancock said morosely. "I need scarcely tell you, General, that the morale of the people has reached a low point. The Battle of Long Island, followed by the occupation of New York by the British, was a terrible blow, and your retreat through New Jersey didn't help."

"We're not in any way holding you to blame," Sam Adams added hastily. "On the contrary, the few men in the Congress who know something about military affairs insist that your withdrawal has been masterly, and you deserve great credit for keeping your army intact."

"Thank you," Washington murmured dryly.

Jefferson laced and unlaced his long fingers. "We've had altogether too much casting of blame onto one or another of our leaders," he said. "It's a useless pastime. The facts of our situation unfortunately speak for themselves."

"That's correct," Hancock said briskly, and began to enumerate points on his manicured fingers. "The spirits of the American people have reached an all-time low. Not only are they failing to contribute money, food, and other essentials to the cause, but recruiting for the Continental Army has come to a virtual standstill."

"Something must be done to turn the tide!" Sam Adams thundered. "Either that, or the cause of the American patriots is lost!"

General Washington tried successfully to hide his exasperation. "What do you suggest, gentlemen?"

They looked at each other uncertainly, and Jefferson, by far the most diplomatic member of the trio, replied. "It's very difficult, General. You lack adequate manpower. You have insufficient supplies of arms and munitions. Even your artillery is in short supply. Your transportation corps has been in a shambles for months. And yet we have the audacity to ask you to perform a miracle."

"Have you read Tom Paine's pamphlet?" Adams asked. "He wrote, 'These are the times that try men's souls.' He put it very aptly. We've come to you, General Washington, because we, in our desperation, have nowhere else to turn. We're asking you and your seven or eight thousand troops to accomplish something sufficiently miraculous to arouse the country from its lethargy and to produce a new spirit, a new willingness to fight toward victory."

"If we're asking too much," Hancock said, "it's best by far to find it out now, rather than fool ourselves and have the world collapse around us later. If you say the word, General, we'll make our peace as best we're able with the British right now and obtain the best terms from them that we can arrange. But I don't hold out much hope for independence or even a measure of freedom. King George is vindictive, and we can be certain that he'll exact the last ounce of retribution from us."

"You want me to accept responsibility for our capitulation to the redcoats? Well, I can't, and won't, do it, gentlemen," Washington said. "I didn't become the commander in chief of the Continental Army to supervise the disintegration of a freedom-loving people into a cowed rabble. You've asked me to accomplish the impossible for all of our sakes. I don't know that I can do it. I can only promise you that I'll try my best."

Generals Greene, Knox, Sullivan, and Putnam, summoned to meet with the commander in chief, arrived to find strict security precautions in effect. Armed guards surrounded the house and lined the hallways leading to the parlor. General Washington closed the door and then explained the situation created by the visit of the delegation from the Continental Congress.

Israel Putnam laughed wryly. "I think the Congress has need of a magician, not a collection of generals," he said.

"I don't need any of you to tell me why this mission can't be accomplished," Washington told them. "I've already discussed that with the committee from the Congress. What I want from you is information that can lead toward a successful and significant mission. Please inform me as soon as you can as to the amount of effective manpower you can put into the field immediately and how you're situated for arms and ammunition. And in your case," he added to Knox, "I want to know the state of your guns and how you can move them with relative ease."

"Do you have a plan of action in mind?" General Sullivan asked.

"Not yet. It will depend in part on what you report to me. Beyond that, I'm going to rely on our scouts to learn where the British are most vulnerable." He stood, went to the door, opened it, and called, "Colonel Hamilton! Please bring Ghonkaba of the scouts' company here as soon as possible."

When Ghonkaba arrived a short time later, he found the army's top-ranking generals gathered.

Gracious as always, Washington put him at ease. "Ghonkaba," he said, "I have a special mission for your entire company that takes precedence over anything else. I want them to study every position held by the enemy within a day's march of us in New Jersey. They're to pay particular heed to the vulnerability of redcoat garrisons. I want reports in full detail on the exact location, strength, and available support troops of every enemy garrision."

Ghonkaba refrained from asking the questions that flooded his mind. "Yes, sir," was all he replied.

"Make haste carefully," Washington said with a smile. "If you send your men out into the field tonight, give them twenty-four hours to accumulate the data, and then you can spend the remainder of tomorrow night putting the information together. I'll expect a full report at breakfast the day after tomorrow."

Ghonkaba was surprised by the urgency of the mission, but again only one reply was allowed. "Yes, sir," he said, and was dismissed.

His mind seething as he hurried to join his scouts, he realized the men assigned to the farthest reaches on the Delaware River must leave at once, rather than wait for nightfall. Washington had made no mention of his reason for wanting the information he sought. Ghonkaba realized that if the mission was to be concluded in the greatest of secrecy, it was all to the good that he knew nothing that he could inadvertently pass along to his subordinates. He would delay his own departure until early evening.

Ena didn't care whether she slept on a bed of young evergreen boughs or corn husks covered with a blanket, or on a featherbed. Her sleep was sound and untroubled, regardless of where she rested. This night, she was determined to retire early.

Clad in a nightgown similar to that worn by Americans, she burrowed beneath the covers of her four-poster bed and soon was fast asleep. She dreamed that she was in a clearing in the forest, wearing Indian attire. She heard approaching footsteps, and looking intently, she saw a man coming toward her. Strangely, he was semitransparent at first, and she could see the bare branches and trunks of the trees behind him. Gradually his body became increasingly opaque, and at last he was whole.

He wore the war paint of a Seneca, and on his head was a feathered headdress of a chieftain similar to that worn by her grandfather, Ja-gonh.

It dawned on her that the man had pale hair, much paler than that of the elder of her brothers, and his skin was white, but heavily tanned. His most arresting feature was the color of his eyes, a piercing light blue. He seemed to be looking right through her, into her innermost being.

"Good evening, girl-child," he said, speaking in the tongue of the Seneca. "Do you know who I am?"

With a sudden shock of recognition, she realized that she knew him, even though she had never seen him. She bowed her head to him. "You are the great Renno, my great-grandfather," she murmured.

"That is correct," he replied. "Raise your head and look at me, child. You bear the name of my mother, and you are of my own blood, my direct descendant. So I shall do my utmost to protect and guide you in this world, and when you grow old and ultimately join us in the land-across-the-great-river."

Ena had to use her whole willpower to raise her eyes to his, and she was comforted to find that he was smiling at her. His smile was benign, and his eyes were soft and kind. She knew, however, that when circumstances warranted it, he could have a terrible wrath and that his anger could shake the entire Seneca nation.

"My father, Ghonka, and I have observed you for many months," he said.

Ena's blood ran cold.

"We have watched with great interest as you have learned the ways of the forest. Never have we encountered a female of the Seneca nation who has learned the art of tracking and avoiding being tracked. Never have we encountered a scout among the women of the Seneca."

Ena was abashed. "I meant no harm, O Renno," she murmured. "If I have erred and I have caused you distress, I beg your pardon."

To her surprise, he chuckled. "Have I said that we disapprove of what you have done? We do not! We are very proud that we have a female descendant eager to carry on the traditions of our family and of our nation."

Her relief was great. "I thank you for feeling as you do," she said. "I have worried for a long time that I've been doing the wrong thing and that my father would be angry if he knew."

"Your father will withhold his approval," Renno told her, "until you prove to him that you are competent to act as a real scout, in a real war situation."

Her eyes widened, but she did not dare to speak again.

"My father and I," Renno went on, "have confidence in your spirit and abiding faith in your talents. Now the time has come to prove your real worth."

"You—you have a mission for me?" she asked, as her voice quavered.

"I have no mission for you, nor does Ghonka. It was your own will that was responsible for your learning the tricks of the wilderness that ordinarily are learned only by the braves of our nation. The manitous allowed you to learn them because they were pleased by your spirit and your willingness to endure discomfort for the sake of knowledge. Now, for the sake of those to whom you owe fealty, the time is at hand for you to use that knowledge. You cannot long keep your father in the dark regarding your activities. The time has come for him to learn of them. Provided you remember well the lessons that you have learned in the wilderness, Ghonkaba will not be displeased, but will be very proud."

Ena was still deeply concerned. "Do you think I am qualified to put into practice what I have learned?"

Renno replied soothingly. "If I were not convinced of your skills, I would not have come to you in this way, and would not suggest that you risk losing your life in combat with the British."

"Then you approve that we have joined forces with the American patriots?"

"I approve, as does Ghonka, because it is right for Ghonkaba and right for you to do what you are doing, just as it would be wrong for Ja-gonh and No-da-vo to abandon the British."

Ena grasped the point of what he was saying. "What is it that the great Renno wishes his descendant to do?" she inquired humbly.

"Ghonkaba is about to embark this very night on a difficult and perilous mission," Renno told her now. "Rise up and follow him."

"Am I to accompany him and act as a scout?" she asked, feeling bewildered again. "Am I, then, to employ my wilderness skills on behalf of the Continental Army?"

"Rise up and follow Ghonkaba!" Renno repeated. "Follow him to his destination, and he will direct you in what you are to do."

To her consternation, his figure grew dimmer. "Wait!" she cried. "There's still so much that I need to know!"

His figure continued to grow fainter, and soon she found herself alone in the clearing.

Ena awoke with a jolt. She was completely alone in the four-poster featherbed in her room on the second floor of the farmhouse outside Philadelphia. But the dream had been so vivid, so real, that she was drenched in perspiration.

Her confusion was swept away. She remembered everything she had dreamed, and she believed implicitly in the validity of that dream. Leaping out of bed, she dressed quickly in a buckskin shirt and trousers. Then she donned her moccasins to be used for wilderness tracking, tied her hair in a knot atop her head, and cautiously left the house. Her brothers were asleep in their room, and no sound came from her parents' bedroom, where her mother, too, was asleep. She was not surprised to see that her father was not present.

The night was bitterly cold and very dark, the moon and stars being concealed by a thick blanket of impenetrable clouds. Nevertheless she stayed in the shadows of buildings as she made her way quickly to the bivouac area of her father's company of scouts.

When she drew near the site, she peered through the screen of evergreens and saw that only a few members of the company were on hand. Her father's frequent companions, the four sergeants, were absent, as were almost all of the Seneca warriors.

Ghonkaba was one of the few who remained in the area. As his daughter watched, he shook hands with three of his comrades and then slipped away.

With Renno's repeated instructions ringing in her

ears, she followed him, keeping at a safe distance because she knew his hearing was extraordinary. It would be most unfortunate if he heard her behind him.

When he reached the shore, she saw him making his way toward three canoes afloat and tied to posts driven into the bank beneath the water.

Scarcely daring to breathe, Ena watched as he untied one of the canoes, stepped into it, picked up a paddle, and began to maneuver out into the swift-flowing river. As he inched his way across to the Jersey shore, Ena recalled anew the instructions of her great-grandfather. She must follow at all costs.

She reached the waterfront, making no sound in spite of her haste. Untying another canoe, she climbed into it, picked up the paddle, and moved quickly into the stream. As soon as the current struck the craft, she had to fight to keep it on course and was forced to use all her strength to keep her father within sight. She knew he was heading toward enemy territory, and wave after wave of apprehension engulfed her. Suffused with fears for her own safety and that of her father, she nevertheless took comfort in the thought that she was doing as her great-grandfather had bidden. She realized that he had mentioned the extraordinary risks and had made her no promise that she would be safe. But it was too late now to think of possible consequences. She knew only that she had to finish what she had started, and she used her paddle with grim determination, battling the current with all her might as she tried valiantly to keep her father in sight.

Chapter VII

As he neared the New Jersey shore, Ghonkaba was concentrating his attention on searching for signs of the enemy. His eyes penetrated the darkness, and he searched the smudged terrain ahead. No redcoats were visible. Because the British military did not take advantage of the terrain, their sentries stood out in bold relief.

The few scouts who had been left behind to carry out their routine duties were under the command of Ranoga, whose loyalty and dependability always could be counted on. He was deeply disappointed not to be

140

included in Ghonkaba's mission, but as a Seneca warrior he was more than adequately disciplined to carry out his assigned duties, whatever they might be, without complaint. Ghonkaba valued him for all his many fine qualities.

Approaching the shore, Ghonkaba sensed—rather than saw—that something or someone was behind him, and he looked over his shoulder and let his eyes sweep across the water. Because the night was very dark, the need to watch where he was going was paramount. Seeing nothing behind him, he dismissed the thought as only his imagination and instead concentrated on what lay ahead.

The canoe swept up onto the deserted shore, and he leaped onto the ground, dragged the craft after him, and deposited it in some thick, high bulrushes, where it would be available to him on his return. Now he was very much aware of the sound of another canoe being paddled, and he crouched low behind a thick young spruce tree as he saw the other craft land and watched the occupant drag it ashore with some difficulty, conceal it well in the rushes, and then start after him.

Ghonkaba drew his knife and waited patiently. Suddenly he threw himself forward, knife poised, and bore his pursuer to the ground.

The most astonishing of shocks awaited him, and he stared in disbelief at the slender figure he had pinned to the earth. "Ena!" he whispered. "In the names of all the manitous, is it really you, Ena?"

Afraid that she would disgrace herself by weeping, Ena could only nod.

A wave of cold anger washed over Ghonkaba. He was engaged on a mission of the greatest importance to General Washington, and this was no time for his children to be interfering. "What's the meaning of this?" he asked in a forbidding tone.

Ena was trapped and realized she had no way to

escape. She was being forced to admit the whole truth prematurely, before she had had an opportunity to prove herself, but she knew this was no time to try to deceive her father.

Speaking rapidly, she blurted out her whole story, telling in detail about the months she had spent learning to familiarize herself with the forest and the ways of becoming at home in it.

Ghonkaba's patience was worn thin. He faced an impossible dilemma: he had either to abandon his mission for General Washington or to place the life of his daughter in grave jeopardy.

Seeing her father's expression and expecting an outburst of temper at any moment, Ena made an attempt to soften the blow by telling him of her dream, in which her great-grandfather had ordered her to follow her father.

His eyes narrowing, Ghonkaba listened intently. She had already demonstrated her ability to foretell the future in her dreams. "Are you quite certain," he demanded sharply, "that you've been truthful in relating this dream? Do you swear that you actually dreamed what you have now related to me?"

"I swear it, my father," she murmured with telling sincerity.

He stared long and hard at her and was satisfied. His children had been drilled to tell the truth, and he had no choice but to believe what she told him. This changed the entire complexion of the situation. He was willing to place his complete trust in her dream and to abide by the advice of his grandfather. Renno was never wrong, and Ghonkaba suspected that those on the far bank of the great river were privy to information not available to mortals.

Having arrived at a conclusion, he acted abruptly. "Very well," he said. "You may come with me."

Ena's world came alive again. Her father was giving her a chance to demonstrate her capabilities, and she rejoiced. "Thank you," she whispered, and lowered her head.

Ghonkaba placed a knuckle beneath her chin and forcibly raised her head until her gaze met his. "Don't thank me," he said. "You're going to be in extreme danger, where one mistake can mean your death and mine. We shall see how much you've learned and how well you've been taught, because I have no choice. We shall find out soon enough whether your dream was valid, as I trust it was. Come along."

Swiftly and silently he began to make his way through the thick evergreens, with Ena following. Never had she traveled so rapidly in the wilderness, particularly at night when visibility was vastly reduced. Certainly her father was not favoring her, and her jaw jutted forward as she made up her mind that she would never disgrace him. On the contrary, she was determined to make him proud of her before the night ended.

For what seemed like an hour Ghonkaba moved steadily through the woods, his pace never slackening.

Ena remained close behind, following doggedly, her silence matching his.

She realized they were no longer in the wilderness but in a park on the outskirts of a town. Beyond the confines of the wooded section were many buildings, and at last—before moving into the open—Ghonkaba halted.

Directly ahead was a large L-shaped building of wood, two stories high, completed so recently that it still lacked paint. Four sentries, each standing at a "parade rest" position, were stationed outside its entrances, and they remained motionless while other soldiers hurried in and out, emptying several carts and carrying the contents inside.

Ghonkaba wanted to know the meaning of the

activity, and motioned to his daughter. Ena silently
went to him.

"Mark the scene up ahead carefully and well," he
said. "I'm eager to know the contents of those bundles
and packages and the meaning of all the bustle. I suggest you sneak over to one of the windows and peer in.
If you're careful, no redcoat will even see you. I ask you
to do this because I believe the British are far less likely
to suspect what a girl may be up to, whereas a man
such as myself would be immediately accosted, searched,
and arrested. If, however, you should be captured,
pretend you speak no English and answer all questions
in the langauge of the Seneca. Then be patient, and I'll
rescue you if I possibly can." He gripped her shoulder
affectionately. "I am sure you can do it."

Ena crept forward, her heart pounding in her chest.
When she came to an open space, she knew she would
be certain to call attention to herself if she tried to cross
it stealthily, so she straightened up and walked casually
toward the windows. By sauntering at so leisurely a
pace she became relatively inconspicuous.

Breathless as she peered into the nearest window,
she found that it opened on a sitting room, and as she
watched a half-dozen redcoats inside, her breathing
gradually became normal. She found it little short of
amazing how easy it was to spy on an enemy position.
Redcoats came within a few feet of her as they repeatedly walked outside, took more bundles from the wagons parked there, and carried them inside. She could
almost have reached out and touched them, but concealed as she was by both darkness and some shrubbery,
not one of the soldiers even saw her.

After she had observed enough to give her father a
full report, she found the situation radically altered.
Suddenly, as she started back across the open area
toward the wooded park, she felt as though the eyes of
every redcoat were suddenly fastened on her.

Only by exerting great self-control was she able to prevent herself from running and thereby undoubtedly attracting attention. Her nerves screaming, she managed to walk at a slow pace, doing nothing to create any interest. By the time she reached the evergreens and rejoined her father, a thick film of perspiration was on her forehead, and she was breathing hard.

Ghonkaba's hand on her shoulder soothed her. He simply allowed it to lie there quietly until he felt certain that she was calm and her breathing again was normal. Then he beat a retreat into the woods, where he finally halted, well out of earshot of anyone near the new building.

"The redcoats," Ena told him softly, "seem to be preparing for a great feast. They have many puddings and pies, such as our relatives in Virginia serve at the Christmas season. They were also unpacking many wreaths of laurel and evergreen. Most of all, though, they were opening bottles of spirits. I saw some large casks that were clearly marked 'rum' or 'gin.' Smaller containers looked as though they would hold brandywine, but I couldn't be certain what was in them."

Delighted with her information, Ghonkaba smiled at her. "You've done well, my daughter, exceedingly well," he said. "If anything untoward should befall me before we return to our headquarters, be sure that you go to General Washington—no one of lower rank will suffice—and tell him what you saw."

She nodded, her eyes wide. "What was the meaning of what I saw, my father?"

He brushed aside her question. "There's no time to explain in detail now. I'll tell you all there is to tell later. We've learned what I came to Trenton to find out, and the important thing now is to get back intact."

Again he led the way through the forest toward the waterfront, with Ena close behind, and once again he was pleased that she was able to travel through the wilderness in absolute silence.

After a time she leaned toward him and whispered, "We're being followed."

Ghonkaba listened, too, and discovered she was right. He was deeply chagrined to realize he had been so intent on reaching the canoes that he had paid insufficient attention to his surroundings. Drawing his knife, he rapidly cut a length of vine about four feet long, and then motioned to his daughter to stand behind him.

She had no idea what he meant to do, but obeyed with alacrity and concealed herself in the underbrush. After no more than several seconds, she heard a noise nearby and then saw a redcoat approaching through the woods. Having heard faint sounds, he was bent upon investigating them.

Ghonkaba crouched low behind a hemlock, the ends of the vine wrapped securely around his two hands. When the redcoat came even with him, he sprang forward, dropped the vine over the soldier's head, and then crossed his hands and pulled with all his might.

Ena had been spared the sight of violence and death in the war, but she could not be shielded now. She gasped, then lowered her gaze while her father choked the man to death, using the length of vine to garrote him.

Ghonkaba threw aside the vine, picked up the dead soldier's musket and bayonet, and motioned his daughter to follow him.

Ena retained enough presence of mind to ask, "You are not going to take his scalp as a prize?"

He smiled but shook his head. "I don't want to let the enemy know that this deed was perpetrated by an Indian. All things being equal, his body should be found some time tomorrow. The skin isn't broken, and no shots have been fired, so I hope they will be able only to speculate on why he died. In that way we'll spread a measure of terror through their ranks at no cost to ourselves."

Ena realized anew that her father was wise without measure in the ways of waging war.

"Wait here," Ghonkaba said, speaking softly. "I'll return for you."

Ena was surprised. "Where are you going?"

"The redcoat I just killed was not the only British soldier in the immediate vicinity," he said. "Haven't you heard others?"

She shook her head.

"Perhaps your hearing will improve as your ears become more attuned to the alien sounds in the forest," he said, realizing that she still had much to learn about the wilderness. He then disappeared among the trees.

Ena found the spreading branches of a bush that had lost its leaves for the winter but was dense enough to provide her with adequate cover. She crawled into the bush, made herself comfortable, and prepared to await her father's return.

After a few minutes, she heard footsteps in the distance and listened intently. They were drawing nearer, but they seemed to lack decisiveness. Whoever was wandering in the forest apparently had lost his way and was going first in one direction, then in another, meandering aimlessly. Rising to a crouching position, she drew her tomahawk and waited tensely.

Soon a young man—a boy, actually, of about Ena's own age—came into sight, limping slightly. He was no redcoat; in fact, in spite of the cold, he was clad only in ragged shirt and trousers. He was hatless, and his hair was very pale. She caught a glimpse of his eyes and saw they were intensely blue. It was too bad that he must die, but she could afford no needless risks.

Raising her tomahawk above her head, she leaped to her feet.

He jumped backward, raised one arm defensively

to shield his face, and then muttered, "Oh my God! Indians! That's all I need."

Only her curiosity prevented her from killing him instantly. "Who are you?" she demanded, taking care to speak softly.

"I'm Clem Dawkins of Trenton," he said. "The redcoats captured me and were holding me prisoner because I wanted to cross the river and join the Americans. I may not be old enough to join the American Army, but the redcoats figured I'd tell the Americans all I knew of the British positions. Well, I got away about ten days ago, and I've been wandering around in these damn woods ever since. I've had almost nothing to eat, I'm half frozen, and I'm telling you right now that if you intend to turn me back to the redcoats, you may as well put that little ax of yours into my brain. I'll never be a British prisoner again."

Ena looked at him carefully, judged that he was telling the truth, and slowly lowered her arm. Perhaps she was wrong to dispose of him. If he wanted to join the American forces, he might even be worth saving.

"If you are trying to escape from the redcoats," she asked, "why are you wandering about in the inland forests? Why aren't you down at the river?"

"Because," Clem Dawkins replied bitterly, "I've lost my way. I haven't the vaguest idea how to navigate through these confounded woods. I grew up in New York, and when my parents died in the plague last year, I came to Trenton to live with some relatives. But they're outspoken loyalists, so we never got along. Then when I escaped from the British, I got lost. I'm a town boy, and I know nothing about this blasted wilderness!"

Unexpectedly, she felt sorry for him. "Maybe I can help you a bit," she offered. "Are you strong enough to follow me?"

He looked at her, a spark of hope reluctantly appearing in his eyes. "You lead," he answered grimly. "I'll follow."

Ena waved him out of her way, then gathered a number of sticks and small stones, which she quickly arranged on the ground in an odd pattern.

As the youth watched her, he was overcome with curiosity. "What are you doing?"

The meaning of her activity was so evident, at least in her own mind, that she couldn't help but feel annoyed. "Obviously," she said, "I'm leaving a private message for my father, telling him the direction that I'm taking. Then he'll know where I've gone and will be able to follow."

She started off, but quickly found that she was going far too rapidly for her companion, who was limping more noticeably and falling farther and farther behind, so she slowed her pace considerably.

The youth was in far worse condition than she had assumed. His step was wobbly, he had difficulty keeping his feet, and his progress was painfully slow. Apparently one leg was paining him greatly. Occasionally he had to halt and lean against the trunk of a tree, where he stood panting, trying to regain his breath.

Ena took pity on him. Draping one of his arms across her shoulders, she put an arm around him and helped support him as he walked. In spite of the clumsiness of the effort, they made much better time than when they went separately.

They moved steadily for at least an hour. Then Ena halted and put her ear to the ground, but could hear nothing.

"What are you doing now?" Clem asked.

She silenced him with a sharp gesture and continued to listen for a time, but could hear no sound of any footfalls in the vicinity.

"We're not being followed," she said at last, "so we'll have a chance to rest and eat."

Clem couldn't understand how she could determine they were not being followed. She didn't appear to be carrying any food, so he had no idea what they might eat, but he refrained from asking.

She motioned the tired, bewildered youth to sit. Propping his back against a tree, he sighed wearily.

Noting a small stream nearby, Ena went to work at once. She cut a length of a supple vine, then carefully removed a large thorn from a bush, onto which she skewered a worm she had dug up. Then, finding a long, slender stick to use as a rod, she attached one end of the vine to it and threw the other end, with the thorn, into the water.

Exactly as she had anticipated, she did not have long to wait before she caught a fish about ten inches in length.

Ena rebaited her makeshift hook and lowered it into the water again. Within a few minutes, she managed to catch three more fish.

The meal was ready in a very short time. Ena removed a long, very sharp knife from her belt and cut off the heads and tails of the fish, then split them and removed their center bones, as well. "Here you are," she said, putting the raw fish in front of Clem.

"Eat!" she instructed, pointing to his food with her knife, "and as you seem not to have eaten anything recently, don't gulp it. Chew very slowly and swallow even more slowly. That's the only way you'll keep a meal down."

Clem did as he was bidden. The fish seemed the most delicious he had ever eaten, and he consumed every bite in front of him.

Then, following her example, he bent low over the stream, cupped his hands, and drank the icy water with pleasure, then he splashed more onto his face.

Kneeling on the ground beside him, Ena twisted

her face toward him and smiled shyly. "Not too bad, was it?" she asked.

"Not bad? It was wonderful! You're truly a magician."

She shook her head. "I am no *shaman*," she said.

He looked at her blankly, "*Shaman?*"

"A *shaman*," she explained, "is what we call a medicine man."

"Oh!" At last she was beginning to make sense to him. Ena had no idea how much time had passed; it had rushed by much faster than she had realized. She thought it strange that her father had not yet shown up, but she wasn't really worried about him. She had every confidence that he would appear soon. Until then, however, she realized it was futile to attempt to cross the Delaware and try to approach the American lines. She had infringed enough on Ghonkaba's authority, and she knew she would have to wait for him now and place herself under his orders again. He would be surprised when he saw her companion, but she was unworried about his approval. He was fair in all things, and she had little doubt that he would accept the presence of Clem Dawkins as necessary.

Pending her father's arrival, she knew that rest was essential. She felt weary, and she could see that Clem was drooping. She had fed him the only decent meal he had eaten in many days, and now he needed healing sleep.

Again busying herself with her knife, she cut a number of young pine boughs and made a soft bed of them. Then she beckoned to him. "You need sleep," she said, "while we wait here for my father to find us. In order to obtain the best possible sleep, you should have a fire beside you to ward off the chill of night. Unfortunately, too many enemies are near at hand, and I dare not build a fire. But this pine bed will not be uncomfortable, and you should have no difficulty in dropping off to sleep."

He moved onto the boughs, and his expression

became beatific. "I was wrong when I said you were a magician, ma'am," he said. "You're an angel." He stretched out and made himself comfortable as best he could.

Ena watched him and became apologetic. "I wish we had a blanket to cover you, but I have none," she said. "For this I'm most sorry."

"What about you?" he demanded. "Don't you need a bed and a blanket, too?"

She shrugged indifferently. "I will manage," she told him.

Ena now could only keep watch over him. She sat where she could make out his face in the darkness, and waited patiently for her father. His failure to appear did not worry her, but she felt increasing annoyance.

Clem sighed, started, and then shivered.

Ena couldn't blame him for being cold. She was in the best of health, and she found the December weather numbing. Snow crunched underfoot, her nostrils stung every time she inhaled, and the lack of feeling in her hands and feet warned her that she needed to exercise them or suffer painfully.

Removing first one moccasin, then the other, she massaged her feet until her skin glowed and her hands, too, felt warmer.

She had more than herself—much more—to think about now. She had accepted responsibility for Clem Dawkins, a fugitive from the redcoats, and she had to protect him, as well as look after herself.

Feeling herself growing chillier, Ena stood, stamped her feet vigorously, and waved her arms for some minutes. She felt better while active, but as soon as she stopped the creeping chill began again.

Considering the immediate problem she faced from every conceivable angle, she knew she had to be sensible. Her well-being was at stake. Clem lacked the strength and stamina to stay on his feet all night, to continue

walking until Ghonkaba found them and took them to
the river where the canoe awaited. Clem would be
unable to tolerate such rigors.

Only one possible course of action was open to her.
Ena knew that in order to prevent herself and her
companion from freezing, she must lie down beside
him. By sharing their bodily heat, they might avoid
injury from the cold. She saw no alternative.

Why, then, was she hesitating? Surely she had no
interest in Clem Dawkins as a male.

Her one desire was the same as it had been as long
as she could remember: she wanted to be a Seneca
scout, second to none. Surely she was unlike other girls
of her age, whom she regarded with disdain because of
their constant interest in young men.

Very well—that settled the matter. She knew what
had to be done and she would do it.

Moving with determination, Ena deliberately climbed
onto the bed of boughs beside Clem and lay down next
to him. Then she moved closer to him until their bodies
touched.

He was half asleep. Sighing gently, he threw one
arm around her.

She snuggled closer still and put an arm around
him in return. Gradually, to her relief, she began to
grow warmer and could feel that he, too, was far less
chilly.

Surely nothing could be wrong in what she was
doing; no moral stigma attached to an act performed
simply to preserve life in bitter weather. Why, then,
were Ena's cheeks aflame? Why, too, was she so very
conscious of Clem's proximity, of his breathing, of every move he made? She had no answer.

To her consternation, she realized that Clem was
not yet fully asleep. He opened his eyes wide and
looked at her.

Her eyes were open, too, and as she returned his

gaze, she had the sensation that they were peering deep into each other's souls.

They closed their eyes simultaneously, and he moved his head forward a few inches, intending to kiss her.

Ena moved away, but she was not fast enough. Later when she attempted to analyze every move, she concluded she had known he was going to kiss her and deliberately had not withdrawn in time. She'd been curious about kissing, and as a pure experiment, wanted to try it. No, that was wrong—she had no interest in kissing as such, but this boy already was assuming a special relationship with her, and she could not bear to disappoint him any more than she could disappoint herself.

Their lips met and Ena's world spun giddily. Nothing she had ever known had prepared her for such an experience, and her reaction was equally unfamiliar. She breathed more rapidly, and found that he, too, was breathing faster. She pressed hard against him, discovering a strange yearning to become a part of him, and sensing that he wanted her.

They clutched each other convulsively, their kiss becoming more impassioned, until Clem broke the spell. Muttering that what they were doing was "not right," he drew back and began to gulp in long draughts of cold air. Ena did the same, and gradually their equilibrium was partly restored.

Clem slid his other arm around her, she put both of her arms around him, and they drifted off to sleep, unaware of the forest and its dangers, of the proximity of redcoats, or of numerous other dangers that might threaten them.

Four British soldiers, members of a heavy infantry regiment, were making their way back to the barracks in Trenton after being relieved from sentry duty. Thoroughly chilled, they hurried because of the prospect of standing before a blazing log fire in the regimental common room.

Three of the soldiers were light on their feet and moved gracefully. The fourth, who crashed through the underbrush as he brought up the rear, was definitely under the weather. For the cold, he had provided his own remedy, which had come in a bottle, and he had consumed enough of it to have it affect his thoughts, his speech, and his movements.

"Not so fast, lads!" he called thickly. "Wait for me!"

As it happened, the trio halted impatiently only a few feet from the pattern of sticks and stones that Ena had placed on the ground as a signal to her father.

The intoxicated infantryman, stumbling as he lurched forward, joined his companions. Two of them caught his arms and helped him to resume his walk. Neither he nor they noticed that he had kicked the arrangement of stones and sticks and had transformed it into a meaningless jumble.

All grew quiet again, and half an hour passed. Then Ghonkaba made his way silently, tentatively, through the forest to the place he had designated for his rendezvous with his daughter.

He realized at once that she was not on hand, and seeing an arrangement of symbolic stones and sticks on the ground, he moved forward to examine it.

His heart sank. The arrangement had been disturbed, and the resulting muddle was meaningless. Seeing the boot prints in the snow, he knew precisely what had happened. Someone, presumably a British soldier, had inadvertently kicked the arrangement, destroying whatever message Ena had left him.

Ghonkaba studied what was left of the arrangement for some moments, his mind racing. When he turned away, he knew what needed to be done. He had to scour the entire forest and find his daughter before he returned to the American camp. He never could go back without Ena. She was not to blame for her failure to reveal her whereabouts to him. For some reason, she had found it desirable to move on rather than to wait in the spot where he had left her, and she had done the right thing in leaving him a Seneca message.

It was urgent that he return to headquarters with a message of vital interest to the high command concerning the redcoats' activities. But it was equally urgent that he find his daughter. He would be unable to face Toshabe, much less himself, if he left without Ena. Accordingly, he set off after her.

From time to time he ate a small handful of parched corn or chewed on a strip of smoked venison. He wasn't hungry, but he knew he had to keep up his strength until he found his daughter. At last he came upon a scene that left him staring in openmouthed astonishment.

Lying on a bed of pine boughs, clasped together in a tight embrace, were Ena and a tall, yellow-haired boy. Both were sound asleep.

Ena opened her eyes and then smiled at Clem. Gradually, becoming conscious that someone was standing behind her, she looked over her shoulder.

A feeling of paralysis assailed her when she saw her father. She cautioned herself that her explanation of her intimacy was natural and she need not be afraid to speak the truth.

Clem stirred, opened his eyes, and smiled at Ena.

For a breathless second she was afraid that he intended to kiss her, and she pulled back hastily but gently.

Whatever his intentions, he caught sight of Ghonkaba at that instant and immediately began to separate himself from the girl. They both managed to rise to sitting positions.

Ghonkaba looked at them wryly. "The redcoats disturbed your signals, Ena," he said. "I've been searching for you, as you might assume. Apparently you've been in safe hands."

Stammering, hating herself for being so flustered, the girl introduced Clem Dawkins to her father and explained the circumstances.

Ghonkaba was immediately interested. "You have been in Trenton in recent days?"

"Yes, sir." Clem marveled at the Indian's command of English. "I escaped several days ago—maybe as many as ten. I'm not sure of time."

"The redcoats were busy tonight," Ghonkaba said, "piling up supplies of all kinds for what appears to be a very large party. Can you tell me anything about it?"

"I believe I can, sir. That's going to be their Christmas party."

"When is this party to be held?"

"On Christmas Day."

"You're certain it isn't to be held on Christmas Eve?"

"Reasonably, sir," Clem replied. "Of course, some of the soldiers—the Hessians—were speaking German among themselves, so I couldn't understand everything that was said. But then I heard one of them speak to a British officer in English about a celebration on Christmas Day."

"Will you be willing to see General Washington with us and corroborate what we have to tell him?"

"Will I ever! There's nothing in the whole world that I'd rather do." Clem was ecstatic.

Ghonkaba reached into the leather pouches he carried suspended from his belt and doled out parched corn and jerked venison to his daughter and Clem.

It was the first time the youth had tasted such fare, but he found it delicious.

"How many summers have you?" Ghonkaba asked.

Clem looked blank.

"My father asked you," Ena said patiently, "how old are you?"

"I'm seventeen, sir," he replied.

Ghonkaba thought for a moment. That made him a year older than Ena, and without doubt the two young people had established a rapport. He assumed from their innocent attitudes that they had slept together for warmth only, and that sex had not entered into their relationship. In fact, he felt ashamed of himself for having been suspicious.

"Come along," he said. "We've got to try crossing the river."

They went through the forest in single file, with Ghonkaba in the lead, Clem in the middle, and Ena bringing up the rear.

To her surprise, they arrived at the waterfront so close to the canoes they had left that they could almost step right into them.

"Take the paddle you used coming across," Ghonkaba directed as he deliberately punched several holes in the bottom of the canoe she had used. It began to sink. It soon would be gone and could never reveal that anyone had come across the river.

"Now," he said, "climb in."

Ena quickly did as she was bidden, and Clem followed her.

Ghonkaba raised his head and listened. He and Ena heard the same sounds, those of someone wearing boots and crashing through the underbrush. They exchanged a quick glance.

Motioning Ena and Clem to lie low in the canoe, Ghonkaba took up a position behind a fir tree. This time he gripped the rifle, holding it in such a way that he could use the bayonet as a spear.

When the redcoat came into sight, Ghonkaba struck without hesitation, jabbing with all his might.

His bayonet gleamed in the dim light as it approached its target.

The redcoat was agile, and managed to sidestep the blow.

Ghonkaba didn't want to fire his musket or allow the soldier to discharge his. The sound of gunfire from that location would alert the redcoats, and that was to be avoided at any cost.

Again Ghonkaba jabbed hard and swiftly with his rifle. This time his aim was true. The bayonet found its target again and again.

The sight of flowing blood made Ena ill, and she wished herself far from the scene. Clem clenched his fists.

The canoe began to move, and she opened her eyes too soon. The ashen face of the redcoat her father had just killed was staring up at her from the bulrushes. She hastily looked elsewhere.

"Paddle!" Ghonkaba commanded, and began to wield his paddle.

Neither spoke again as they headed for the far shore, paddling in unison. The canoe shot up onto the land without being challenged. Ghonkaba tied up the craft and then looked at his daughter in grim satisfaction. "You are not too tired, I hope, to finish the job you started with so much enthusiasm."

She tried to stifle a prodigious yawn. "No, my father," she murmured. "I am ready."

Smiling proudly, Ghonkaba motioned her to come with him, and he started at a trot across the camp toward the farmhouse where Washington was quartered.

Lieutenant Colonel Alexander Hamilton was on duty. "I'm sorry to ask this of you, Colonel," Ghonkaba said, "but perhaps you'll be good enough to call General Washington."

Hamilton blinked at Ghonkaba, his daughter, and Clem and then shook his head and pointed to a clock on the mantelpiece. "The commander in chief is not yet awake. Don't you realize it's barely daybreak?"

"I'll take full responsibility for waking him. Please tell him I've returned from the Jersey shore and have urgent information."

Hamilton mounted the stairs to the second floor. He was gone only a short time.

"You're to go up to the sitting room adjoining his bedchamber," Hamilton said, "and may the Almighty pity you if you don't have urgent news for him."

Following her father up the stairs, Ena felt confident. Whenever he was present she felt safe from all harm. Clem trailed along behind her, overcome by awe.

A fire burning in the sitting room grate took the chill off the air. General Washington entered the room and looked inquiringly at Ghonkaba. He raised an eyebrow when he saw the young woman and ragged youth.

"This is my daughter, Ena, whom you've met previously in the company of my other children, General," Ghonkaba said. "She followed me to the New Jersey shore during the night, and I'm very grateful that she did. I was angry with her at first, but when you hear of her accomplishments, I believe you'll be agreeably surprised. As for the young man with us, he has his own story to tell."

General Washington regarded her curiously, steadily, as he sat in a rocking chair near the fire.

Ghonkaba took a seat nearby, then motioned Ena closer to the fire. "Tell the general what you saw in the redcoat barracks, Ena," he directed.

Still unaware of the significance of what she had seen, Ena repeated in detail the story of the laurel and pine wreaths, the casks of liquor and bottles of brandywine, and the many puddings and cakes she had watched the redcoats unpack as they'd come indoors from wagons.

General Washington reacted much as her father

had done. His knuckles whitening as he gripped the arms of his rocking chair, he leaned forward tensely. "Are you certain that you saw all these things, Ena?" he asked sharply.

Ena wondered why Washington, like her father, had become so excited after hearing her news. "Yes, sir," she replied simply. "I tell you what I saw with my own eyes, and I tell you nothing else."

A slow smile spread across Washington's face. "I think the Almighty has favored us," he said to Ghonkaba. "We have borne more than our share of misfortune, and now the tide may have turned in our favor."

Now it was Clem's turn. Washington questioned him at length, and received cogent and full responses. Eager to join the Continentals, he had determined to escape across redcoat lines. He had been intercepted and made a prisoner about eight weeks earlier.

Finally, more than a week ago, he had made good his escape and had been wandering in the wilderness until Ena had found him and saved his life.

He corroborated all that she had told the general, saying that the British were making extensive preparations for a huge Christmas feast and party, which he believed would be held on Christmas Day.

Washington listened, then went over many of the points several times to make certain that Clem's responses were consistent.

"I can certainly sympathize with your desire to join the Continental Army," he said, "and because of the example you'd be setting for so many older persons, I wish we could accept you. However, I can see that you are not in the best physical condition. Life in this army is very rugged and demanding. I would not recommend, or even permit, your enlistment until your health is up to snuff."

"I really want to serve with the Continentals," Clem replied stubbornly and rather forlornly.

Washington smiled at him, revealing his own tiredness at the same time. "I can't say I blame you for feeling as you do. What I can do for you is rather limited. If you wish, I can assign you to General Greene's division as a drummer boy or a mascot. I'm not certain that I'm doing you any favor, however."

"I regard it as a very great honor and as a tremendous favor, sir," Clem replied eagerly. "If you could make such an arrangement, General, I'll be grateful to you always."

"Consider it done," General Washington said, and reached for a sheet of paper and a quill pen, which he dipped in an ink jar; then he scribbled a note. "For the first time since I accepted this command," he said to Ghonkaba, "I believe I can detect a glimmer of hope ahead."

"I thought you'd feel that way, sir," Ghonkaba said.

"You've done well," Washington told him, and turned to Ena. "As for you, young lady, you've performed remarkably, and I shall issue you a commendation, although because there is much that we want to conceal from the enemy, it will mention no details. That will encourage you to employ your extraordinary talents again, perhaps at some future time when they may be needed."

Blushing and tongue-tied, Ena didn't know how to respond adequately.

"Get some rest," Washington told Ghonkaba, "and when your scouts return, let them do the same. By the time you awaken at about noon, I will have further instructions for you."

"Very good, sir." Ghonkaba stood, saluted, and took his exit, first ushering Ena and Clem from the room.

Colonel Hamilton was waiting downstairs and looked at the trio questioningly.

Ghonkaba grinned at him. "You may relax, Colonel," he said. "Your position is safe." He left the house and headed for his own dwelling, his arm around his daughter's shoulders.

On the way, they parted company with Clem Dawkins. A sergeant from General Greene's division, responding to the commanding general's note, caught up with them and offered to escort Clem back to division headquarters.

Clem shook hands with Ghonkaba and then with Ena; he held the girl's hand longer than was necessary.

To her own surprise, she did not mind in the least.

"I don't know how I say thank you for saving my life," he stammered, "but I'm going to try. May I call on you in the future?"

Ena was about to give her consent but first looked questioningly at her father.

To him, it was plain that Clem was smitten and that Ena was similarly affected. He wanted to wait and discuss the matter with Toshabe, but could see no reason to withhold his approval now.

Although it was difficult for him to realize, Ena was growing up and was suffering in the throes of what might be her first romance. It was better, he knew, to let the relationship develop under parental guidance than to put obstacles in its path.

"By all means," he said heartily, "you're always welcome at our house."

Clem finally released Ena's hand, and as he started off with the sergeant, father and daughter again resumed their walk toward their house.

As they approached it they saw the light of an oil lamp burning in the parlor, and then the front door opened and Toshabe peered out. She stared hard at her daughter and then looked at her husband; in spite of her lifelong training, she was near tears. "I thank the gods that you're safe," she told Ena, and swept the girl into her arms, hugging and kissing her.

Ghonkaba closed the front door behind him and followed his wife and daughter into the parlor.

"I happened to awaken," Toshabe said, holding fast to the girl, "and when I discovered that Ena wasn't here, I blamed only myself. I knew that she was trying out her skills as a scout, and I was furious with myself for having concealed the truth about her activities from you for all these months."

Ghonkaba replied soothingly. "Never mind. She behaved superbly and has just received a commendation from General Washington himself for her work tonight. Ena is the most accomplished scout in my command," he added with a quick smile.

Toshabe was so overwhelmed she could not speak.

Ghonkaba turned to their daughter. "Are you hungry, Ena?" he asked.

"Ravenous, my father."

"I thought so," he said with a chuckle. "You're a true scout in every sense of the word, Ena. It's customary to eat one's fill after returning from a mission. The activity—perhaps the danger—creates an unparalleled appetite. If your mother's willing, we can see what's available in the larder."

Toshabe preceded them to the kitchen. "I have a mixture of corn and broad beans," she said. "I can heat it in a very short time."

"I prefer it cold," Ghonkaba said.

"Me, too," Ena chimed in.

"There's also the broiled filet of a large fish that El-i-chi caught in the river. It's left over from supper."

"We'll share it," her husband said promptly.

Toshabe took the food from the larder and served it.

Ghonkaba was impressed by the attitude his daughter displayed. Instead of boasting to her mother about her exploits of the evening, she did not mention the escapade and refrained from revealing where she had been or what had occurred. Toshabe asked no questions, and as far as Ena was concerned, the subject appeared to be closed. Justifiably, Ghonkaba was additionally proud of her.

After she had taken the edge off her appetite, Ena smiled at Toshabe. "I'm sorry, my mother, that you were needlessly worried about me."

"I don't think it was unnecessary," Toshabe replied with a sniff.

"I'm afraid it was. I had a very vivid dream early in the night. I dreamed that my great ancestor Renno appeared and ordered me to follow my father to his destination and that he would direct me in what I was to do."

Ena folded her hands in her lap and volunteered nothing more about her dream. She was satisfied that matters had worked out in the way that Renno had predicted, and she believed the substance of her dream was a strictly private matter to be repeated to no one.

Her parents realized it, too, for they refrained from questioning her.

Ghonkaba relaxed, enjoying a great sense of wonder and relief. The manitous plainly had taken Ena under their care and were protecting her; as long as she obeyed their precepts, she would come to no harm. It was odd, he thought, that she, rather than her brothers, was to be the chosen member of her generation, but how the manitous reached their decisions never would be known. It was enough that Ena was favored by them. They were helping her and, through her, the cause of American independence.

On the day before Christmas the Continental Army was heartened when Major General Townsend Whiting arrived with a division of twelve hundred men, whom he had sworn in as volunteers and had led south from New England. They had avoided the redcoats and their Mohawk allies in New York, had sidestepped the many British regiments in New Jersey, and had reached Washington's lines without having fought in a major battle.

General Whiting conferred privately and at length with the commander in chief. Then the other generals were called in and met for several hours behind closed doors. When the conference ended, Whiting went in search of Ghonkaba, whom he found with his four sergeants eating a simple meal of boiled beef.

They received the general politely, but showed no awe of his rank, in contrast to the strict discipline of the British Army, in which a general was received with a reverence far greater than even his rank warranted.

Ghonkaba led his friend away from the bivouac of the sergeants, and they started toward the house occupied by the Seneca and his family.

They exchanged inquiries about the health of their wives, and then Whiting said, "I gather that your daughter has been unexpectedly busy of late."

Ghonkaba stiffened. "What have you heard?"

Whiting slapped him on the back. "Never fear," he said. "General Washington described her accomplishments in some detail in a meeting of the general officers. The information she gleaned is going to be put to great use, I assure you."

"I thought that the Continentals were going to act on the information that she gathered last night, but apparently the commander in chief has decided upon a delay?"

"That's right," Whiting replied and lowered his voice. "He wants to make dead certain that the redcoats are enjoying a full celebration of the holiday before he strikes. The only time he can be certain that the British regiments and the mercenary Hessians will be relaxed is on Christmas night—tomorrow evening. That's when we're now scheduled to act, which is just fine with me. My men can enjoy a rest of a day and a half before they go into actual combat."

"I've received no notification of that as yet," Ghonkaba told him.

"You will, never fear," Whiting said. "From the strategy the commander in chief described, your scouts will play a major role in the attack, but I think it's only proper that we wait and let General Washington tell you the details himself."

"By all means," Ghonkaba replied.

He did not have long to wait. In midafternoon he was summoned to Washington's headquarters. An aide-de-camp ushered him into the study, where Washington, studying several sheets of paper spread out before him, was frowning intently. Ghonkaba saluted, waited until he was bidden, and then took a chair.

"You've undoubtedly been wondering why I've delayed our attack on Trenton," General Washington said, "but I am not a gambling man by nature, and the mere fact that we're going into battle with numerical odds of at least two to one against us is quite enough of a handicap. I wanted to make certain that the enemy would be celebrating and would be caught off guard. Brigadier General Anthony Wayne, whose Pennsylvanians include a great many men of German descent, checked with his subordinates and came back with the positive information that the Hessians will be celebrating Christmas tomorrow night, rather than tonight, as we Americans are likely to be doing. Then, when General Whiting arrived today, he assured me that the British troops in the Trenton garrison could be expected to do the same thing. A celebration on Christmas Eve is practically unknown to them, so as closely as I can judge, the best time for our attack will be tomorrow evening."

Ghonkaba understood and expressed his approval.

"I'll want you to transfer your company of scouts to the New Jersey shore after sundown tomorrow," Washington said. "How long do you estimate it will take you to find out for certain whether the enemy is holding its celebration at that time?"

Ghonkaba engaged in some rapid mental calculations. "To be on the safe side, General," he said at last, "I'd say it will take us about an hour and a half."

Washington seemed pleased by his answer. "In the event that no party is in progress," he said, "you'll send your men back across the river and the attack will be called off at once. We'll allow another half hour for the crossing, so that gives you two hours in all to complete your mission and determine whether the assault takes place."

"That's ample time, sir," Ghonkaba assured him.

"Only if the enemy is having a Christmas party," Washington reiterated, "are you to permit the attack to take place as scheduled."

"Yes, sir," Ghonkaba said.

"In that event, your company will be gathered again near the waterfront, and as our troops come ashore, they will be guided to the enemy's bivouac area by a scout. If you assign one scout to every battalion, that should be the right ratio."

"May I inquire, General," Ghonkaba asked, "how large a force you intend to employ?"

Washington's reply was a trifle rueful. "I'm assigning every infantry unit in the Continental Army, without exception, to this task, including General Whiting's division. We'll number between seven and eight thousand men. The only part of the army that will not participate will be General Knox's artillerymen. It will be too difficult to ferry the heavy guns across the river and maintain the necessary degree of quiet."

Again Ghonkaba did some rapid calculations. "Ena

and I," he said, "figured that the redcoats have twelve to fifteen thousand men in garrison in Trenton."

"That's the estimate I'm using," the commander in chief replied. "I've had no cause to change your figures."

"With all due respect to the Continentals as fighting men, how do you expect them to beat a corps that outnumbers them by two to one?"

"I'm relying exclusively on the element of surprise," Washington told him. "I've said that I'm not much of a gambler, but I'm afraid I was exaggerating. I'm gambling with the entire future of our people, and I'm risking everything on one throw of the dice. I'm banking solely on the hope that when we do strike, the enemy will be taken completely by surprise and will be in no condition to fight back. Only in that way can we hope to achieve even the most limited of victories. If I've miscalculated in any way or if the British and Hessians get wind of our intention to attack, it will mean the end of the American people's magnificent dream of liberty."

Chapter VIII

The area beyond the fringe of trees concealing the land along the Pennsylvania waterfront of the Delaware River was teeming with Continental soldiers. As dusk fell, the divisions moved into place, the battalions moving in single file. The troops maintained absolute silence as they went into position. All were aware that after having been on the defensive for so long, after having taken blow after blow, at last they were going to take an initiative of their own and strike back.

The scouts moved forward through the ranks of their comrades, every two men carrying a canoe. They were grim and silent, each aware of the grave responsibility that he bore. They alone would determine whether an attack on the Trenton garrison would take place.

As Sergeants Ryan, Ginsberg, MacDavid, and Muller launched the leading canoes, Ghonkaba shook hands with General Washington, who wore a long cape over his uniform, and with several subordinate generals. Then he climbed into the prow of a canoe as some of his men pushed it into the water, and with MacDavid behind him, he began to paddle for the opposite shore. The other sergeants fell in behind MacDavid, and then came the rest of the company of scouts, strung out until they seemed to bridge the Delaware.

Arriving on the eastern bank, Ghonkaba allowed his sergeants to hide the canoes, and he immediately struck out for Trenton. Soon he could hear the faint sounds of the entire company falling in behind him. He substituted caution for speed as he approached the town. Conscious that he could run across armed redcoat or Hessian sentries at any moment, he moved with extreme care, often holding up a hand to halt those behind him as he listened intently for any sound of sentinels. But to his surprise no sentries appeared to be abroad. The weather was cold; the light snow that had been falling had changed to a freezing rain. The pellets stung his hands and face, but he paid no attention and worked his hands frequently in order to get rid of the numbness that crept into them.

At last he came to the little park adjacent to the L-shaped barracks that he and Ena had discovered, and seeing no British or Hessian sentries on duty outside the oversized building, he sent MacDavid and Ginsberg ahead to investigate. He was apprehensive that the enemy, knowing or suspecting what Washington had planned for that night, were setting a trap for the Americans.

The two sergeants appeared to encounter no

difficulty, and when they beckoned their comrades, Muller and Ryan moved across the open space and joined them. All four took turns peering in through the windows, and then, to Ghonkaba's astonishment, they all began to wave to him.

He started forward, feeling conspicuous in the open space between the park and the barracks.

As he approached the windows, he heard shouts, laughter, and snatches of song from within the building. The sergeants moved away from the nearest window in order to give him the opportunity to look inside, and as long as he lived he would never forget the sight.

Liquor was flowing freely from casks and bottles in two rooms inside the barracks. In one, redcoats were gathered, their tunics unbuttoned, their weapons nowhere to be seen. Huge quantities of sliced ham, cold fowl, and Christmas puddings of various kinds were piled on tables, but no one seemed interested in food. Redcoats eagerly filled and refilled steins and glasses and, in some cases, put their mouths directly below spigots, which they then turned on full. The British Army was noted for its discipline, but no discipline of any kind was being observed this Christmas night. Sergeants major fraternized with enlisted men of lower ranks, and no officers were in sight anywhere. Ghonkaba assumed that they were having a party elsewhere.

The other room was crowded with Hessian mercenaries, even more under the influence of liquor than were the redcoats. They were unaccustomed to drinking hard liquor, and many of them were sleeping peacefully. Some tried to sing in unison, but succeeded only in making braying sounds. Others were staggering, and only a few seemed to be sober. Even they were disheveled, however, and the tunics of their green uniforms were open at the neck and their crosswebbing was awry.

Ghonkaba had seen enough. Conditions were perfect for General Washington's assault. He retreated hastily to the edge of the wilderness, and his sergeants followed him one by one. Slowly the entire company made its way down to the waterfront, where they dispatched a scout in one of the canoes to tell Washington that the attack was on. Then they settled down in high spirits to await the arrival of the Continental Army.

The wind became stronger, blowing sleet with gale force into the faces of the shivering scouts. Even though they could anticipate a victory, they were miserable and stamped their feet repeatedly to keep from freezing.

At last they saw an armada of small vessels, including fishing boats, pleasure craft, and supply ships, bearing down on them from the Pennsylvania shore. The Continental Army was on the move.

General Washington stood amidships in the first boat, so that as many of his followers as possible could see him. His cloak was wrapped around him as a protection from the sleet, cold, and biting wind, but nevertheless he was thoroughly chilled by the time he reached the New Jersey shore.

Ghonkaba was on hand to greet him when he stepped onto dry land. "Your gamble is paying off, General," he said. "They're celebrating, all right. I've never seen so much liquor being consumed!"

Washington reacted as Indians did in moments of great stress: his face betrayed no emotion, and his voice was calm, almost indifferent, as he thanked his chief scout. Looking at him and listening to him, no one would have realized the tremendous strain he had been under ever since the idea of attacking the Trenton garrison had been conceived.

Ghonkaba led the commander in chief and his staff through the forest to the park opposite the barracks. There they settled down to await the rest of the attack corps.

General Sullivan's division, which had absorbed the brunt of so many attacks, had been chosen to move in first, so the men advanced now to surround the barracks. They were followed by the men of General Greene's division, who had the task of going inside and driving the defenders into the open. Held in reserve were the newcomers of General Whiting's division, who were ordered to prevent the enemy from organizing once they were driven outside.

General Washington, observing the entire operation as coolly as though watching a stage play from a box seat in the theater, gave the signal that set the battle in motion.

The Continentals poured into the building, and the battle was decided before a single shot was fired. The redcoats and Hessians were caught completely off guard, expecting no action on Christmas night.

Many were too befuddled to offer serious resistance, and they began to surrender by the hundreds.

Then a battalion of Sullivan's division flushed out the redcoat and Hessian officers from a separate wing of the barracks. A number were glassy-eyed, but even those who were quite sober were helpless to turn the tide, and they were forced to give up their swords and to accept incarceration. Washington was elated when he discovered that seven enemy generals had been captured.

A few British troops were sober enough to try to put up a fight. Banding together, they opened fire on their attackers.

But the Americans, eager for combat, returned the fire so vigorously that the British were soon overwhelmed and raised a white flag. The mercenaries, who were ordinarily brave enough in combat, had no desire to lose their lives unnecessarily, and they surrendered by the company and by the batallion.

When the inevitable confusion of battle was sorted

out and order of a sort was restored, the Americans were astounded to learn the magnitude of their victory. Eight thousand British and Hessian troops had surrendered, and at least five thousand more had fled to the north in the desperate hope of gaining sanctuary behind General Howe's lines in New York.

The American victory was by far the greatest since the start of the war. The Continentals moved on to occupy a number of warehouses. These included depots where muskets, bullets, and gunpowder were stored and other buildings filled with crates of dried beef, barrels of pickled fish, and sacks of rice, potatoes, and other food supplies.

The following day promised to be fair, and as the sun rose, Washington and his senior generals were convened in the living room of a barracks suite that had belonged to a British colonel. The commander in chief's orderly found a supply of excellent, aromatic tea from India, and having the good sense to mention his discovery to no one, he prepared large pots of tea for the generals, who had not tasted such a delicacy for many months.

Real hens' eggs were available, as was a large side of bacon, and the generals anticipated a memorable breakfast. While it was being prepared, they disappeared two by two in order to shave, obtain fresh garments if possible, and make themselves presentable at the breakfast table. General Washington, as they knew, would be immaculate in appearance and would expect nothing less from his close associates.

Tired after a sleepless night and lulled by the luxury of food they hadn't tasted in a long time, the generals sat in front of a blazing hearth in the British colonel's drawing room and gradually became more and more sleepy.

The commander in chief finished his bacon and eggs and smiled. "Gentlemen," he said, "I know most of you are eager to return to your bivouacs and get in a few hours of sleep. But I think it's imperative that I take up an urgent matter of strategic planning with you immediately."

His listeners, most of them middle-aged men like him, managed to shake off their fatigue and devote their full attention to him.

"You don't need me to tell you that we won a signal victory last night," he said. "Soon every patriot's household, from Maine to Georgia, will be buzzing with the good news, the first that we've offered them. I propose to double that good news, at the very least."

No one in his audience was surprised. His generals had learned that whenever he had the opportunity, he was audacious in his planning, in spite of his seeming conservatism.

"I think we've succeeded in destroying the better part of the enemy forces in New Jersey," Washington said. "I doubt if Howe has many more Hessians under his command, and he certainly has lost a substantial portion of his heavy infantry. I propose that we strike yet again while the iron is hot and complete the task that we've begun with such notable success."

Putnam and Sullivan exchanged grins. Nathanael Greene chuckled and slapped his thigh, and even Whiting, the newcomer to the group, had to smile.

"Of course," Washington said, "we can't let Henry Knox miss all the fun. The first order of business will be to send the scouts across the river to bring Knox and his entire artillery corps across."

"He'll be delighted," General Greene said, "when he learns that we've captured a number of fair-sized cannon and the ammunition that goes with them. Henry is going to be that much stronger."

"So are we all," Washington assured him. "What I propose is very simple. We waste no time resting. We consolidate our victory, leave our older and partly incapacitated men behind to guard our prisoners, and after taking all the supplies and equipment that the enemy left behind, we set out in search of a major redcoat force."

"Do you have any idea where we're likely to find such a force, General?" Whiting inquired.

"At the moment I have no idea, General," Washington replied. "But I have full confidence in Ghonkaba's scouts, and I propose that they fan out ahead of us until they locate a sizable enemy force."

"What do we do when we come head to head with the enemy?" It was Putnam's question.

Washington replied in a deceptively mild voice. "I should think we'd give them a battle that they'll remember for a long time to come. I'm not saying that we're going to win another victory. We guessed right last night, and our challenge paid big dividends. Perhaps the troops are sufficiently inspired now to give their all in another battle and to fight harder and more professionally than they've ever fought previously. If so, we'll astonish the foe by defeating him again. If not, however, I'm determined that we shall give an exceptionally good account of ourselves, so the country will be lifted permanently out of its terrible lethargy, and recruiting for the Continentals can begin again in earnest. I suggest that you rest yourselves and your troops until noon, and at that time we'll be on the march north through New Jersey."

The company of scouts rested, and the men passed the time by napping, fishing, and eating. Ghonkaba, however, took advantage of the respite to cross over to the Pennsylvania shore in order to bid farewell to his wife and children. The reason for his exertion soon became evident.

After speaking privately and at length with Toshabe, he went to the door of the parlor and summoned their daughter. Ena was so wide-eyed, her expression so innocent as she came into the room, that she was immediately suspect.

Her father motioned her to a chair. "You've heard, I assume, that the army is on the move, following our victory last night."

Ena nodded, but did not reply.

Ghonkaba glanced at her. "You've been thinking," he said, his tone gently accusing. "You had a major hand in our victory last night, and I'm the first to admit it. But the mission given the scouts today is far different from that in Trenton."

Ena looked at him inquiringly.

"We're obliged to fan out in advance of the vanguard regiments and discover the locations and sizes of any redcoat units that we encounter as we go. The members of the company will be in constant danger, and as only a portion of the territory is wooded, they'll be exposed at least part of the time. Our casualty rate may run very high. It all depends on the cunning and expertise of the individual scouts."

Ena was sober-faced now.

"Knowing you," he said, "you've had the bright idea of somehow crossing the river and joining us after we start north from Trenton. Don't do it! You've had no combat experience of any kind, and this mission requires experience under fire if one is to carry out one's assigned role successfully."

"How can I acquire that experience if I don't take risks?" she asked.

Her question put Ghonkaba in a quandary, and he pondered for a moment. "I'm afraid I have no idea," he said firmly. "I see no reason why you need to gain actual combat experience. You've accomplished far more than anyone has the right to expect of a female, so be good enough not to push your luck. Not only will the manitous disapprove of your accompanying the scouts on the march north, but I disapprove so heartily that I forbid it."

Ena opened her mouth to reply, thought better of it, and closed it again.

Looking at her intently, Ghonkaba was less than satisfied that his words were having any effect. "I require you to swear—on the memories of your noted ancestors—that you will remain here with your mother, and will make no attempt to join the scouts or to usurp any of our functions in the campaign that we're beginning today."

Ena realized that he meant every word and that she had no escape from the inevitable. "As you wish, my father," she murmured reluctantly. "I swear on the memories of all my ancestors that I will make no attempt to join your company or to usurp any of your functions in the military campaign that you are starting on this day."

Ghonkaba turned to Toshabe. "I think it fairly likely now that you'll encounter no problems with Ena while I'm gone this time. See to it that she prays to the manitous to make her wise in the ways in which women are wise and leaves the functions of warriors to those who are braves."

A regiment of sharpshooters from Connecticut and Rhode Island, members of Major General Nathanael Greene's division, led the cautious northward advance near the Delaware. Ahead of the regiment ranged the company of scouts, stretching eastward from the wilderness on the riverfront.

Every scout was on his own, bearing full responsibility for his sector. The American frontiersmen and Seneca warriors who composed the bulk of the company were confident of their abilities and moved far more rapidly than did the army behind them.

Ghonkaba seemed to be everywhere, traveling from

west to east and then heading west again as he and his subordinates moved northward. He had divided the territory to be covered into four zones, putting each of them under the overall supervision of one of his experienced sergeants; they, in turn, reported to him as he covered the ground ceaselessly and without tiring.

When the vanguard regiment halted at sundown, the scouts continued to push forward for a time, and then they, too, halted, retracing their steps until they were able to form a screen of sentries for the entire army behind them.

Ghonkaba inspected the positions taken by his men, approved them, and then went back to join General Greene, who was eating supper with Colonel Donald Davis of New Haven, the regimental commander. The pair were dining more than adequately, if not sumptuously, on food captured from the British in Trenton, including dried beef, cold potatoes, and an overly sweet pudding. Colonel Davis offered Ghonkaba a plate as he sat down with them.

"You must be exhausted, Captain," he said. "You've walked at least three miles for every mile that our troops have covered today."

Ghonkaba shrugged, but refrained from saying that he was not in the least tired after his day's efforts. What he had done was in no way unusual for a Seneca warrior, and he knew that his subordinates, his Seneca brothers, felt precisely as he did. They had not even begun to tap their reserves of energy.

He began to eat in silence, following the Seneca custom of pausing for a time between each mouthful. In this way, not only could he consume more food, but it seemed to do him far more good than would have been the case had he given in to his natural desire and gulped the meal.

General Greene looked at him. "What luck did you have today, Captain?"

Ghonkaba smiled. "My men are thoroughly bored, General," he said, "and if the truth be known, so am I. We saw no sign of redcoats or Hessian mercenaries anywhere. It was as though a giant broom had swept them all away."

"Our victory at Trenton appears to be even greater than we realized," Greene said. "It's my own hunch that Billy Howe felt his Trenton garrision was isolated and therefore vulnerable, so he concentrated his principal strength in New Jersey there."

"At the expense of lesser garrisons here and there, you mean?" Ghonkaba asked.

"Exactly so," the general replied. "By putting all his available troops into one garrison, Howe felt reasonably certain his unit had too much strength for us and that we'd be overwhelmed in a confrontation with them. It didn't occur to him that we would be able to neutralize every advantage that they held."

Ghonkaba pondered for some moments. "If your theory is right, sir," he said, "we should be able to travel the better part of the way to New York before we encounter any redcoat strength in significant numbers."

"Exactly so," Greene replied. "The farther north we travel, the more secure our hold on New Jersey will become."

"I saw that for myself today," Colonel Davis interjected. "Every time my troops came to a farmhouse—which the scouts quite naturally had avoided—they were greeted rapturously by the farmers. They had been desperately unhappy under the British occupation, and they were delighted to find that they now are in territory controlled by the Continental Army. I might add, sir, that their opinion of General Washington's troops was vastly improved."

The situation continued to grow increasingly favorable to the American cause as the new year, 1777, came. The scouts continued to find no sign of British or mercenary troops anywhere, and the inhabitants of farms and of villages who were encountered on the march were elated when they learned that the area to the south had been cleared of enemy troops.

The citizens of New Jersey had a tendency to hail Washington as a hero, but he refused the role they would have assigned to him. "It's premature by far to claim a victory," he told his personal staff. "First, we've got to meet and tangle with the enemy, and only if we succeed in driving him back will we earn the right to be called heroes."

On the year's second day, the army came to an abrupt halt in the deep woods south of Princeton. There the probing scouts had discovered a redcoat and Hessian force of considerable consequence.

Ghonkaba and his scouts conducted reconnaissances while the army silently took up positions in the woods. After the veterans had made their reports to Ghonkaba, he hurried to Washington with the accumulated information.

"The British have maintained a garrison of considerable strength in Princeton for a number of months," he said, "and General Howe has reinforced it strongly since he lost Trenton. My sergeants and I have made separate estimates of the enemy strength, and our figures are virtually identical. We estimate the present garrison consists of approximately six thousand redcoats and three thousand Hessians. Almost all are infantrymen, as they've had no opportunity to move artillery weapons from New York to this area."

"In that event," Washington said, "Knox's guns have a natural advantage. For once the tide of artillery has turned toward our side."

"Yes, sir," Ghonkaba agreed.

The commander in chief looked at him. "Captain,"

he said, "how well do you suppose your scouts can emulate the Pied Piper?"

"That depends, General, on how many redcoats you want us to tempt into following us."

"Of the nine thousand enemy troops in the area, I'd like to depend on your scouts to inveigle as many as possible into following them."

Ghonkaba nodded. "It won't be easy, sir, but we'll do our best. What do you have in mind?"

The commander described a simple but daring plan. "One main road leads south from New York through Princeton and cuts through the woods south of the town," Washington said. "What I have in mind is stationing my entire corps of Continentals deep in the woods on either side of the road. I'd like to back them up with artillery and keep the infantry units more or less flexible. The ideal situation would be for your scouts to act as a magnet pulling all nine thousand of the enemy into this forest. Most of our Continentals are very much at home in the wilderness, but it's been my experience that the redcoats have learned nothing from history and are totally unable to take advantage of the art of concealment in deep woods. Do you happen to know who the commander of the redcoat garrison is?"

"I think so, sir," Ghonkaba replied. "He's a major general and is one of Howe's deputies. I have reason to believe that he's Lord Cornwallis."

Washington smiled slightly. "Splendid!" he said. "I certainly hope you're right. Cornwallis has had no experience whatever at fighting in the New World and knows nothing about the conduct of a wilderness campaign. Don't misunderstand me. He's an extremely competent soldier, but he fights strictly in the European manner, like General Braddock did in our campaign against the French."

"How soon do you want my men to start their flirtation with the enemy?"

Washington glanced up at the sky. "It's too late to initiate any action today, so it's fortunate that the British are unlikely to discover our proximity. Get your men in readiness in advance of Colonel Davis's regiment and let them begin their operation at daybreak. I'll have the entire corps in battle formation by that time."

Ghonkaba saluted and returned to his unit.

The scouts were thrilled when Ghonkaba told them of the role they were to play in the forthcoming battle.

"In order to attract as many of the enemy as we possibly can," he said, "you'll need to fire very rapidly and make every shot count. We want to give the redcoats the impression that we're a much larger body than we actually are. I hope that every last redcoat and every Hessian in Princeton will follow us into the forest, hoping to annihilate us. It will be our job to set them up so that the Continentals can do their part. We have a chance to achieve a substantial victory, far more significant than the one in Trenton. Everything depends on your ability to playact and to make your shots count."

The veteran scouts rolled up in their blankets after taking a position in the woods just outside Princeton, and in spite of the tensions created by not knowing what the morning would bring, they slept soundly.

They were stirring an hour before daybreak and ate an Indian breakfast of jerked meat and parched corn while resting on their rifles. Then they spread out at more than arm's length, with Ghonkaba and his four sergeants anchoring the center of the line.

A messenger came forward from Colonel Davis to notify the scouts that General Greene's entire division was now on both sides of the road, ready for action. Presumably the remainder of the corps was behind them, and the artillery, too, was ready for action.

As the night sky of midwinter began to turn from deep black to progressively lighter shades of gray, the scouts crept forward until they were close to the limits of the forest. Peering out between the branches of the evergreens, they could see the enemy's extensive camp, pitched in the open. Cooking fires were already being built up in preparation for their breakfast.

Ghonkaba's rifle spoke, and immediately the fire of numerous other rifles sounded up and down the long line. The Battle of Princeton was under way.

The sky was still so dark that the enemy was prominently revealed by the flaring cooking fires, and the troops made superb targets. The scouts, long accustomed to wilderness warfare, wasted no bullets and inflicted heavy damages on their foes. Following their captain's instructions, they reloaded swiftly, then fired again. The sound of rifle fire from the edge of the woods was constant.

The redcoats and Hessians suffered heavy casualties, but being no novices in warfare, they organized swiftly and began to retaliate, pouring a concentrated fire into the edge of the forest.

The scouts responded by retreating deeper into the underbrush, taking cover behind trees and bushes.

Following the skilled example of Ghonkaba and his sergeants, they kept up a steady, lethal fire. So accurate was their marksmanship that the British were convinced that at least a full regiment was taking part in the assault.

Lord Cornwallis promptly assigned a full division to dispose of the "regiment" of rebels.

The self-discipline exercised by Ghonkaba and his men was remarkable. They retreated inch by inch, with tantalizing slowness, still making every shot count, and the British consequently committed more and more men to the struggle.

General Washington had been exaggerating, of course, when he had said he would be pleased if the enemy general committed his entire force to the struggle.

But the British did send two full divisions, or more than twenty-five hundred men, in pursuit of the company of scouts, and Ghonkaba had every reason to feel proud of all his troops. They were still taking a heavy toll of the enemy and suffering almost no casualties when Knox's artillery opened fire, signaling the beginning of a new phase in the battle.

The little mortars sent iron balls hurtling high into the air and then raining down death and destruction, while the heavier cannon cut deep gaps in the ranks of the redcoats.

The massed Americans in the forest held a decided advantage: they could see their foes plainly, while the British could not. The Continentals could shoot at will and make every bullet count.

The British were forced to shoot wildly into the woods, and most of their fire was far too high, soaring harmlessly over the Americans.

The redcoats appeared to be faltering, and Cornwallis sent two divisions of Hessians after them to bolster their lines. They made the mistake of marching in stiff formation, advancing in the hollow squares that were traditional in European battles. Every regiment was accompanied by its own drummers and flag-bearers. With its ranking officers in front of the first lines, it resembled a unit on parade.

The Americans were merciless. Remembering the many humiliations they had suffered in the Battle of Long Island and in the engagements that had followed since that time, they poured fire at their erstwhile tormentors, and when the redcoats and Hessians became confused they increased their fire.

The fighting became much more intense, and Washington's wish was satisfied as the enemy committed more and more units to the struggle. By the time a watery sun rose in a cloud-speckled sky, the entire British force appeared to be engaged in combat.

The scouts, withdrawing deep into the Continental lines, had lost all direct contact with the foe. The sergeants made a casualty check, and the report to Ghonkaba was encouraging; three of his men had been wounded, none seriously.

Sergeant MacDavid spoke for the entire company when he said to Ghonkaba, "Captain, I surely trust that we haven't left the battle to a bunch of amateur soldiers. We were just getting warmed up in the fight when we moved out of shooting range of the enemy. I hope we're going to get another crack at them."

Ghonkaba realized he was in a strange position. His men had performed well, brilliantly carrying out the mission assigned to them, and for all practical purposes their part in the battle was ended. But it would be unfair to ask them to avoid the confrontation they had been at such pains to establish. Ghonkaba reported directly to the commander in chief, and therefore he bore no allegiance to any division commander or other authority. He reported only to General Washington, and though outranked by numerous officers in the Continental Army, he was not required to obtain their permission to participate further in the battle. If he chose to reenter the fight, no one could refuse him permission.

"Mac," he said with a grin, "we haven't been in a fight for so long that I can hardly remember when we last flexed our muscles. I guess this is too good a chance to improve our skills for us to miss. We'd better stop going backward before it gets to be a habit. Pass the word to the company to reverse itself and start forward again."

The scouts threw themselves back into the fray with renewed vigor, seemingly with joyous abandon. Actually, they were too wise in the ways of battle to take unnecessary risks.

They set an example for the adjacent units as they

hugged the ground, taking care to conceal themselves in the brush as they moved to a forward position and engaged the enemy in a head-to-head confrontation.

Three of the American division commanders paid the scouts the highest of compliments in their reports to Washington after the battle. Each commented that his men had learned from them and had followed their example in battle, much to their own advantage.

The outcome was not in doubt from the outset. The Continental Army, though outnumbered, had taken the initiative from the very start and held it throughout the morning. Some British and Hessian units fought brilliantly and deserved the highest praise, but the majority floundered like amateurs and had an extremely difficult time gaining any momentum.

Meanwhile, Henry Knox and his expanded corps of artillerymen, many of them engaging in full-scale combat for the first time, behaved with the skill and aplomb of veterans. Most important of all, men from Massachusetts, New York, and Pennsylvania fought side by side with men from Georgia and South Carolina and Virginia. State and regional quarrels and differences were forgotten as the infantrymen remembered only that they were Americans fighting for the liberty of their entire nation.

By noon Cornwallis realized that his cause was hopeless and his losses severe, and he ordered his entire corps to retreat to New York.

The northern movement of redcoats and Hessians out of the forest soon resembled a panicky retreat, and the confusion was so great that with very little effort the Continentals were able to capture more than a thousand prisoners.

The full results of the battle did not become evident for several days. Then it was learned that Sir William Howe had suffered a severe shock, never having dreamed that Washington's army was capable of inflicting a heavy blow on his forces. He withdrew his entire army from New Jersey into New York and abandoned the state to the Continentals.

In the combined actions at Trenton and at Princeton, General Washington had won the most significant victory of his career. The country reacted precisely as the committee from the Continental Congress had hoped. Recruiting for the Continental Army picked up momentum, and young men everywhere enlisted for the duration of the war. The states were no more generous with their funds, but Benjamin Franklin, who had been sent to Paris as a special ambassador for the United States, reported that for the first time the French government was considering seriously the possibility of openly recognizing the American rebels and forming an alliance with them.

The distant hope of freedom entertained by two and a half million Americans was drawing closer to realization.

Toshabe heard the knock at the door shortly before noon, and when she hurriedly answered the summons, she was not surprised to find Clem Dawkins on the threshold. It was the first time he had ever called so early in the day. She'd met him on several occasions, agreeing with her husband that he and Ena should be gently encouraged in their relationship, rather than frustrated by being kept apart. She smiled a greeting.

"Morning, ma'am," he said politely. "Is Ena at home?"

"Indeed she is. Won't you come in?" Toshabe knew that at the sound of his voice Ena had appared miraculously at the head of the staircase. Now she raced down to the ground floor, paying no attention to the fact that her behavior was quite unladylike.

"These here are for you," he said, and held out his knitted yarn cap to her. It was upside down, and from the manner in which he gingerly handled it, apparently something delicate was inside. "They're duck eggs," he explained.

Ena blinked at him in astonishment, having expected no such gift. "Duck eggs?" she asked blankly.

"It seems this here duck got left behind," he said, "when all the others went south. I don't know exactly how it happened, because I wasn't around at the time. Anyway, the fellers in my battalion kind of adopted it, and they've been giving it a warm place to sleep and feeding it every day with bits of corn and dry bread. Seeing as how I don't have to stand guard duty or nothing, I got put in charge of the duck, and all of a sudden, a few days ago, she began laying eggs, one every day. A full battalion has so many men that what one duck puts out ain't enough to feed them, so the fellers decided I could do what I wanted with the eggs." His face shone with pleasure and anticipation. "So I been saving them until I got enough for a decent-sized present, and here they are. They're for you."

Overwhelmed, Ena could only stammer her thanks.

"I hear tell that duck eggs make a mighty tasty omelet," Clem said.

Toshabe came to her daughter's rescue. "We'll soon find out," she said, and took the knitted cap containing the eggs from him. "You'll stay and eat with us, I hope, Clem?"

He was moved to protest. "That wouldn't be fair!" he said vehemently. "These eggs are supposed to be a present!"

Toshabe reacted as though she didn't hear him. She looked at his lean frame and gaunt face meaningfully. "What did you have for supper last night?" she demanded.

He found it exceptionally difficult to lie gracefully. "I—I don't remember."

"You'll stay for dinner," Toshabe told him, and the

note of finality in her voice precluded further conversation on the subject.

Soon she called her children to the kitchen table. Renno and El-i-chi were in high spirits, having trapped a pair of rabbits that morning, but were surprised and disappointed that their mother elected to save the brace for supper. The boys were served fish that El-i-chi had caught, and Toshabe had the same on her own plate. Then she brought in a large omelet, which she proceeded to cut in half and serve to Ena and to Clem.

The boys watched their sister and the yellow-haired youth as they ate.

"The duck omelet looked like it was very good," young Renno observed.

"It was more than good," Ena declared. "It was delicious."

"How would you know?" Renno retorted.

As he said later to his mother, "All she and Clem did was sit there, making eyes at each other the whole time they ate. I swear it! I don't think they even tasted the food they put into their mouths."

Chapter IX

Having proved the worth of his army to the entire United States and to Great Britain as well, early in 1777 General Washington moved with his Continental veterans and an ever-growing body of recruits into winter quarters at Morristown, New Jersey.

The site was an impregnable natural fortress that could not be easily approached by an enemy from any side. Here the army settled down for the winter, while Mrs. Washington and a number of other ladies, including Toshabe, moved to a cluster of farmhouses not far away.

Sir William Howe remained bottled up in his winter quarters in New York, fuming because of the mortification of the twin defeats he had suffered at Trenton and Princeton. At the War Office in London, energetic steps were taken to bring the war to a successful conclusion, but the optimism of the top-ranking leaders of the British Army and of Parliament was giving way to a more unstable and questioning attitude. America had displayed her latent strength for the first time, and farseeing Englishmen were able to catch a glimpse of the handwriting on the wall. They could envision the day when the American colonies would sever relations with the mother country irrevocably and finally.

Ghonkaba's scouts, together with several small cavalry units, were given a special mission. Free to roam beyond the immediate area, the scouts were ordered to find any convoys of supplies being transported by the British and to confiscate them, as food was desperately needed by the army in Morristown.

On the night before the unit's departure, Ghonkaba was summoned to the commander in chief's house. There, to his great surprise, he found his wife, sons, and daughter present. Along with other guests, they were shepherded into the drawing room for a brief ceremony.

General Washington amazed and delighted Ena with a handsome gift acknowledging her contribution as a scout. He gave her a collapsing telescope, such as a ship's captain might use. It was small enough that she could carry it easily.

Overwhelmed by the gift, she vowed she would always carry it in the future and declared she would fashion a case of leather so it could hang around her neck. Ghonkaba, although he feared for her future safety, nevertheless was inordinately proud of her. She gave promise of carrying on in the proudest of family traditions.

During the social hour following the presentation

to Ena, Ghonkaba approached the commander in chief. "General," he said, "I've been wanting a few words with you."

"Certainly," Washington replied, and withdrew into the adjacent dining room, where refreshments soon would be served.

"I'm grateful for the assignment you've given my scouts, General," Ghonkaba said. "It will be far better for the spirits of the men to be roaming through the countryside, looking for the British supply convoys, than to be doing nothing here. All the same, I'm wondering if I can't leave the unit temporarily in the capable hands of my sergeants."

"I suppose that could be arranged," General Washington replied. "What do you have in mind?"

"To be honest with you, sir, I think our exploits at Trenton and Princeton warrant a special visit to the land of the Seneca. Now that we have sufficient cause to raise our heads and boast, I'd like to present the facts to the Seneca council and to the Great Sachem of the Iroquois. I think the time has come for the nations of the Iroquois League to reconsider their stand and join forces with you."

Washington couldn't help but laugh. "Of course, I grant my permission freely for such a venture. But aren't you taking a great risk that you'll be held captive once you reach the land of the Seneca?"

"I think not," Ghonkaba replied. "I intend to take my daughter and the elder of my sons with me to witness whatever is going to occur there, and I feel certain that my father and my uncle would not dream of taking me prisoner, especially in the presence of my children."

"All I can tell you," Washington said, "is to go with my blessing. We need all the help we can get, and may you be successful in your venture."

*   *   *

Ghonkaba led his daughter and son northwestward by the most direct route, which took them through the land of the Erie. Although the Erie and the Seneca were both allies of the British in the present war, the two tribes remained implacable enemies of each other. Ghonkaba took every precaution to prevent his children's falling into the hands of the Erie, who would hold the grandchildren of Ja-gonh for a high ransom. If it were not paid promptly, they would not hesitate to execute both Ena and Renno. They moved at a good pace. Renno, as was expected, demonstrated a greater stamina than did his sister.

Ghonkaba was fascinated by the differences in the attitudes of his daughter and son. Renno showed promise of becoming a solid warrior who could be depended upon. Ena, on the other hand, had the indefinable air of one thoroughly at home in the wilderness. It held no mysteries for her, and she was totally unafraid.

Alternating in choosing their resting places each night, the young people were extremely careful and always chose well-protected sites where they could have maximum concealment.

On the fifth day after leaving the winter quarters, they were about to enter a territory nominally under the control of their allies, the Mohawk. They were trotting in single file, with Ghonkaba in the lead, when suddenly Ena tapped him on the shoulder.

They halted and she raised a finger to her lips.

All three immediately dropped to their knees and placed ears to the ground. Ena was right; they heard the soft approaching footsteps of at least two men.

Fully prepared for such an emergency, Ghonkaba pointed to the upper branches of twin oaks; Ena and Renno understood and obeyed with alacrity. Ghonkaba concealed himself behind the thick trunk of one of the oaks and removed his tomahawk from his belt; grasping it firmly in his right hand, he waited.

Two Erie appeared, advancing cautiously. Ghonkaba noted at once that they were young, broad-shouldered, and husky. In the physical prime of life, they not only outnumbered him but had the advantage of youthful physical strength and stamina.

What they lacked, however, was the experience gained through long familiarity with deadly combat. They were searching the ground for footprints, broken twigs, and other signs that people had recently passed this way. Ghonkaba realized that he or his companions had carelessly left tracks that could be followed. That meant it was too late to take evasive action.

He knew that he would have to kill or be killed. In any confrontation between the Seneca and the Erie, no quarter was given.

Leaping into the open before his hiding place was discovered, Ghonkaba raised his arm and brought down the tomahawk, putting all of his strength into the blow. He decapitated one of the Erie warriors, who pitched forward onto the ground and lay still, the earth turning reddish-brown as it absorbed his blood.

Before the second Erie could recover from his shocked surprise, Ghonkaba twisted toward him and released his tomahawk. His aim was perfect, and the weapon lodged itself in the warrior's throat. He was dead by the time he reached the ground.

Ena and Renno descended swiftly from above, admiration for his father's skilled exploits plain in Renno's eyes.

In simple pantomime, he told them he wanted them to scalp the two dead warriors. Ena hesitated briefly, but Renno went to work at once. Adept with his hands, he performed the operation neatly and with dispatch, wielding his knife with the expertise of a veteran warrior who had scalped countless defeated foes. Ena delighted her father by controlling her repugnance as she, too, went about her task with crisp efficiency.

Giving them the right to carry the scalps, Ghonkaba motioned them back onto the trail. They had lost very little time.

Ghonkaba thought it inconceivable that anyone wearing the war paint of the Seneca would be subjected to an attack by close allies, but he couldn't help but feel that they were under false colors as they made their way through the land of the Mohawk. He realized that any Mohawk seeing him as he passed through their territory with Ena and Renno would assume that he, like the majority of his nation, was a supporter of the British. For once the fortunes of war shielded him, and for that he was wryly grateful.

When they came to the land of the Seneca, the nation proved to be as alert as always. No sooner did they move into Seneca territory than the war drums of the unseen sentinels in the deep forest became active. Listening to the messages, Ghonkaba was hardly surprised to hear it related that he and two of his children were traveling swiftly through the forest, apparently making their way toward the town. The messages mentioned that no trace of belligerence showed in his demeanor.

Ena and Renno felt mounting excitement as they went through the familiar wilderness where they had received their earliest training. At last they could see the high, spiked wooden palisade of the town in the distance. They reached the area where in summer the Seneca women grew corn, beans, and squash, but the fields were barren at this time of year. Beyond them, standing outside the palisade, were Ja-gonh and Ah-wen-ga. Ena and Renno raced across the frozen, hard-packed snow and, ignoring the customs of the Seneca, enveloped their grandparents in hugs.

Ghonkaba acted with greater dignity and raised his arm in a formal greeting. His father returned the gesture, but his mother stood staring at him, her arms around her grandchildren as she blinked back happy tears.

Her son took her in his arms and kissed her fondly. Then he and his father clasped each other by the shoulders and smiled in complete understanding.

A worried look was in Ah-wen-ga's eyes, and Ghonkaba recognized the reason for her concern. "Toshabe and El-i-chi send you their love," he said, "and they are sorry they could not come on this journey with us. But it was necessary that I make as good time as possible, so I brought only the two elder children with me, as they could keep up my pace."

Ja-gonh laughed, then asked jocularly, "Can Ena be adept at wilderness travel?"

His son nodded somberly. "I will gladly enter her in competition," he said, "with any warrior in this nation. When you hear what she has accomplished, you'll be able to understand why General Washington places a value beyond compare on her talents."

"We have much to hear," Ja-gonh said as he ushered them through the gate and started striding toward his house.

"Yes," Ghonkaba added pointedly, "and we have much to discuss."

Ja-gonh looked at him sharply, realizing he had not come home on a purely social visit.

They were joined by Ghonkaba's aunt and uncle, Goo-ga-ro-no and No-da-vo, the sachem of the Seneca.

The women, assisted by the two young people, began to prepare a celebratory supper, and while they worked, Ghonkaba regaled them with a full account of what Ena had accomplished preparatory to the Battle of Trenton. He also revealed that Ena had acquired the mysterious ability to foretell the future in her dreams.

Her grandparents were deeply impressed, as were her great-aunt and great-uncle.

"You should rejoice, Ena, because you have won the favor of the manitous," Ja-gonh said. "I, too, have enjoyed the favor of seeing the future unfolded before me in my dreams, and I can tell you that you bear a grave responsibility, as well as enjoy a great privilege. You must be alert to the messages you receive. When you have news of consequence to impart, be sure you pass it along, without delay, to those to whom you are related and others directly concerned. Above all, never use this talent for selfish purposes. The gods, acting through the manitous, have singled you out as a messenger between their world and the world of living beings. Your duty is to use the gift wisely."

Sobered by her grandfather's admonition, Ena promised to do her best to live up to the faith placed in her by the manitous.

While supper was cooking, No-da-vo inquired about the battles of Trenton and Princeton, saying that the news of Washington's twin victories had been received in recent days.

This was an opening that Ghonkaba had awaited, and he recounted in glowing terms the activities at Trenton and Princeton, which had led to American victories. He emphasized the importance of the victories to the American cause, stressing that the British had been driven out of New Jersey.

He timed his remarks nicely, and just before they moved to form a circle around the cooking fire, he concluded with a subtle plea.

"I make no farfetched claims for the Americans," he said. "I do not for one moment say that they will win only victories from now until their independence is assured. But there can be no doubt that they will achieve their freedom. There's no doubt that eventually

Great Britain will become tired of losing and will retire across the Great Sea to her own territory."

His mother had remembered his favorite foods, which she served for supper, and she did not forget to end the meal on a note favored by the young people, who loved her corncakes and maple syrup.

After the meal the men retired to the principal room of the house, where they sat on the floor, and Ja-gonh lighted a long pipe, which they passed from hand to hand.

Ghonkaba was satisfied that he had given his father and uncle much food for thought before supper. He had observed both of them carefully and had noticed that they were often preoccupied. So he deliberately picked up where he had left off.

"I have often thought about the fate that awaits my people," he said. "For a time it appeared that my father and my uncle were right to have kept their alliance with the British. It seemed that the redcoats could do nothing wrong and that they would win every battle. But that is not so. The Americans are gaining strength, and they remind me of the Seneca in their tenacity, their stubbornness, their will to win.

"What will become of the Seneca," he demanded, "when General Washington has driven the redcoats into the Great Sea? Then the British will return to their own distant homes and King George, the most selfish of monarchs, will abandon his allies to their fate. I cannot believe that the American men-at-arms will treat the allies of their foes with kindness and a willingness to forgive."

Ja-gonh broke his silence. "You think they will seek vengeance against those who were their foes?"

"Would the Seneca seek such vengeance in like circumstances?" Ghonkaba asked. "Of course we would! The Americans are similar to the Seneca in many ways, including the way they fight. They have learned the lessons of the wilderness, and none are more expert in the firing of muskets. They remember their friends, and they do not forget those who have been their enemies."

Ja-gonh and his brother-in-law exchanged an uncomfortable glance. No-da-vo was the first to break their silence. "Why do you tell us these things?" he asked. "Do you seek to frighten us by giving us threatening information?"

"I have no wish to frighten you," Ghonkaba said. "Neither do I threaten. I have been absent from my people for many moons, but that has not diminished my love for you, my greatest concern in this world. I shudder when I think of the revenge that the victorious Americans will want to exact from their foes. The British will be far away, and the only enemies near at hand will be the Seneca and the other unfortunate nations of the Iroquois League that made the wrong choice of allies in this great war." He was deliberately exaggerating, hoping they would come to expect the reaction of the Americans to be similar to that of the Seneca in like circumstances.

Ja-gonh puffed on his pipe. "You have been associated with the Americans for many moons, my son. What do you advise that we do?"

This was the opportunity that Ghonkaba had been awaiting from the outset.

"My father," he said, "is an honest man. He is known throughout the nations of the Iroquois League as one who always keeps his word. Surely he will never go back on what he has sworn during his father's last moments on this earth. He promised that the Seneca and the other nations would indeed sign a sacred treaty of alliance with Great Britain, that the enemies of the British would be their enemies. This my father has done. But I believe I can see ways of altering that state without breaking his word."

"I'm afraid," Ja-gonh replied wearily, "that I can find no way to solve my dilemma. No-da-vo and I, like all the warriors of our people, have felt a natural, instinctive sympathy for the Americans. But we have been prevented from joining them by the need to keep my promise. What does my son suggest that we do now?"

"The Iroquois," Ghonkaba said boldly, "have not had to take an active role in the war, but have sat in the background while the British and Americans hurl their forces at each other. Now, as the British lose more and more battles to the Americans, they will try to rely more heavily on the Iroquois. As you already have decided, the Seneca and their Iroquois brothers should not respond as the British wish but should remain inactive."

Ja-gonh's face began to clear as he listened. He was pleased with Ghonkaba's comments on the situation.

"The Americans," Ghonkaba said, "have no need for the active alliance of the nations of the Iroquois. The Continental Army grows stronger moon by moon, and soon it will be able to fight all its own battles. Active opposition by the Iroquois could be too much, however, for the Americans to tolerate, and I strongly urge that you continue your policy of avoiding direct conflict in battle with them. It was a wise decision, I am convinced."

"You have given us much more to ponder, my son," Ja-gonh said. "I will think on it, and I charge No-da-vo to do so also. We will discuss it further between us, and then before you must leave, we will inform you of our decision. You will decide whether or not you should tell the Americans of our strategy."

What Ghonkaba failed to realize was the depth of the opposition he faced from his old foe, Tredno, whose ambitions were boundless. The sly warrior remained firmly but secretly opposed to everything that the ruling family was trying to accomplish.

Regarded as unreliable by the Seneca high command, he stood high in British favor because of several raids he had led on American settlements. Now that Ghonkaba had arrived for a visit, Tredno discreetly remained in the background. Absenting himself from the town, he spent most days hunting and fishing, and he avoided meetings at which war chiefs ordinarily were expected to be present. He kept his views strictly to himself.

Although experience had taught him that he could do his subversive work most efficiently when Ghonkaba was not on hand, he fretted with the inactivity, while consoling himself that Ghonkaba's days were, after all, numbered. He saw it as inevitable that they would meet again in battle. When they did, Tredno was determined that he would take the life of his sworn enemy.

Even while realizing that Tredno's opinions were more than ever bitterly opposed to his own, Ghonkaba failed to regard those views as significant and he discounted Tredno's influence. Despite the antagonisms of the past—even taking into account Tredno's firing at him during the Battle of Long Island—it never entered his mind that the rival war chief could be so treacherous as to connive to oust Ja-gonh and No-da-vo from their posts. He assumed that because of his own fall from grace in the Seneca hierarchy he no longer would be a target of Tredno's bitterness. In short, he instinctively felt that he had much more important matters to consider and decide than any brave's personal enmity. This, as he came to realize later, was a grave mistake on his part. In the meantime, he shrugged off the occasional chill that overtook him, like the chill he had felt when sitting convivially with friends around a campfire. Sometimes he momentarily pondered the possible meaning of these feelings, as he had then, but he saw no reason to consider them a major factor in his life.

*   *   *

The sachems of the other Iroquois nations were summoned by the Great Sachem to a secret meeting. After they had all arrived, Ja-gonh requested that Ghonkaba repeat his comments before the assembled visitors.

Ordinarily, Ghonkaba would not have been present at such a high-level conference, but Ja-gonh had decided that a full range of views and opinions should be represented at this critical gathering. Several other Seneca warriors, including even Tredno, were on hand by this special dispensation.

Ghonkaba would speak first, and then after an opportunity for discussion the Seneca warriors would be dismissed before the sachems held their private session, at which decisions would be reached.

Midway through his quite brief remarks, Ghonkaba was interrupted by a raucous voice that came from one side of the council chamber, contemptuously disregarding the time-honored proprieties of such a serious situation and the wishes of the Great Sachem. It was Tredno, who shouldered aside nearby warriors in his haste to make his presence known and his voice unmistakably heard.

"What you have been hearing is nonsense!" he shouted at the Iroquois sachems. "It is completely full of false thinking given to you by one who already has proven his disloyalty to all that we stand for—"

He was glaring wildly about him and so was unprepared for the heavy hand that No-da-vo clapped upon his right shoulder from behind. As the Seneca sachem's grip tightened, the taut voice of Ja-gonh was heard above the developing hubbub.

"I must express to my brothers," he declared, "the regret that I so deeply feel at this unseemly interruption in our proceedings. To the warrior Tredno, who is abusing the privilege I granted in permitting him to be present, I speak now with an admonition that I can only hope he will take as fully to heart as he should. I must, indeed, insist on his recognition, before all of you gathered here, that he has transgressed and acknowledges this as a grievous offense as we explore together our course of action."

Ja-gonh's piercing gaze riveted Tredno, who stared back at the Great Sachem coldly even as he spoke a few words of slight, grudging apology.

Additionally irritated by Tredno's continued display of arrogance and surliness, Ja-gonh spoke again, even more harshly.

"No war chief of the Seneca, no matter how valorous he may be known to be and no matter how vehement his opinions, is permitted to disturb the proper order of proceedings of this council," he said firmly, never taking his eyes off Tredno. "I would have expected much better deportment by such a person, especially one who professes to see what proper behavior on a much larger scale should consist of. Again, I must express my personal regrets to each of our visitors for an unseemly incident. We will have no more of it, I assure you!"

Throughout this, Tredno had stood motionless, his gaze unflinching but seemingly unseeing. His entire body was rigid, his attitude unbending. But though he revealed no sign of humiliation at the public rebuke, he was sensitive to a disgrace beyond any he had felt all his life. Blinded by anger, he was repeating to himself, over and over, that his vow to put an end to the leadership of Ja-gonh's family now was more important than ever before. First to go would be the treacherous Ghonkaba!

Ja-gonh seated himself once more and in a calm manner called the meeting to order again. He instructed Ghonkaba to resume his remarks, which were then quickly finished. Though he had intended to have a general discussion that would include the Seneca warriors, he instead dismissed them all.

Taking up where Ghonkaba had left off, the Great Sachem spoke to the other sachems feelingly, putting the untoward incident out of his mind.

"My brothers," he said, "as you may know, but as my son does not, I recently returned from a strategy meeting in Canada. There I learned of the British War Office's plans for what they regard as the principal campaign for this year. They have proposed an invasion from Canada by way of Lake Champlain to gain control of the line from the lake down to the Hudson River. In this way New England could be isolated and the American forces divided and crushed piecemeal. According to the secret War Office plan, General John Burgoyne will lead a strong column of British troops into New York from Canada, by way of Lake Champlain. Meanwhile, Colonel Barry St. Leger will lead a force of loyalist refugees and our own Iroquois warriors along the Mohawk River, and we are supposed to unite with Burgoyne near Albany. In the meantime, troops also will be detached from General Howe's army in New York and will march north to give Burgoyne additional support."

"We were given no voice in the determination of this plan," No-da-vo added. "We were simply informed of what is to be and of the role we are assigned."

"What led the British to believe that we would obey and do their bidding?" the sachem of the Oneida demanded.

"That is the British manner," Ja-gonh said. "They never react as the American colonials did when we were in partnership with them. The officers commanding American troops always sought our advice and listened to what we suggested when they made their battle plans."

"We are not colonials, and we do not owe allegiance to the British throne," the leader of the powerful Mohawk said angrily. "I don't see how they can assume that we will just jump to obey their commands."

"That is their way of dealing with those they regard as inferiors," Ja-gonh said.

The sachem of the Mohawk made a wry face. "The more I hear, the more inclined I am to agree with the words of Ghonkaba."

"We cannot reply to the British request with a refusal to serve," Ja-gonh said flatly. "Then they will claim we have gone back on our word and they will send many regiments of both infantry and artillery to teach us a lesson. Our warriors are courageous men, but they would have no chance in battle against superior rifle and cannon power."

"If we should decide to remain neutral when this great battle is fought," No-da-vo said, "we must keep that fact to ourselves, in a secret compact. We cannot let the British—or even our own warriors—learn our intentions."

"We must show that we expect to live up to whatever the treaty technically calls for," Ja-gonh added. "But the manner in which we carry out our obligations will make Colonel St. Leger and General Burgoyne realize that we are not the mere pawns of the British."

After a long silence, the sachem of the Tuscarora spoke. "Can we call ourselves honorable men if we in any way appear to break our agreement with the British?" he asked. "Can we face ourselves honestly?"

Ja-gonh was ready with a logical and effective answer.

"First of all," he stated in a deliberate tone as he looked separately at each sachem present, "let us keep uppermost in our minds that each of us—and especially the Great Sachem of all Iroquois—must strive above all else to ensure the survival of our people. I consider this to be true regardless of alliances, present or former. In this new age, with its complicated and unprecedented alignments of power, we Iroquois risk being crushed between two great factions of white men who choose to go to war—the British and the Americans.

"Even if it appears cowardly, we must choose the course that is best for us and our future ability to live our own lives. In this new age, we are required to respect new rules. No longer is it enough for us simply to run at the side of our allies, fighting when they fight, conquering when they conquer.

"In striving to protect the future of our great people, we must know that the manitous have willed this to be so. If some of our actions do appear cowardly and dishonorable to others who, now or later, may observe them, that is only because they do not see things as clearly as we must—as clearly I am persuaded that I am now seeing our future.

"This is no time for passions to run riot. We must act coolly. And history will be the judge of our wisdom."

He scanned the faces of his comrades again, and seeing the remaining looks of uncertainty, he resumed with matters of more immediate tactical concern.

"Before the war between the British and her colonies began," he told them, "I was visited by a high representative of King George, who promised ten thousand rifles for the warriors of the Iroquois if we would join forces with Britain for the duration of the war. We have kept our word. But the British have not kept their word. We have joined them and they have benefitted from our alliance. But we have discovered that of the ten thousand rifles that were delivered to us, nearly seven thousand are useless because bolts and other vital parts were omitted from them. We have been left to fight with whatever weapons we possessed previously. The British think they have outsmarted us. By refusing to give us rifles that can be effective in battle, they think that we will be harmless if we ever turn against them. I regard that action on their part as dishonorable, and one that frees us from any obligation to do their bidding at whatever time they may choose to call upon us. I propose that at no time during the remainder of this war do we raise our hands in war against the Americans. I propose that we indicate our acceptance of the role we have been asked to play, but that in actuality we remain neutral. My own conscience thereby will be clear. I hope that you, my brothers, will feel as I do."

After another silence, the sachem of the Mohawk spoke up. "I stand with my brother, Ja-gonh, in this matter!"

A shout of acclamation greeted his words, and the vote was unanimous. The nations of the Iroquois would do nothing overt to rupture their alliance with Great Britain or disavow it, but would also do nothing to further the British cause and would remain neutral for the rest of the war. Because a supposed ally had treated them falsely and played them for fools, they need not and would not honor the ostensible obligation to fight along with that ally. Accordingly, they could expect that it would be a long time before another nation treated them like children. By taking matters into their own hands, they would be serving proper notice and just reward on the canny British, and they would be preserving their honor.

Ja-gonh decided to wait until Ghonkaba was about to rejoin General Washington before revealing the position of the Iroquois to him.

"You have succeeded in your mission, my son," he said. "The warriors of the Iroquois will lift no hand against the Americans."

"You will not regret having made this decision, my father," Ghonkaba replied. "The Seneca undoubtedly are the finest warriors in all the world, but you can put no more than fifteen hundred braves into the field at any one time without straining your resources. The Americans, however, have a large population that they can rely upon, and as they gain in strength and draw closer to independence, they will sweep before them any who oppose them. I am convinced that by adopting this stance toward Britain, you have assured the peaceful future of this great nation."

The eager recruits who joined the Continental Army following Washington's twin victories in New Jersey discovered too late that they were exposed to all the rigors of winter at the army's quarters.

In spite of the successes of the troops of cavalry and the company of scouts in intercepting British supply trains, food was in short supply. Frequently the entire army went hungry for several days at a time until Captain Harry Lee of Virginia or one of the other commanders managed to intercept a British convoy.

Mrs. Washington and the other women who occupied the farmhouses nearby settled down to a hard winter, too. Fortunately, supplies of wood were ample to make fires in the many hearths, so the women and the children at least were warm.

Martha Washington set an example, quickly followed by others, of asking for no special privileges and sharing the army's rations. This meant that the commander in chief and several division heads whose wives had accompanied them into winter quarters lived on very meager fare. No one complained.

Time hung heavily on Toshabe's hands with her husband and two children absent. El-i-chi, her younger son, sharpened his wilderness skills by spending several hours each day in search of edible roots in the marshy areas of the forest. By virtue of covering himself with bear grease before he ventured out of doors, he suffered far less from the cold than did the troops. Often he returned with roots to which snow still clung, but which were useful in augmenting the slender fare.

Toshabe knew she had no cause for complaint. She lost weight, and her figure was as slender and supple as when she was a girl. She read every book in the tiny library of the small farmhouse, and housework occupied very little of her energies. The lack of food meant even less time spent in cooking. Frequently she went to the window looking for any sign of Ghonkaba.

Now, she caught sight of an officer wearing a frayed blue and buff greatcoat with the epaulets of a lieutenant colonel struggling through the snow toward the house. She knew all too well why he had chosen to call on her, and panic assailed her. She was alone in the house; El-i-chi would not return for another two hours, and she could count on no one but herself to fend off Alexander Hamilton.

Exercising supreme self-control, she managed to calm herself and concentrate on her task. She did not want to become involved in an affair with any man— including Hamilton. Realizing he was both ruthless and quick-witted, she knew he would not be put off easily, and she searched for some way to evade him. Suddenly an idea that was both outrageous and daring occurred to her.

The door knocker sounded, and Toshabe had no opportunity to weigh the thought and to plan its execution. She would have to do her best and hope she would succeed.

Hamilton removed his helmet and stamped snow from his boots. "I hope I'm not disturbing you by appearing unexpectedly in this way, without an appointment," he apologized.

"That's perfectly all right." Toshabe welcomed him with a broad smile. "As it happens, I've been thinking about you all day."

He was pleased, as she had known he would be. "Really? I hope they were pleasant thoughts."

"Of course," she replied, half closing her eyes and regarding him through long, lowered lashes. She had not flirted with anyone for a great many years, but the knack was not lost.

"I am flattered," Hamilton said, and followed close behind her as she led him into the parlor. He went to the hearth, where a blazing log fire was burning.

He extended his hands toward the fire, then rubbed them together. "This is delightful."

"Isn't it, though!" she replied cheerfully. "I'm so glad there's no shortage of firewood. I can tolerate almost any inconvenience except being too chilly."

"I know of many ways to overcome a chill," Hamilton told her suggestively.

"I am sure," Toshabe murmured, and changed the subject. "Would you like a glass of wine, Colonel Hamilton?"

"Very much," he said, pleased with the way his visit was going.

Toshabe went to a sideboard where she poured a glass of wine concocted of fermented juice of snowberries, to which she had added various herbs.

He glanced at her questioningly. "Aren't you going to join me?"

She shook her head, her manner demure. "I'm afraid not, sir. At times I find it difficult enough to keep myself controlled, without having to fight off the added stimulus of wine."

She knew from the smug expression on his face that he had leaped to the conclusion she had expected.

He sipped his wine, then tried to sound casual. "This is delicious. What is it?"

"It's a Seneca wine that I make from an old recipe that belonged to my husband's great-grandmother. The family has served it on important occasions for many years."

"Do you consider this an important occasion?" he asked, a teasing note in his voice.

She looked at him innocently, her huge eyes luminous. "It well could be," she said. "It depends on many factors."

Hamilton was encouraged. She seemed to be inadvertently disclosing her liking and admiration.

He seated himself on a divan and patted the cushion beside him.

Looking guileless, she shook her head. "I—I don't dare."

Hamilton looked at her with an expression of mock injury. "Are you intimating that you don't trust me?"

Toshabe contrived to look very innocent and young. "It isn't you," she said. "It's myself I don't trust."

Feigning impatience, he reached out, caught hold of her hand, and tugged. She lost her balance and landed close beside him on the divan. He managed to keep hold of her hand.

"Oh, dear," she murmured, straightening her skirt and trying to sit upright.

Still holding her hand, he exerted a subtle, gentle pressure on her arm so that she moved closer to him, until their shoulders touched. "There," he said, "that isn't so bad, is it?"

The moment on which the success or failure of her scheme depended had arrived.

Raising her face to his, she looked like the essence of ingenuousness as she murmured, "Certainly not. It's what I've known it would be. It's just wonderful!"

As she had anticipated, he took the bait. Bending his head, he kissed her gently.

Fighting and conquering a strong feeling of revulsion, she forced herself to return his kiss. The experience was so distasteful that she dug her fingernails into her palms to prevent herself from wrenching away from him and screaming.

His touch gentle, his timing perfect, Hamilton slid an arm around her.

Toshabe laid her head on his shoulder, unmindful of the epaulet that scratched her cheek. She knew the time had come; by waiting she would be risking complications. *Now!* she told herself.

Staring into the fire, she murmured, "You're very brave."

"How so?" he asked, tightening his hold.

"Not many men of your background," she told him glibly, "are willing to face an experienced Seneca warrior in deadly combat."

He was only half listening, concentrating instead on the logistical problem of moving her from the divan to a bedchamber. "What do you mean?" he asked idly.

Inventing as she spoke, Toshabe replied sweetly and with apparent sincerity. "It has long been a custom of the Seneca," she said, "that when a wife and a man other than her husband fall in love with each other and inform him of this state, the husband challenges the other man to a fight to the death. They wear only loincloths, and both are armed with long knives. It can be a fatal fight, to be sure, but I might have known you would not shrink from it."

She hoped she sounded convincing. No such custom existed among the Seneca. But she spoke with such quiet certainty that she hoped he would believe her.

Colonel Hamilton, unfamiliar with the customs of the Indian nations, drew a deep breath and quietly moved his arm from her waist to her shoulders. "Do you think it's necessary," he asked tentatively, "to inform your husband of our feelings?"

Here was the chance she had been awaiting. "Certainly!" she said with great fervor. "Nothing is clandestine or unclean about what we feel toward each other. I admire you additionally because you are facing the dissolution of your marriage so calmly and are prepared to accept the termination of mine, as well. I can tell you, though, that I'm glad I'm not a man. Ghonkaba may appear to be equipped with all the graces of your civilization, but at heart he is a ferocious barbarian who will stop at nothing to gain his ends." She was afraid to look at Hamilton now, for fear that she would giggle.

The parlor became very quiet, and they could hear no sound but the crackling of the burning log.

Hamilton stirred slightly and gently extricated himself from their embrace. He removed his arm from Toshabe's shoulders and inched away from her on the divan.

She knew beyond all doubt now that her scheme had succeeded. She had avoided becoming intimate with Hamilton and yet had handled the relationship in such a way that he could neither blame her nor resent her reactions.

A clock chimed on the mantel. Hamilton immediately rose to his feet. "I had no idea that it was four o'clock already," he announced. "You'll have to forgive me, my dear, but I'm afraid that duty calls me."

"Of course," she replied. "I'd be the last to come between an officer of the Continental Army and his duty."

He hurriedly donned his greatcoat, picked up his helmet, and clicked his heels as he bowed. "We shall meet again soon, my dear," he said, and was gone.

Toshabe felt weak. She leaned against the wall, laughing silently, and was comforted by the knowledge that she had defeated Alexander Hamilton at his own game.

Gradually her amusement faded. She wiped her mouth vigorously with the back of a hand, went to the fireplace, and spat into the hearth. The expression in her eyes was far from ingenuous or sweet. She resembled a savage, and if the colonel could have seen her at that moment, he would have realized she was capable of the action that she had attributed to Ghonkaba, that of viciously plunging a knife deep into his heart.

Already inundated with troubles, the people of the United States were contending with the coldest winter within memory. In the northern states the sun shone infrequently, the temperature remained far below freezing for many days on end, and snow fell often, piling up on arable land and on roads and trails.

But Ghonkaba, Renno, and Ena paid scant heed to the chill while making their way back to Morristown. Clad only in shirts and trousers of buckskin, they shared the Seneca secret of keeping warm in the coldest weather: each wore a light covering of rendered animal fat. Consequently, they encountered little difficulty as they hurried through frozen wastelands.

Travel through such terrain offered both advantages and disadvantages. Others who were abroad could not conceal their presence, because their steps were quite plain in the deep snows. In turn, however, it was impossible for Ghonkaba's party to hide their own presence, though they did enjoy one solid advantage. Few others ventured abroad in such inclement weather, and they had the wilderness to themselves. Therefore, they could progress as rapidly through the snow as they could manage.

They had no need to forage for food, as Ja-gonh had been exceedingly generous in giving them supplies before they departed. They carried more than enough with them to eat well.

Ghonkaba was pleased with the ease with which Ena and Renno adjusted to their difficult surroundings. They were able to keep up with him, they knew enough of the ways of the wilderness to select dry wood for their campfires, and they were frugal in their use of food.

One morning when the sky overhead was leaden as

usual, he was particularly pleased when both Ena and Renno picked up the tracks of a deer that had crossed their trail.

"It's unusual," Ghonkaba said, "for a deer to be wandering about through the wilderness in adverse weather like this. Wait here. We're comfortable in this clearing, your campfire is built, and you need only to add wood to it. What's more, no other humans are within many miles of us."

"You're going after the deer, my father?" Ena asked.

"If it isn't too scrawny a beast, I'll bring it down, yes. Although our supplies of jerked meat are more than adequate, I relish the prospect of the taste of a fresh venison steak. This cold gives me a huge appetite."

"Me, too," Renno said.

"I'll follow these tracks and see where they lead," Ghonkaba said. "I shall travel swiftly, so I want you to stay right where you are and wait for me here. When I return, I may or may not be bringing fresh venison for us to eat." He departed at once, making his way silently through the forest as he followed the tracks of the deer. Renno added another armful of wood to their fire, and then he and Ena settled down to wait.

The youngsters sat close to the fire, facing each other, and enjoyed its warmth. To assuage their appetites, they ate some parched corn and jerked meat.

Suddenly they froze. In the woods behind Ena they heard the crackling sound of someone—or something—approaching through the snow, occasionally stepping on a dead branch that cracked underfoot.

Looking about quickly for some means of protection, they grasped their tomahawks and braced themselves. Their tension grew second by second until finally through the snow and the underbrush a wild boar appeared. The beast was lean, but large enough to weigh some three hundred pounds. Just behind its snout were two wicked tusks. Its eyes were tiny, red, and malevolent.

Apparently the boar had smelled them or their meal and had come in search of food.

Finding itself confronting humans, its natural enemies, the boar stopped and considered. It looked first at Ena, who was closer to it, then at the flames leaping high into the air.

Ena handled a tomahawk adroitly, but knew she could not kill the boar with a single blow. That would be an accomplishment far beyond her capacity. Thinking swiftly, she reached behind her, tossing the weapon toward her brother, who could wield a tomahawk better than she could.

"You're more adept with a weapon than I am, Renno," she told him. "You see that branch of the oak tree above my head? When the beast starts forward again, I'm going to hoist myself up beyond its reach. Then you'll have a clear shot at it."

"Are you sure you can get out of its path?" Renno asked in great concern.

She laughed wryly. "If I don't succeed, I won't live long enough to know the difference!"

The boar pawed the ground, sending sprays of snow cascading behind it, and snorted four times, its head lowered as it prepared to attack.

Ena measured the distance to the branch. Then, just as the boar started forward, she leaped, her terror giving her added strength.

She caught hold of the ice-glazed branch with both hands and managed to pull up her feet and legs, which she also wrapped around the branch. She had forgotten that it would be covered with ice and snow.

The boar, demonstrating remarkable agility and speed, barely missed her and charged through open space.

Ena was so cold on the branch that she was almost forced to let go. But her fear gave her added resources, and she clung with all her might.

The boar halted and looked around in myopic confusion. Its enemy had suddenly vanished, but it could still smell human beings.

Observing the beast from the relative safety of the far side of the fire, Renno gripped Ena's tomahawk. Remembering everything his instructors had taught him, he let fly with it.

His aim was fairly accurate, and the blow landed on the side of the animal's head, inflicting severe damage to one ear.

Bleeding profusely, the boar gave several anguished grunts and began to paw the ground. It had caught sight, dimly, of another human foe on the far side of the fire, and was determined to kill its enemy.

Renno still had his own tomahawk. His bow, made for a boy rather than a man, was large enough to bring down small game but would be ineffective against so massive a beast.

Ena, clinging to the branch overhead, shouted encouragement. "Shoot now, Renno!" she called. "Throw your tomahawk, and aim for the place between its eyes. Don't be nervous, and don't miss!"

Renno measured the distance to the boar, staring at an invisible target between its tiny, bloodshot eyes. Then, as he exhaled, he threw the tomahawk with all his force and skill.

His aim was true; the sharp blade penetrated between the boar's eyes, and the animal, bleeding heavily, collapsed. The snow around its head turned crimson as it died.

Before Ena could disengage her hands and drop to the ground, Ghonkaba stepped into the clearing. He held his heavy bow in one hand, and with the other dropped a stout arrow back into its quiver. "You did well with the tomahawk, my son," he said. "That's because you positioned yourself properly before you threw it. Your first shot wasn't more effective because you had forgotten something you've been taught; your feet were improperly balanced." He reached up, caught hold of his daughter, and said, "Release your hands very slowly, Ena. Don't pull or jerk them, because you'll only succeed in tearing off chunks of flesh. Open them little by little, and when they come free from the tree, I'll lift you down."

Ena did as she was bidden, and when her father lifted her to the ground, she threw her arms around his neck, hugged him, and kissed him. "You saw everything that happened!" she cried.

Her brother found his voice. "You were off in the woods watching us!"

Ghonkaba smiled. "I saw the deer," he said, "but it was too scrawny, so I didn't even try to bring it down. When I came back, I saw the boar preparing to attack, and I immediately armed myself with my bow. But I refrained from using it until I saw how you two behaved."

Ena giggled, but her brother looked unhappy.

"You did well, Renno," Ghonkaba said, "even though you needed two tomahawks to complete the task that should have been done with one. Fortunately for both of you, your sister gave you her weapon."

Renno looked down at the ground. "I owe a debt of thanks to my sister, and I must apologize to you, my father. I broke the first law of a Seneca warrior with my initial throw. I was so rattled that I failed to remember to take a proper stance."

"You remembered it in time," Ghonkaba said reassuringly, "and that's what matters. As for you, my daughter, you showed great presence of mind, as you always do, when you leaped up to catch the branch. Your only mistake was in forgetting that it was icy, and when you discovered it, you almost released your hold. Fortunately, you were too afraid of the boar for that."

"How do you know what I had in mind and what I forgot, my father?" Ena asked.

"That was plain to see by your expression. At least you didn't injure your hands badly. I hope both of you will ponder the lessons that you've learned today, and in the meantime we'll celebrate, if you will, by butchering the carcass, and we'll have hot boar meat for our midday meal before we resume our journey."

Chapter X

Ghonkaba toured the encampment as soon as he had reported to General Washington. He was astonished at how living conditions had deteriorated since he had left to visit his parents.

But despite their damp, chilly quarters and inadequate food supplies, the men remained in high spirits. Veterans and recruits, numbering over fifteen thousand, were determined to see the winter through to an end and then to take the field again against the enemy.

Washington had told him that desertions were very few. The veterans had suffered the taste of bitter defeat in battles, beginning with the clash on Long Island, and had then known sweet victory. They were determined, as were the new arrivals, to continue their victorious ways and were willing to make any sacrifice necessary.

Money to purchase rations for the army was still lacking. The Continental Congress had failed to persuade the states to give it the power to levy taxes. Consequently, the frenzied quartermasters encountered many difficulties in buying enough food to feed fifteen thousand hungry men.

As Ghonkaba quickly learned, the army depended completely on the bands of cavalry and on the scouts for their food. When these units intercepted British supply trains, the army ate. When they did not, the army went hungry.

A scant two days after Ghonkaba's return, he and his family were eating a simple supper when they were interrupted by a ringing of the doorbell.

Renno answered the summons and came into the dining room moments later. "Captain Lee of Virginia is here to see you, my father," he said. "He's anxious to speak with you in private."

Ghonkaba hurried into the parlor. As a boy he had spent his summers with Captain Henry Lee of the cavalry, a member of the renowned Lee family of Virginia, where Ghonkaba had visited relatives on his grandmother's side of the family.

He and Lee greeted each other warmly, with hearty handclasps and slaps on the back.

"I hear you went up to the land of the Seneca and back just for practice in wilderness travel," Lee said jovially.

"You've been exercising your horse by catching British food convoys, the way I hear it," Ghonkaba replied. "You don't look a day older than the last time we met."

Toshabe entered the room and got the men tumblers of brandywine before taking her leave again. The old friends settled near the fire burning in the parlor hearth.

"I remember when we were about eight or nine," Lee said. "We were going to play a game of 'Settlers and Indians.' You refused to be one of the Indians, which at the time I thought was very unfair."

"You've always had definite ideas, Harry, and from what I hear, you still do."

The smile faded slowly from Harry Lee's face. "I'm not a know-it-all," he said, "but I do have a fair idea of what's needed to get the job I've been assigned done. Your scouts have been a big help during the time that you've been absent, Ghonkaba, and I thought we might put our heads together for the benefit of the whole army."

"By all means," Ghonkaba replied.

"I've enjoyed reasonably good luck," Lee said, "in intercepting British food convoys, but I think we can improve our methods. Every convoy travels with a strong armed guard of redcoats these days. I'm quite sure they're acting on Billy Howe's orders. The problem we face is that by the time we've fought off the armed guard and reduced them, at least a portion of the convoy escapes, and we're lucky to capture part of the supplies they're carrying. What I have in mind is to work out a new system with you that will enable us to seize a whole convoy without losing a single wagon that carries any food."

"Sounds fine, Harry," Ghonkaba said. "What have you got in mind?"

"I worked with your scouts on three or four occasions during your absence, and I have a specific use for them. Your four sergeants in particular are rather wonderful characters who can deceive anyone into believing what they want believed."

"Begin at the beginning, Harry," Ghonkaba said. "So far you're just confusing me."

"What I have in mind is something quite simple," Lighthorse Harry Lee replied. "When we know that British convoys are operating in a certain area and we've set our sights on which one of them we want to capture, we use your scouts as decoys. Your four sergeants appear in the open on the road and claim that they're loyalists who've been robbed by rebel marauders. When they've attracted the attention of the convoy's armed guard, the rest of your scouts attack from the woods on either side of the road. They're aided, of course, by the sergeants, and they put up a whale of a battle. While the fight is going on, my cavalry swoops down on the convoy and takes charge of the food wagons and drives off with them. Then my men double back, and together with your scouts they dispose of the enemy's armed guard."

"As I see it," Ghonkaba replied thoughtfully, "the greatest difficulty for us will come when we launch our initial attack. We'll have to hold the armed redcoat guard off indefinitely until your troop of cavalry can rejoin us."

"You're quite right. We'll need to coordinate our activities carefully."

They agreed to meet again, the next time with their principal noncommissioned subordinates. The idea was well worth developing, and they needed no authority but their own to put the plan into effect. General Washington had given them carte blanche to serve as they saw fit through the winter, and all he asked in return was solid results.

The meeting took place several days later at Ghonkaba's quarters after his scouts and Lee's troop of cavalry had returned from their previous assignment. Ghonkaba had no commissioned officers serving under him, his four sergeants having steadfastly refused to accept promotions to lieutenant. They and one of the Seneca war chiefs were the senior noncommissioned officers of the company. Lee's aides included two lieutenants and four sergeants, all of them cut from the same mold: without exception they were superb horsemen, all were passionately devoted to the patriot cause, and all were reckless and willing to take almost any risk.

While other scouts surrounded the house and permitted no outsider, no matter what his rank, to approach, Lee and Ghonkaba presented Lee's idea to their subordinates. The response was overwhelming. Representatives of both the scouts and the cavalry approved the scheme. Ghonkaba pointed out that his scouts would be forced to bear the brunt of the fighting with the redcoat guards until the horsemen were able to spirit the captured supplies out of the immediate vicinity. This, he pointed out, might take quite some time, and he did not know how long his scouts could sustain an attack unaided.

At the suggestion of one of Lee's lieutenants, the cavalry contingent withdrew for a private discussion, and after a brief absence, they returned with broad smiles.

The largest convoys encountered to date had consisted of fifty wagons, and the cavalrymen estimated that seventy-five horsemen, acting in unison, could control the movement of these wagons in any direction they pleased.

That left another seventy-five horsemen who could be thrown into combat with the British armed guard without delay.

"That means," Lee said, "that we'll be a mighty sorry lot if we can't chomp up the redcoats as fine as hominy grits in no time!"

The cavalrymen and scouts cheered his remark.

After the assemblage grew quiet again, Ghonkaba

had a few words to say. "This scheme we've worked out sounds as though it should be very effective. Certainly I believe it will be, if we keep the plan completely to ourselves. I see no need for anyone at the commander in chief's headquarters to learn of it, and there's certainly no need to notify any of the divisions of what we're doing, either. It will be more than enough if we bring back the food the troops need. In other words, keep your mouths shut! Don't talk about the tactics we're going to employ with anyone who isn't going on the mission. Our success depends on our ability to maintain absolute secrecy about our operations, so we'll keep our plan to ourselves!"

Captain Lee had established a network of informers, including several who worked at the wholesale food market in New York. At irregular intervals these men were able to inform him of the movements of food convoys out of British-occupied New York to various outposts where redcoats were stationed.

After hearing nothing from his informers for more than a week, Lee went to Ghonkaba in an excited state. "There's a huge convoy about to take off," he said. "They're going to leave New York next week, and after crossing the Hudson, they're going up the river to an outpost on Bear Mountain. If my information is correct, as many as one hundred wagons may be in the convoy."

Ghonkaba whistled under his breath.

"This is going to be somewhat more complicated than we expected, however," Lee went on. "I'm also told they'll have an escort of two hundred and fifty veteran redcoat light infantrymen."

"We're incapable of coping with that strong a force unless we have ample reinforcements," Ghonkaba replied instantly. "There's only one place we can get them."

They went promptly to the commander in chief's dwelling and asked to see General Washington.

"Why do you want to see him?" Colonel Hamilton asked in a challenging voice.

Lee, who didn't like the colonel, replied tartly, "We seek admittance to his presence on a strictly military matter that's entirely our own business and his. We can't mention its substance to anyone else, and that includes you, Colonel."

Hamilton flushed but went to Washington with the request, and within a short time the two officers were shown into the general's study. As soon as the door closed, Lee told the general of the message he had received.

Washington was impressed, but he looked hard, first at Lee and then at Ghonkaba. "As I see it, you lack the strength to face two hundred and fifty redcoat marksmen."

"Exactly so, General," Ghonkaba replied boldly. "We're here to ask for immediate reinforcements. We'll need help if we're to pull this scheme off. I need to double the size of my scout company, and Captain Lee requires double the cavalrymen he commands."

Washington was silent, and Ghonkaba assumed that his request for additional manpower was going to be rejected. But it soon developed that the commander in chief was thinking of various possibilities.

"What would you say," he inquired at last, "if I were to give you a battalion of Dan Morgan's Virginians?"

Ghonkaba and Lee exchanged broad smiles that spoke for themselves. Colonel Daniel Morgan commanded a regiment of frontier sharpshooters who had participated in every major engagement of the war and were the most solid and reliable troops in the entire Continental Army. Not only were they expert shots with their long rifles, but being frontiersmen, they were thoroughly familiar with the wilderness and needed no lessons on getting along in the forest.

Washington saw their faces and needed no other answer. He sent for Colonel Morgan, who was delighted to collaborate, observing that his men were getting out of practice. A company of one hundred men was assigned to Ghonkaba's scouts, while another company of equal size augmented Lee's cavalry. Now the expedition numbered enough men to meet the redcoat guards on equal terms.

They started north that same day, traveling as rapidly as the foot soldiers could march. Lee was in overall command, with Ghonkaba as his deputy. The captains of the two companies of Virginia rifles rounded out the high command. Lee had known the two infantry leaders since boyhood, and Ghonkaba had served with them under Washington when they had been young ensigns in his regiment. A distinct spirit of comradeship prevailed from the outset. By special dispensation, young Clem was allowed to travel with Ghonkaba, under Ranoga's particularly watchful eye.

The Virginians were eager to stretch their legs, the scouts refused to be beaten by more energetic compatriots, and the cavalrymen were anxious to retain their supposed superiority.

Therefore, Lee did not call a halt until late that evening, and the men under his command ate a supper of cold beans and parched corn, jerked beef, and pickled fish.

The four commanders conferred while eating their meal. Ghonkaba, whose scouts were leading the march, had the dominant voice. "As I see the situation," he told them, "when we come to the Hudson, we should stay on the west bank. We'll worry about where to deploy in the wilderness after we get there."

"Do you happen to be familiar with the Bear Mountain area?" Lee asked.

"I've passed through the region," the Seneca said, "but I can't claim any real familiarity with it. However, one of my key scouts, Sergeant Muller, grew up in the area south of Albany, and he undoubtedly knows the entire area intimately. I'm depending on his judgment in determining our ultimate bivouacs."

The others were comfortable with the arrangement. All were familiar with Muller, and they had heard many tales of his prowess.

The march proved uneventful. For several days the weather was quite warm, and the snows melted considerably, leaving the ground muddy. The so-called January thaw had set in.

The Continentals overcame that difficulty by increasing their rate of march, ignoring the sloppy conditions underfoot, and finding relief in the warmer weather.

When the column approached the Hudson, Ghonkaba moved their line of march farther into the wilderness, so they would not be observed from the shore of New York.

At last they approached Bear Mountain, and Sergeant Muller was called in to meet with the high command.

"The British garrison," he said, "is on the far side of Bear Mountain. Only one road leads there. It follows the river and actually goes up much of the mountain. My friends and me, we've been studyin' it for the last hour, and we've found no sign of wagon tracks that would show that the food convoy has come this way. So that means we're in luck. We got here first.

"The big question," he went on, "is where do we intervene and take hold of the supplies? There's disadvantages everywhere. The terrain is better north of Bear Mountain, but that would bring us too close to the British garrison. There's probably a large number of enemy troops stationed there—"

"At least twenty-five hundred, according to the

latest estimate of our espionage agents," Ghonkaba interrupted.

"We sure as shootin' can't take on twenty-five hundred redcoats in one battle," Muller declared. "I'd like to try, but it ain't too practical. That means we've got to stay on this side of the mountain, where any rifle fire wouldn't be heard in the garrison."

"You mentioned disadvantages everywhere," Lee said. "What's wrong with fighting right around here?"

"No open space anywhere," Muller explained. "The road is little more than a trail that cuts through heavy woods. It's great for our concealment, but the redcoats can use it for the same purpose, and we might have our hands full dislodging them."

One of Dan Morgan's captains smiled slightly. "From what I've seen of the British in combat," he said, "they don't take advantage of the terrain the way Americans do. I'd be inclined to take our chances with their prowess, or lack of it, in the forest."

The others tended to agree with him.

Ghonkaba, however, still had doubts, being imbued with the natural caution of the Seneca. "Let's assume," he said, "that the redcoats assigned to guarding the food train are more accustomed to the forests than are most British troops. Purely for the sake of discussion, let's say that they're the exception and are completely at home in the wilderness. They might be considerably harder to dislodge than most redcoats, it's true, but I can't see us failing to rout them out in the long run. Men who have just learned how to use the wilderness can't possibly be a match for men who've known the forests all their lives."

That settled the issue, as the group decided unanimously to accept Ghonkaba's appraisal. The raiders would take up their positions on the south side of Bear Mountain.

The expedition's high command inspected the terrain where they expected to deploy their troops and were well satisfied. Although the leaf-bearing trees were bare, ample numbers of evergreens would afford sufficient concealment. The scene was set for one of the most daring feats yet attempted by the Americans in the war.

After the departure of Ghonkaba's scouts and Lee's cavalry troop, the approaches to the Morristown camp remained deserted. No one left the bivouac area, and following a heavy snowfall, no one visited the Continentals' bivouac area.

That was all the more reason why the officers in command were disturbed two nights later when someone aroused the sentries by snooping nearby. When daylight came, a large number of booted footprints were found in the snow.

The incident was reported to General Washington, who took it seriously enough to investigate in person. He followed the footprints for some distance beyond the head of the valley and then returned somberly to his quarters nearby.

Toshabe was surprised and flustered when, as her children were eating their morning meal, El-i-chi shouted that the commander in chief was coming up the path.

She received the general as graciously as circumstances warranted, apologizing because she had no Dutch green tea on hand and could offer him only a brew made with acorns.

General Washington sipped the "acorn tea" as though it were the finest brew imported from India; gradually, he explained his strange problem to Toshabe. "Your husband's absence with all his scouts leaves me unduly shorthanded here," he told her. "My troubles are compounded by the absence of the two companies of frontiersmen from Dan Morgan's regiment."

"I see," Toshabe replied, having no idea of what he had in mind.

"Your daughter," Washington said, "impressed me greatly with her skill and knowledge when she performed a scouting mission for us in Trenton. I attribute our victory there to the information she provided. I wonder whether—with your permission—she'd be interested in a similar and possibly simpler feat now."

Before Toshabe had a chance to reply, Ena, who had been eavesdropping, burst into the parlor, her face glowing. "I accept, General," she cried enthusiastically. "You mean you really want me to do scouting for you again?"

Her mother laughed helplessly. "I don't seem to have much voice in this matter," she said. "All I can ask is that she not be assigned to a mission that's going to put her in physical danger."

"To the best of my knowledge," General Washington said, "only minimal danger attaches to this assignment. But I must be honest with you. In wartime it's impossible to distinguish the safe from the unsafe, the dangerous mission from the routine. I think the risk will be minimal, but I must stress to you that's only a belief, not fact. I wouldn't ask this favor if I had any available men competent to perform the task."

Toshabe did not flinch. "I understand," she said, and turned to her daughter.

Ena did not hesitate. "I'll be ready to go with you in a very few minutes, General," she cried, and dashed upstairs to apply animal grease to her skin before venturing out of doors.

She returned shortly, her hair descending down her back in a neat pigtail, her face shiny with grease. She looked almost absurdly young, innocent, and vulnerable. She blew kisses to her brothers and murmured something that sounded like, "Don't worry, my mother," to Toshabe. Then she faced General Washington: "I'm ready, sir," she said.

He stood, still disturbed by his need to rely on a young girl for the information he needed.

With two of his aides leading the way, the General escorted Ena to a point where he could show her the tracks in the snow to which the sentries had called his attention.

Ena followed the tracks for a short distance and then returned to the general's side. "These are prints left by many men. What's more, they were armed. Note these marks." She pointed to a number that were identical. "Those were made by the butts of rifles rested on the ground. From this quick examination, it appears that a large number of armed men were involved."

"What do you mean by a large number?" he asked, speaking gently so that he didn't alarm her.

Ena thought for a moment. "I should say at least thirty, but perhaps many more. It's impossible to tell unless I now follow the trail they left in the snow."

"Do you want anybody to come with you?"

She peered ahead into the thick tangle of trees and bushes ahead. Someone unaccustomed to wilderness travel would slow her up. "Thank you," she replied, sounding demure, "but I think I can manage better by myself."

The commander in chief began to suffer doubts about the mission he was giving her. "Perhaps it might be best," he said, "if you were to let it drop here and now."

Ena's jaw jutted forward stubbornly. At that moment she bore an almost uncanny resemblance to her great-grandfather, the noted Renno. "I'm intrigued by it now," she said, "and I intend to get to the bottom of it."

Before Washington could halt her, she darted away, following the marks in the snow that led into the wilderness.

The general was on the verge of calling out to her,

but thought better of it. Moments later, she disappeared into the evergreens and was hidden from view.

The scouts rested at their ease in the forest on the south side of Bear Mountain as they awaited the British convoy. Next to them was a company of Morgan's infantry, who also were completely at home in their wooded surroundings. Both units were relaxed, eager for combat.

Ghonkaba held a key position in the line, with his four sergeants stationed nearby. He alone was to give the signal that would start the attack on the convoy.

Familiar with the wilderness, the men could hear the thud of approaching infantrymen's steps, the creaking of harnesses, and the grinding of wagon wheels.

Ghonkaba counted one hundred and twenty-five redcoated infantrymen, each carrying a musket with a bayonet attached. Behind them, moving slowly, came the first in a long line of large wagons, each pulled by two oversized workhorses.

The commander of the wagon train did not understand the nature of wilderness warfare and was not anticipating a battle before he reached his destination. Ghonkaba was delighted to observe that he had split his defense force in half, putting some in the vanguard and the others far behind in a rearguard. In this way the Continentals could attack separately, rather than face the combined power of the entire British force.

Pointing toward the slowly advancing British foot soldiers, he began to move rapidly through the forest.

Preferring his bow and arrow to firearms, Ghonkaba notched an arrow into his bow and released it. It made a slight singing noise as it shot swiftly through the air, caught a redcoat lieutenant beneath the base of his helmet at the rear, and sent him pitching headlong onto the ground.

Half of the scouts saw and responded instantly.

Led by Ranoga, the dozen Seneca warriors followed
Ghonkaba's example and used their bows and arrows.
The American patriots resorted to their rifles. Clem
Dawkins, unable to actively participate, did his utmost
to help the soldiers keep their fire up. No effort was too
much for him as he ran from man to man, assisting in
the reloading, bringing water, and carrying out other
tiring and onerous, as well as dangerous, chores.

The rifle fire acted as an alert to the scouts on the
other side of the trail and to Dan Morgan's riflemen,
who were situated in the woods ahead of the scouts.
They immediately opened fire, and the whole forest
came alive.

The ambush caught the British completely by
surprise, but they nevertheless responded with courage
and speed. They began to return the fire, necessarily
shooting blindly into the woods on either side of the
trail.

Lee, concealed on higher ground with his cavalrymen, heard the shots and gave an order that sent the
entire troop careening down the slope toward the trail,
firing as they rode.

The drive of the cavalry was the only encouragement the scouts and Morgan's sharpshooters needed.
They redoubled their efforts behind the redcoats, while
the cavalry bore down on them from the front, and
between the two forces the British were in danger of
being crushed. They tried to fight their way out of the
hole in which they found themselves, but it was too
difficult and too late.

The British tried to conceal themselves behind
tree trunks, evergreens, and bushes, but they had little
opportunity to hide properly. The horsemen routed
them out, and the infantry marksmen and the scouts
did the rest.

After a fierce, one-sided engagement that lasted no
more than a quarter of an hour, the British line broke,

and the redcoats milled about in confusion as they tried to flee.

Lee needed no further encouragement to put the heart of the battle plan into motion. He led his cavalry up and down the long line of wagons that were the object of the attack. The individual drivers, isolated on buckboards with no support from anywhere, surrendered quickly. With ruthless determination, Lee's men forced them to turn the wagons and retreat southward, virtually as captives. They had no choice.

This maneuver now placed the British infantry at the rear of the column into the forefront, and as they struggled to gain some idea of developments, they were attacked by the other company of Morgan's sharpshooters.

By prearrangement these American troops were soon joined by more from Morgan's first company, and the two units of marksmen sent countless volleys at the remaining redcoat infantry.

Lee's cavalry had only one task to perform, and they concentrated on it with singleminded devotion. They were solely responsible for moving the supply wagons in the right direction, and they kept them going smartly, threatening the frightened drivers with the flats of their swords and insisting that the workhorses move at a rapid clip.

In the meantime, the scouts had the most difficult assignment, one that required the greatest ruthlessness. They were responsible for ensuring that not one redcoat escaped to reach the British garrison. That undoubtedly would mean that they would have twenty-five hundred men on their trail, intent on overtaking and overpowering them.

Every enemy soldier who tried to escape had to be pursued and shot down. The scouts spread out thickly through the forest and took up positions, with most of them concentrating on the area near the single trail. Fortunately, it was almost impossible for anyone unfamiliar with wilderness travel to make his way across Bear Mountain without using the trail. That meant that any British soldier who tried to get away would be almost certain to use the path.

Ghonkaba's orders to Ranoga, which he passed along, had been explicit: "Don't let a single man escape to the north. Any time you capture someone who wears a scarlet uniform, that will be useful. But if you can't capture them, shoot them down on sight."

The scouts responded to the challenge without wavering, and the Seneca in particular were merciless, shooting down many redcoats as they tried in vain to flee. One of the scouts who particularly caught the eye of Ghonkaba was Casno, a warrior who seemed to show many leadership qualities.

In the meantime, the company bringing up the rear of the caravan was encountering an exceptionally difficult time. The young officers in charge had no idea what had happened at the head of the march and were bewildered by the turnaround of the supply wagons. Their ranks were being decimated by unseen foes on both sides of the forest trail. Nevertheless they fought with stubborn courage and a determination that caused the Americans to admire them as opponents.

Many of the British had suffered wounds. The veterans fought on until they were killed, and their casualties were enormous. Nevertheless, they continued to refuse to surrender.

The British force suffered a defeat because of the shortsighted policy of their army, which insisted on confining all information to commissioned officers. Knowing this, Lee and Ghonkaba systematically saw to it that every ensign, lieutenant, and captain in the redcoat guard was killed. The troops who survived had no idea how close they were to the garrison or that the escape of only one man could turn the entire balance in favor of the British.

The soldiers who managed to escape fled south instead of north, and the overwhelmingly strong British garrison remained ignorant of the battle. Those who went south scattered in the wilderness and did not emerge to make their way back to New York until long after the Americans had marched away in triumph with their captured wagonloads of provisions.

They moved rapidly toward Morristown, with the supply wagons safely in their possession, having suffered remarkably few casualties. Their victory, as Ghonkaba and Lee assured one another, was one of the signal triumphs of the war. Most important, they brought with them enough food to supply the army for a full month.

It was small wonder that both Lee and Ghonkaba were promoted to the rank of major by General Washington on their return. Commendations went, upon Ghonkaba's heartfelt suggestion, to Ranoga and several other scouts. As for Clem Dawkins, to him it was a first taste of glory.

Chapter XI

Ena made her way happily through the forest, following the distinct trail in the snow. She walked in the footprints so that she would make none herself. She moved rapidly and was only vaguely conscious that she was traveling a considerable distance from the encampment.

She was certain of one thing: although the identity of those who had been spying in an effort to obtain information about the Continental Army's winter bivouac was still unknown, a reconnaissance in force had been made by both infantry and cavalry.

What confused Ena was the seeming familiarity with the wilderness that the intruders showed. They stayed close to the trail, never straying from it, and they had done precisely what she was doing, using each other's footprints in the snow so that it was impossible to determine the exact number who had approached the American camp.

To the best of her knowledge, no British troops and no Hessian mercenaries in the pay of King George were that wise in the ways of how to deal with the forest.

Pausing briefly when she came to a small clearing, Ena caught a glimpse of several thin columns of smoke rising from the forest a considerable distance ahead—a certain sign that the travelers had stopped and were cooking a meal. Now she proceeded with far greater caution.

In addition, she realized to her chagrin that she had left without taking any food because she had been so anxious to comply with General Washington's request for help.

Eventually she caught the delicious aroma of beefsteak cooking over an open fire, and she told herself that whatever these men might be, they must be suffering no shortage of food.

Increasingly cautious as she drew closer and closer to the campfires, she successfully eluded two sentries and finally paused behind a large, hollow log and peered through the evergreens and dead underbrush at the fires.

A large group of men—later she estimated their number at at least fifty—were gathered around the cooking fires. What bewildered her was their appearance. They wore dark green uniforms, unlike any she had ever seen, and it was obvious that these were no makeshift outfits. Their greatcoats of thick wool, heavy gauntlet gloves, and high boots of supple, fine leather warded off the cold. Ena suddenly knew their identity, and a chill crept up her spine.

These were loyalists, Americans who had remained faithful to their pledge of allegiance to the Crown, had offered their services to the British Army, and had been enrolled in a special unit. No wonder they had seemed familiar with the wilderness! They knew it every bit as well as did other Americans, from whom they differed only in their loyalties.

Of all the enemies of the American patriots, by far the most dangerous were the loyalists, who were familiar with American ways, knew the forests, and were difficult to deceive.

Ena was so stunned by her discovery that she forgot her stance; one foot slipped and came down hard on a dead branch. It cracked, making an explosive sound like a pistol shot. The noise immediately attracted the full attention of the loyalists.

Ena knew flight was impossible. Desperate for a place to hide, she dropped to the ground and crawled into the hollow log, inching her way down as she became covered with bits of dead wood and snow.

She concealed herself none too soon. Within seconds, she could hear the loyalists roaming through the woods on all sides of the log.

"I don't see anybody, Captain Ned," a man with a deep baritone voice called.

"Neither do I, and I'm damned if there's any sign of footprints in the snow."

Ena was glad of the precautions she had taken to conceal her presence.

The voices and scuffling sounds continued for a time.

Then someone with a high baritone voice, obviously an officer in a position of authority, called loudly, "We'll take no chances, men. Spread out in the forest over as wide an area as you can, and search every inch.

If someone has been eavesdropping on us, I damn well want to know it, and we'll take him prisoner!"

The sounds faded and absolute quiet reigned.

Realizing she had very little time, Ena poked her head cautiously out of the hollow log, then quickly crawled into the open, brushed herself off, and simultaneously decided to escape by the route from which she had approached. She had more than enough information now, and it was vital that she return as rapidly as possible to General Washington with her findings.

The steaks continued to sizzle over the fires, and Ena, sorely tempted, took her all-purpose knife from her belt, speared a huge slab of beef, and rapidly retreated into the forest, taking care to use only the footprints in the snow. Not pausing, she cut a narrow slice from the meat and chewed it as she withdrew.

When she had gone nearly a mile from the campfires—she could not be certain of the precise distance—she heard a rustling sound in the underbrush and froze when a shaggy-haired animal appeared directly in front of her.

The beast was a dog, and plainly it had been on a stringent diet. It was painfully thin and had been attracted by the odor of beefsteak. It stood now directly in front of the girl, blocking her path and growling menacingly, teeth bared.

Ena recognized it as a shepherd dog, and her fear vanished. She realized the dog was ravenous, and though her hunger was far from satisfied, her heart went out to it. "Here," she said softly, speaking in the tongue of the Seneca. "You may have this." She held out the whole steak.

The dog approached gingerly and was surprisingly gentle as it took the offering from her. Then it proceeded to eat the entire steak in several swift, gulping bites.

Her danger momentarily forgotten, Ena patted the dog on the head.

The shepherd flattened its ears against its head, and its tail wagged from side to side. It had found a new friend.

"I shall call you Lyktaw," Ena whispered. In the language of the Seneca it meant "forest lion."

The dog continued to wag its tail.

Aware of her dangerous situation, Ena hastily resumed her retreat. She was no longer traveling alone. The shepherd trotted close behind her. Glad of its company, she made no attempt to send it away.

A burly figure in a green uniform suddenly loomed up directly ahead. "Who goes there?" he demanded. "Halt!"

Before Ena had a chance to move, much less reply, the dog sprang at this being who dared to menace its new friend. With a growl emanating from deep within its throat, it sprang and landed full force on the man's chest and knocked him backward onto the ground. He lost his grip on his musket. The dog stood with its front paws on the man's chest, its continuing growl suggesting that it would not mind ripping open his throat.

Working with frantic haste, Ena removed the rawhide laces from the man's uniform boots and bound his ankles securely, then tied his wrists behind his back. Cutting a large chunk of the lining from his greatcoat, she stuffed it into his mouth as a gag.

The pain, frustration, and disgrace that the loyalist was suffering were evident in his eyes. As Ena worked, she figured that he was thinking of what he would be made to suffer when he revealed to his superiors that he had been rendered helpless by a slip of a girl and a shepherd dog.

Certain now that he would not give an alarm that would send his comrades searching in earnest for her, Ena began a hasty retreat, breaking into a run as she followed the trail of footprints in the direction of the encampment. Lyktaw loped happily beside her. With him nearby she felt infinitely more secure.

Her version of the Seneca trot was far more rapid than the speed achieved by many Iroquois warriors. Unlike a warrior, however, she was not able to sustain her speed indefinitely, and after running for about an hour, she thought her lungs would burst. Panting silently, she halted.

The dog halted beside her, looked up at her, wagged his tail, and then began to lick up snow, the run having created a substantial thirst.

Ena was filled with gratitude for his loyalty, and throwing her arms around the his neck, she hugged him impulsively. Lyktaw's tail thumped enthusiastically.

When she had regained her breath enough to resume the journey, Ena was sufficiently relaxed to travel at a more leisurely pace. Listening carefully, she could hear no one behind her and reasoned that she was relatively safe.

The dog sensed her more relaxed outlook and no longer stayed close beside her, but ran around her in loose circles, sometimes dropping as far as a dozen paces behind her, then racing ahead on the trail and waiting until she caught up before starting to play again.

Dusk was falling when Ena reported to the sergeant of the sentry guard on duty. She told him she had news of importance for the commanding general, and she was escorted at once to Washington's quarters. Lyktaw went along uninvited.

Colonel Hamilton protested when Lyktaw started to follow Ena into the commander in chief's study, but Ena immediately objected. "He comes with me," she said, and put an arm around him.

Lyktaw made his own views on the matter eminently clear by baring his teeth and growling at the colonel, who decided to ignore protocol and allow the dog to accompany his mistress.

George Washington, who habitually took note of every detail in the appearance of those with whom he dealt, observed that Ena seemed exhausted and that the dog was very tired, too. Before allowing Ena to tell her story, he sent for a glass of milk for her and had Colonel Hamilton bring in a bone with meat on it for Lyktaw. The dog stretched out at Ena's feet and contentedly gnawed on his bone. Conscious of her dirty hands and face, her streaked hair, and the bits of rotten wood that still clung to her apparel, Ena drank her milk and told Washington the story of her adventures.

The general listened quietly. He bore no animosity against the British troops, who were subjects of the Crown, or against the German mercenaries, but he loathed the loyalists who entered the British Army to serve against the American cause. In his opinion they were American traitors and deserved to be treated with contempt.

Whatever his feelings, he leaned forward in his rocking chair and questioned Ena closely about what she had seen.

Ena's observations had been sharp, and she answered every question accurately, confining herself to the pertinent details.

Well satisfied with her answers, Washington called in Colonel Hamilton and told him to alert General Anthony Wayne's brigade, which had been ordered to augment the sentries beginning that very night. A loyalist attack should be expected, he said, and he ordered Wayne's brigade to be ready to smash it.

Only after giving his orders to his aide did Washington terminate his session with Ena. He thanked her for her information and her efforts and then added, "If you have nothing better to do, perhaps you'll meet me at the parade ground at two o'clock tomorrow afternoon."

Ena murmured happily that she'd be glad to oblige.

Washington's lips twitched suspiciously, but he refrained from laughing. "By the way," he said, "you might bring your dog with you."

Ena headed toward home, the dog at her heels, and when she reached the house, she was delighted to discover that her father had just returned from his mission, having successfully delivered more than seventy-five wagonloads of provisions to the Continental Army.

He and a vastly relieved Toshabe wanted to learn all about her experiences, and her brothers clustered nearby, too, excited because of the shepherd dog.

Ena repeated her whole story, and when she came to the part played by Lyktaw, Ghonkaba was so impressed that he went to the kitchen and returned with a chunk of meat. The dog realized he had made another friend and nuzzled Ghonkaba's hand.

Toshabe, delighted, prepared a celebratory meal; then, bone-tired, Ena went to bed immediately with the dog curled up on the floor beside her. She was awakened shortly after midnight by rifle fire, which continued for some time.

Ghonkaba went to investigate, telling his family to remain indoors until he returned with word as to what was happening.

Returning three-quarters of an hour later, he smiled at Ena. "You made your discovery just in time today," he said. "A whole regiment of greencoats—loyalists—tried to sneak into the area tonight, intending to inflict as much damage as they could on the army. But Wayne's brigade was lying in wait for them. When General Wayne gave the word, his men attacked simultaneously from three sides. The enemy was nicely trapped, and the regiment was all but demolished. Relatively few managed to escape. That's one loyalist regiment that won't be creating any more mischief."

Ena was wide-eyed. "I'm glad," she said, "that I got the information to General Washington in time."

Her parents laughed, and Ghonkaba said, "Yes, I think the general is quite pleased, too."

Ena slept late in the morning and then luxuriated in the bath, where she scrubbed the dirt from her face, body, and hair. She found that her brothers had bathed Lyktaw, whose coat was now soft and shiny. After a large breakfast, which she insisted on sharing with the shepherd dog, they cavorted indoors, as Toshabe refused to let them go out into the cold so soon after having had baths. Then the entire family made ready to go to the parade ground at two o'clock. It had been made known that a special ceremony of some kind was scheduled.

Ena was demure in a lovely silk dress given to her by Mrs. Washington, as well as a warm outer coat. The dog, her inseparable companion, looked particularly handsome with his sleek coat as he trotted beside her. Toshabe, her children, and their dog sat together behind the reviewing stand, where General Washington took the troops' salute.

Division after division marched past the reviewing stand in ragged uniforms, compensating in spirit for what they lacked in polish. Brigadier General Anthony Wayne's brigade was greeted with applause for the previous night's exploit against the loyalists. Then Major Lee and his troop of cavalry came onto the field, followed by Ghonkaba's scouts and the two companies of Colonel Dan Morgan's Virginia sharpshooters. The applause that greeted them was riotous. Everyone in the assemblage appreciated the dramatic increase in rations that they'd enjoyed.

Washington rode out onto the parade ground on his white horse and, taking a piece of paper from his pocket, began to read. Special unit citations were awarded to Lee's cavalry, Ghonkaba's scouts, and

Morgan's infantry companies for valor beyond the call of duty. The commanding officer of each of the companies was called forward and accepted a personal medallion on behalf of his entire unit. Then Anthony Wayne was summoned and was given a similar citation, with his brigade authorized to wear a loop around their right shoulders as a special badge of honor.

Everyone thought the ceremonies were at an end, but soon learned they were mistaken. General Washington put away the sheet of paper, and speaking in a clear voice that could be heard in the far corners of the parade ground, he related a tale about a young woman and a dog who had saved the Continental Army from an attack that could have been crippling, but that had ended in victory because of information she supplied.

Ena was scarlet, and even the lobes of her ears burned as she stared in miserable embarrassment at the snow-flecked ground.

Her discomfiture became unbearable when General Washington called out to her to join him on the parade ground. Looking far younger than her adolescent years, Ena rose to her feet. "Come along, Lyktaw," she muttered. "I guess we're in for it now."

The entire assemblage seemed to explode when she and the dog walked onto the parade ground. The noise that echoed through the surrounding area was so deafening that the birds in the trees flew high in the air and forthwith continued on their journey north.

The commander in chief dismounted and presented Ena with a special citation, which consisted of a pearl and diamond brooch contributed for the purpose by Mrs. Washington.

Ena was barely capable of stammering her thanks.

The applause was still echoing when Washington, a twinkle in his blue eyes, produced a large bone, which he bravely presented to Lyktaw as the animal's "prize" to commemorate his services to the Continental Army's cause.

Ena moved back to her seat amid wild cheers, and the ceremonies were concluded. Ena and Lyktaw were surrounded by well-wishers. She thought she didn't deserve all the fuss being made over her; she didn't feel like a heroine and didn't believe that she deserved all the praise. But she was glad, all the same, that her dog was being treated like a hero. He had saved her life, and nothing was too good for him.

Shortly after Ena returned home, she was delighted when Clem Dawkins came to call. He asked, rather diffidently, if she would walk with him in the open, and when her mother readily gave her permission, she accompanied him.

Without doubt, the terrible winter was coming to an end. Spring was emphatically in the air, and when the sun shone, as it was doing, the breeze from the west was positively balmy.

Ena's conduct was far from that of the self-confident, rugged heroine. She was still wearing her colonial attire, including handsome shoes. Consequently, whenever she came to a place where melting snows made the ground soft and messy underfoot, she clung to Clem's arm. He didn't seem to mind her helplessness in the least.

At last they came to a crest of a hill at one side of the entrance to the valley. The sun had melted the snow on top of a stone fence, and the stones were now dry. Ena expressed a desire to sit, so Clem obediently lifted her to the stones and leaned on one elbow beside her. They looked at each other at eye level.

"If it's all right," he said, "I brought you a little present."

She was thrilled and clasped her hands together. "Oh, Clem! You really shouldn't! What is it?"

"I started making this for you quite some time ago," he said, "when you told me that you and your family are members of the Bear Clan. Then, when you performed this scouting deed for General Washington, I decided the present had to be extra special." He opened his fist; in his palm nestled a carved wooden bear about an inch and a half tall affixed to a slender gold chain. "The chain was my mother's, and I've been carrying it in a wallet in my pocket ever since I left New York. As to the rest of it, I made it."

Ena was breathless. "I've never seen anything so lovely in all my life!" she cried. "Are you sure you want me to have it?"

"Of course," he replied huskily. "I made it just for you."

Ena took the carved figure and examined it. It was true to life in every detail, and she was deeply impressed. "This is perfect," she murmured. "I know of no Seneca artist with such an eye for detail or fingers capable of working magic like this."

Clem looked away diffidently. "It's just a knack I've always had," he said modestly.

She clutched the little bear, beaming, and then turned her back and held up the necklace. "Will you fasten it around my neck, please?"

"You bet!" he replied.

"I much prefer it to anything else that I own, even that lovely diamond brooch of Mrs. Washington's. I shall wear this as long as I live, Clem."

She turned toward him, intending to kiss him on the cheek. Instead, as he bent toward her, their lips met and their arms went around each other.

When they drew apart both were short of breath.

"I—I'm sorry," Clem muttered.

Ena grasped his arm fiercely. "Don't apologize—ever," she told him. "There's never been anything like it before, and it's so wonderful that it can't possibly be bad."

He thought for a time. "I think you're right. It can't be bad, and it can't be wrong."

They looked at each other and became lost in the depths of one another's eyes.

When Ena spoke again, an uncertain note was in her voice. "I never expected to feel toward another human being as I feel toward you," she said. "This is such a huge and unexpected surprise. I don't quite know what to do about it."

"Neither do I," he confessed. "My future is in serious doubt. My battalion commander sent me to General Greene, and he told me flatly that I can't enlist in the Continentals unless I can somehow get rid of this ailing leg. And who can tell how long that may take? They could let me tag along as a drummer boy, but I'm damned if I want to go on serving as a drummer boy. When I'm enlisted, I aim to pick off as many redcoats as I can shoot!"

"I know exactly how you feel," Ena said, sympathizing with him.

"It's not right for me to ask you to marry me, because I have no certain future ahead of me. But I will ask you if you'll wait for me, Ena. I don't know how long it will take, but when the war ends I'll do my damnedest to earn a living for both of us."

"Of course I'll wait," she told him breathlessly.

He threw back his head and sent a loud, crowing whoop echoing through the hills. "That's all I ask," he said. "I can't think of anything more that I want in all the world."

The food supplies captured from the British were running low, and the specter of hunger again haunted the army in bivouac. A number of states had recently indicated their willingness to provide money for the army's use, but it had not yet been forthcoming, and when it would be available was uncertain.

At least, the dreadful winter had come to an end, and with spring at hand the prospect of too little to eat was somewhat easier to bear. The temperature rose some fifty degrees, the grass turned green, trees and bushes and shrubs were budding, and the inadequately clad men no longer had to keep wood fires burning twenty-four hours a day in order to keep warm.

The series of incidents known to history as the "miracle of the fish" began inauspiciously. Several members of Sullivan's and Putnam's divisions were fishing quietly in the swift-moving waters of the nearby Raritan River. They found the water filled with fish, biting readily. Word spread swiftly, and soon hundreds were at the water's edge, armed with buckets and containers of every sort. Fish by the uncounted thousands and tens of thousands were hauled in. No one who witnessed the spectacle had ever seen anything like it, nor did they expect to encounter a similar phenomenon ever again.

Willing soldiers eagerly dug a channel to divert some of the river's water and then broadened it to create a small lake. Fish swam into the man-made lake, thus making it possible for them to be kept alive and fresh until they were needed.

When night came, men lit flares so they could continue to fish. The run continued undiminished for four days and three nights, as the waters remained thick with fish. In the four days, the soldiers managed to extract at least one hundred thousand pounds of fish; some swore the catch amounted to at least a half-million pounds.

As General Washington remarked, precise numbers were irrelevant. What mattered was that every man had ample food to eat and that the supplies would last at least until money from the states arrived and food could be purchased.

Men feasted on fish for breakfast, dinner, and

supper. No complaints were heard about the monotony of the diet. The fish was as delicious as it was plentiful, and recollection of the near-starvation to which the army had been reduced before the miracle was an effective remedy for any dissatisfaction with the meals.

At the same time another miracle took place. Among the foreign officers from European countries who were attracted to the American cause and volunteered their services to General Washington was a high-ranking Prussian officer. He asked for the right to instill appropriate discipline into the army. Washington and the other generals of the high command gave him their blessing. Daily drills began in the Prussian manner. Men spent their entire days marching, doing manuals of arms, and otherwise learning the basic disciplines of European troops.

Gradually the ragged rabble was transformed. The casual demeanor of the war's early years was past. The divisions now demonstrated the rigid discipline that they had sneered at in the British. As they improved, they took a new pride in themselves and in their units.

The army that emerged in the spring was lean but healthy, well fed but not overweight, and imbued with a sharp sense of discipline.

The Continental Congress, by unanimous vote, cited the fish for their valiant contribution to the war effort. The army left its winter quarters, and as Washington remarked, the time had come to take the offensive.

Ghonkaba's scouts, who had grown from a company to a full battalion, had their work cut out for them. They ranged throughout New Jersey, and at their direction, Washington sent out successive units to harass the British and capture or disrupt the redcoat supply trains.

General Howe, vastly annoyed, likened these American activities to those of a swarm of insistent mosquitoes. He determined to end the nuisance by capturing

Philadelphia, and mustered his full force for a drive on that city. As it happened, this coincided neatly with plans of the American high command. The scouts, in particular, fitted into the strategy that Washington projected. They mustered in front of the advancing British, and instead of fighting, repeatedly melted away into the underbrush as the redcoats drove south. Washington maneuvered brilliantly, pretending to take a stand and hold his position, but then abandoning it at the last possible moment.

But Congress, unable to appreciate Washington's sensitive plan, grew panicky and withdrew into the interior of Pennsylvania.

By early autumn, Howe captured Philadelphia. As he soon discovered, this was not the end of the campaign, but the beginning. Having lost the city, Washington adopted a new and effective strategy. His advance troops repeatedly and tellingly attacked the supply trains from New York supporting the enemy with food and arms. These were easy targets for Washington's disciplined veterans. Howe needed his whole army in order to maintain his precarious hold on Philadelphia.

In the meantime, Washington strengthened the army in the north under Major General Horatio Gates by sending the dashing Benedict Arnold, another general, northward with several divisions of crack troops, including Ghonkaba's scouts. They were due to engage General John Burgoyne, who was known to be marching south from Canada into northeastern New York.

General Arnold, short, wiry, and vain, had acquired the reputation of being the "fightingest general in the American Army." As he marched north, he kept in touch with Gates's headquarters by means of a stream of messengers who arrived daily.

Such a messenger arrived one evening, shortly after the column had halted for the night, and interrupted General Arnold's supper by making his report to him. The general summoned Ghonkaba to his tent. "Major," he said, "I've just had a report to the effect that Colonel Barry St. Leger is moving southward, with a column consisting of three thousand loyalist troops and as many as ten thousand auxiliaries. Those auxiliaries reportedly are all Iroquois."

Ghonkaba responded calmly. "I imagine the report is accurate, General," he said. "They're following the plan that my father, the Great Sachem of the Iroquois, outlined when I last visited him."

"How many of those warriors are Seneca?" Arnold demanded abruptly.

Ghonkaba did not need to do any figuring. "Approximately fifteen hundred," he said. "The rest are principally Mohawk and Oneida, and I daresay that all are veterans."

Arnold was very annoyed. "General Washington gave me no inkling of the need to meet ten thousand Iroquois in battle, as well as Burgoyne's army and three thousand loyalists. The troops I've been given are good—damned good—but they can't perform miracles."

"I'm sure no one expects the impossible from them, sir, and that includes General Washington."

Arnold's hard, gimletlike eyes seemed to bore into the Seneca. "What in tarnation is that supposed to mean?"

Ghonkaba's conversation with his father had been confidential, and he had repeated its gist to no one except Washington. He could not reveal it to Benedict Arnold or anyone else. "I think you'll find, General," he said, "that the Iroquois will be no source of trouble for you in combat."

Arnold continued to stare. "What in the devil am I supposed to understand from that?"

"I'm going on a hunch," Ghonkaba said. "I know my people and their Iroquois brothers exceedingly well, and I anticipate certain conduct from them. It well may be that I'll suffer a severe disappointment, but I think that's a most unlikely event. I'd advise you, sir, to put Colonel St. Leger's column out of your mind."

Arnold opened his mouth to retort, but refrained. A niggling inner sense told him to let the subject drop and not pursue it. Certainly nothing was to be gained by cross-questioning the Indian, who evidently had no intention of speaking freely.

The general's poise and charm did not desert him, and he tried to accomplish through friendship what he had been unable to achieve by exerting his authority. He invited Ghonkaba to dine with him.

Ghonkaba was fascinated by his glimpses of Benedict Arnold's character. A sea captain and privateer owner who had made his fortune through trading in the West Indies, Arnold was a natural leader of men. This trait, combined with his bent for militarism, had won him a high-ranking commission at the start of the war, and he had covered himself with honors. Short-tempered and abrupt with subordinates, his first concern appeared to be the glory he coveted at almost any cost.

Ghonkaba found it difficult not to confide in him. Though Ja-gonh had not asked him to keep their last conference confidential, the very nature of it made secrecy essential, Ghonkaba realized. He had no knowledge of what the high command of the Seneca had in mind, and that probably was all to the good, he was aware.

The column finally joined Horatio Gates's army near the little town of Saratoga and were incorporated into Gates's command. Almost immediately, the officers of the combined force were summoned by the generals to meet at an outdoor site near their bivouac areas. Gates and Arnold shared a platform.

The first to address them was dry, matter-of-fact Horatio Gates. "Gentlemen," he said, "I haven't called you together to hear idle patriotic speeches. When you've heard what I have to tell you, I'm quite certain you'll agree that the military situation in this area as it exists today greatly favors our cause."

A stir went through his audience. Ghonkaba was impressed. Gates appeared to be a straightforward commander.

"You'll be glad to learn," Gates went on, "that Colonel St. Leger's forces no longer constitute a threat to this corps. His loyalists have been roundly defeated in a battle at Oriskany. They met a force of militiamen of German descent, who delivered a sharp blow for freedom.

"Oddly," he went on, "although St. Leger was accompanied by a very large band of Iroquois, the Indians took no part in the battle."

Stiffening, Ghonkaba stared straight ahead, his face expressionless. He had known that his father would keep his word and that the Iroquois would not actively enter the war.

"Actually," General Gates went on, a note of incredulity in his voice, "the Iroquois disappeared soon after the battle had reached its climax, and they haven't been seen since. Our informants assume that the Indians have dispersed to their homes, but we can't be sure of that."

Ghonkaba could feel General Arnold's eyes boring into him. He continued to look straight ahead, his face impassive.

"My other news," General Gates was saying, "is that General Washington has been keeping the British in Philadelphia so busy that they've had no opportunity to send troops north to aid General Burgoyne. Therefore, Burgoyne's force will meet us in battle without reinforcements from either Clinton or St. Leger. They'll be meeting us on quite equal terms. On that basis, I feel confident that we can win."

258

Benedict Arnold made an impassioned, fighting, patriotic speech that brought cheers from his audience.

The officers then dispersed. An aide to the commanding general awaited Ghonkaba at his bivouac area. "Major," the officer said, "General Gates would like to see you at your earliest convenience."

That meant immediately, Ghonkaba knew, so he accompanied the aide to headquarters. There he found Horatio Gates in his tent, sipping coffee with Arnold, who was drinking a strong whiskey and water. The difference in their choice of beverages was consistent with their respective characters, Ghonkaba felt.

"Sit down, Major," Horatio Gates invited, waving Ghonkaba to a camp stool. "It's come to my attention that you're related by blood to the leader of all the Iroquois and to the chief of the Seneca."

"Your information is correct, sir."

"Am I correct in believing we're a two-day march from the homeland of the Seneca?"

Ghonkaba considered the statement briefly. "As we Seneca travel, General," he replied proudly, "we're less than two days' distance from the main town of our people."

Gates sipped his coffee, glanced in the direction of Arnold, and then said, "So much the better. You have a number of fellow Seneca in your battalion, I believe."

"Yes, sir. One dozen of them."

"Good! I want you to take them with you as an escort. Go to the homeland of the Seneca without delay and ascertain whether their warriors and those of the other Iroquois nations have returned home. Even more important, I want you to find out—if you possibly can—whether their braves intend to take up arms against us in the course of this war."

It would be unnecessary for Ghonkaba to return home in order to carry out such a mission. He knew that for the Seneca and their brother Iroquois, the war was over. But he could not admit that without revealing more than he wished about his father's position with the British. So he confined himself to a brief, "Yes, sir." At the very least, he would be able to pay another visit to his parents.

Never one to waste time, Gates asked him to leave with his scouts as soon as he found it convenient.

Ghonkaba returned to his own bivouac area, summoned his Seneca colleagues, and left the area with them at once. At a slow run in the true Seneca manner, they traveled without rest for two nights and a day. They had the thrill of hearing the drums of their nation's sentries boom a greeting to them when they crossed from the land of the Mohawk into their own territory.

Soon after they came to the principal Seneca town, Ghonkaba was reunited with his parents.

He was admittedly tired, but he brightened considerably over the hearty meal his mother prepared. After he ate, he and his father talked.

"I have revealed your war position to no man other than General Washington, my father," Ghonkaba said, "and you may rest assured that he will speak of it to no one."

"That is good!" Ja-gonh said. "I hope we can gain the friendship of the Americans when they learn we declined to join forces with General St. Leger."

"Our officers already have been told this news," Ghonkaba replied, "and it is sure to spread quickly through the entire Continental Army. You may be certain that this gesture will be remembered with gratitude by the Americans when the war ends, though I doubt that any recognition could be made of it before then."

"I expect no early recognition," Ja-gonh answered him. "I am motivated in my decisions only by what I deem is in the interest of our people. So far, I have been proved right. The warriors of the Seneca and our brother Iroquois have survived a war in which, as you know far better than I, Americans and British troops have killed each other in large numbers. We have become a minority in our own land, and we must tread softly if we hope to live and to flourish. I mention matters that I had once thought best left unsaid, but mention is necessary because of your present situation."

He looked at his son searchingly. "Have you given any thought to what you will do when this war comes to an end, Ghonkaba?" he inquired gently.

"When I left the land of the Seneca, I believed I was going into exile for all time," Ghonkaba answered. "I could not look clearly into the future then, any more than I can see ahead now. I thought vaguely of settling in Massachusetts or in Virginia. I also thought of crossing the mountains and traveling west in the hope that I could find a new life with some tribe in the territory where few white men have penetrated. But ever since I have learned of your plan to withdraw your support from Great Britain in this war, I have been encouraged to dream. My dream is that when peace comes I will return to the land of my ancestors and that these war years can be forgotten. I expect that the Seneca who serve with me—even though they know nothing of your plan of disengagement from the British—have been entertaining a similar dream."

Ja-gonh looked at his wife, who immediately sat down beside him, her manner as serious as his.

Ghonkaba realized that Ah-wen-ga's attitude meant a serious crisis was impending.

"It has long been a tradition of the Seneca," Ja-gonh said soberly, "that our allies are the same as we ourselves, and their enemies are our enemies. It happened that when you went off to fight against the British, they were the formal allies of the Seneca and of the Iroquois."

"That is so," Ghonkaba admitted.

"And it happened that, technically at least, you and the warriors who went with you to join the American cause were raising your hands against your own nation by raising them to fight the British."

In all fairness, Ghonkaba was forced to say again, "That is so."

"In this matter I have sought the advice of Renno and of Ghonka from their dwelling in the land-beyond-the-great-river," Ja-gonh said, "and they have given me signs to show that I am correct in what I have determined."

Noting again his mother's expression, Ghonkaba braced himself for the worst.

"The ancient tradition of our people," Ja-gonh said solemnly, "has become a law that no man has dared to violate for untold generations. He who becomes an enemy of our allies by that act becomes an enemy of the Seneca. I well realize that no situation such as the one that now exists has ever before arisen in the long history of the Seneca. I realize, too, that our entire nation is now loosening its ties with Great Britain and is prepared, when the war comes to an end, to resume its historic friendship with the Americans. Nevertheless," he added, his voice becoming firmer, "this does not in any way excuse your deed. Your actions have cut you off from our people, and they condemn you and your seed to exile from the Seneca nation for all time."

Ah-wen-ga averted her face and sobbed quietly.

"You have no idea how it grieves me to tell you all this," Ja-gonh said, "but I have no choice. A nation is no stronger than its traditions, especially in times of crisis. The Seneca will disappear from the face of the earth unless they hold firmly to the roots that tie them to their past. When the Americans win this war, they will sweep over the entire continent of North America like a mighty wave, and those who do not make their peace with them will be engulfed and will vanish. This much I can see clearly."

"Your father," Ah-wen-ga said to her son in a barely audible voice, "has sought the advice of Renno and of Ghonka and is abiding by their wishes, as well as his own best judgment. It breaks our hearts to exclude you from our future and from the future of our people, but what is destined to be must be."

"You are free to return here when you wish to visit," Ja-gonh said, "and you will always be welcome on such visits. This also is true for your wife, for your children, and for their children after them. Their past, their heritage, is that of the Seneca. Their present, however, lies elsewhere, as does their future."

Ghonkaba knew he was wrong to feel deeply disappointed. When he had made his choice and had taken up arms on behalf of the Americans, he had expected to have no more to do with the Seneca. It was only after learning of his father's plan to disassociate the tribe from the campaigns of the British Army that hope had been reborn in him. Certainly his loss was not really unexpected, and he resigned himself to its inevitability.

Straightening his shoulders, he asked softly, "My father, do you or my mother have any advice on where I might go to lead a new life when the war comes to an end?"

Ah-wen-ga's bewildered gaze told its own story. She had no idea what would become of her son and his family, and she was deferring to her husband.

Ja-gonh, as usual, replied judiciously. "You have served honorably and well in the army of the Americans, my son," he said, "and I'm sure you will continue to fight with distinction for them. You will be welcomed to live anywhere in the lands that the United States controls. You spoke of settling on a farm, either in Massachusetts or in Virginia. Let me tell you that you are not the first to have had such thoughts. Renno, your grandfather, entertained them because he was married to the daughter of a farm owner from Virginia. When your mother and I were married, we were disillusioned with the politics that separates some nations and binds others together, and we, too, wanted to live our lives peacefully on a farm. But your mother was dissuaded, as I was, by considerations far stronger than we were. It does not matter how many of our ancestors were white and how many had the darker skins of the original natives of this continent. We were reared as Indians. You, too, were brought up as an Indian, just as you have reared your children in that tradition. You—and they—think and speak and act in all things as Indians. You've been made aware, as I was and as my father was before me, too, of what I owe to my heritage as an American of English descent. But you, like me, are first and foremost an Indian. Is this not so?"

"It is so, my father," Ghonkaba replied somberly.

"I am convinced now," Ja-gonh declared, "just as I was convinced when I was younger than you and was forced to make my own choice, that a life on an American farm is not the life for me or my wife or my children. I demanded to live as an Indian. You are being denied your Seneca heritage, which is unjust and is unfair, also, for your sons and your daughter. But I beg you—for the sake of your own happiness, as well as for theirs—seek your future in the wilderness that belongs only to the Indians of North America and is claimed by neither the Americans nor the British. The freedoms that you know and love and want are not those that satisfy the white man."

"Where do you advise that I go in the great wilderness, my father?" Ghonkaba asked.

"It is not my place to say," Ja-gonh replied. "I do not pretend to have information beyond what you possess. When the time comes for you to make your home, you will know where you are to go. You have your own means of communicating with the gods of our people and with your ancestors. Use those means freely, and they will answer and will guide you."

"I feared," Ghonkaba said, "that because I am no longer to be a Seneca that I would not be able to speak again with my grandfather or with his father. I feared, too, that I would be cut off for all time from the manitous of the Seneca and from the gods they represent."

"The blood of your ancestors flows in you," Ja-gonh said. "You are tied to them for all eternity. As for the manitous and the gods beyond them, your faith in them has never wavered, so they will not desert you in your hour of need. Of that you may be certain!"

Chapter XII

Ghonkaba and his escort of Seneca scouts traveled as rapidly as they could on their return to General Gates's command. They completed the journey in the excellent time of thirty-two hours.

This suited them well, because they were in a reckless mood. Through Ghonkaba, they had learned that they were permanent exiles from the land of the Seneca, regardless of the outcome of the war, and although the banishment was no great surprise, they nevertheless were bitter.

Ghonkaba reported to Gates that the Seneca warriors had returned to their homeland and that, in his opinion, Gates need not worry about the Iroquois in the immediate future.

Satisfied with what Ghonkaba had told him, Gates revealed that he expected Burgoyne to initiate hostilities at dawn the following morning.

Ghonkaba went off to join his scouts in their forward bivouac area, and there he found his four veteran sergeants drinking rum. All were in a rare reflective mood.

Sergeant Muller aimed a stream of spittle at a reddish-gold leaf hanging from the branch of an oak tree and sent it to the ground on his first try. "We were snoopin' around behind enemy lines today—you know how curious we get just before a battle—and we ran across the damnedest sight we've ever seen. Tell Ghonkaba about it, Ryan."

"Me and Ginsberg," Ryan said, an element of awe in his voice, "saw this here special collection of tents set aside toward the rear end of the redcoat camp. First of all, we saw a huge cook tent."

"We thought it was for a battalion, at the very least," Ginsberg put in, "but we were wrong! There were two stoves inside, one for firewood and the other for charcoal. And talk about food! I never saw so much fancy food in all my days. Some kind of sauce was bubbling away in a pot on one of the stoves and every once in a while a feller with a high-crowned white hat would add some French cognac to it from a bottle he had."

"Another feller," Ryan added, "picked all the lobster meat out of its shells and mixed it with vegetables and some sort of a fancy sauce. Then he was stuffin' the whole thing back into the shells again. Fanciest food fixin' you can possibly imagine."

"We got so hungry just watching them work," Ginsberg said, "that we got us to hell and gone out of there. We went past maybe four or five donkey carts loaded with French wines of all kinds, and then we saw a truly amazing sight—a huge tent made of silk instead of canvas. It had a floor of hardwood, and over it—so help me!—a real Turkish rug. I even saw a stove in the place to take the chill out of the air. And the bed!"

"You won't believe this," his partner said solemnly, "but it was a genuine four-poster bed that I reckon could be taken apart and put together at will."

Ghonkaba listened intently and kept his opinions to himself.

"The initials 'JB' were on the sheets and pillowcases," Sergeant Ryan said, "so it seemed that all this finery must belong to General Burgoyne."

"We looked high and low for the lady travelin' with General Burgoyne, but we never did see her," Ryan remarked with a wheezy laugh. "We blame near got ourselves caught a couple of times, though."

"The closest we came," Ginsberg said, "was when we ran across her gear. You never saw so much stuff! Clothes boxes and hat boxes and cosmetics cases, and the Almighty only knows what else!"

"So help us," Ryan said in awe. "We saw enough gear to fill three carts, if you can imagine it. What do you make of all that?"

Ghonkaba showed no surprise. "I've heard of British generals who travel in great style," he said, "and it appears that Burgoyne is one of them. If he devotes the same care and attention to his troops that he does to his personal comfort and his mistress, we're in for one hell of a battle tomorrow!"

In spite of Ghonkaba's exhaustion, he had difficulty in falling asleep. He knew the forthcoming battle would be important, because Washington had said as much to him before he had left Pennsylvania, but the significance it could assume in the history of the American Revolution was still unclear to him.

Awake an hour before dawn, he ate a few handfuls of parched corn and a strip of jerked venison. Then he made the rounds of his battalion to assure himself that everything was in order. His scouts, located in front of the patriot vanguard, would bear the shock of the initial enemy thrust, but Ghonkaba found the entire battalion in high spirits. The recklessness that had pervaded the ranks of the Seneca the previous day was catching. Today every one of the scouts had a devil-may-care attitude.

Even after three years of war, the British apparently had not learned the art of initiating a battle in silence. The piercing, high-pitched whistles the sergeants sounded up and down the line were audible throughout the forest. And then the regimental buglers sounded the attack.

A full division of His Majesty's light infantry, resplendent in uniforms of scarlet and gold with crosswebbings of white, advanced into battle in the half-light of early morning.

Dawn had just broken, but General Arnold, commanding the forward sector, was pleased. Already, it was light enough for his purposes. He waited as the enemy advanced; he continued to say nothing as the column of redcoats came closer and closer.

Even Ghonkaba grew nervous as Arnold refrained from giving the order to open fire. Seldom had an enemy approached so near to American lines. Even Washington had ordered his regiment to open fire long before this point when similar situations had arisen.

The faces of the British troops could be seen plainly now. Veteran scouts exchanged looks of consternation at Arnold's delay. But their discipline held, and no man opened fire, no soldier broke faith with his general.

Ghonkaba felt greatly relieved when a clicking sound

off to his right told him that Arnold, concealed behind the trunk of a large elm tree, had just cocked his pistol. Then the bark of his shot sounded, and the entire American front erupted.

The handful of Seneca scouts, Ghonkaba included, sent a shower of arrows into the clearly defined ranks of their enemies. Simultaneously, the other scouts opened fire with their muskets. The redcoats, making no attempt to conceal themselves, were perfect targets and suffered accordingly. Their ranks were quickly and severely thinned.

Dan Morgan's regiment of Virginia sharpshooters, in the vanguard directly behind the scouts, needed no order to open fire with their long rifles. The effect was awesome. A huge, unseen scythe seemed to have mowed down the enemy.

The redcoats halted in confusion, and men in the rear stepped forward to the front ranks to replace those who had fallen. The losses were considerable, but neither the division commander nor any higher officer ordered the advance halted. The British, who had not yet fired a shot, nevertheless were expected to continue their advance and attack.

Ghonkaba's scouts and Morgan's riflemen, together comprising one of the deadliest and most effective units of foot soldiers, continued to pour shots at the foe.

The British division took a frightful beating. Their loss of one man killed or wounded out of every five spelled certain defeat, as it would for any army.

In spite of the beating they were taking, the British light infantry did not give up or panic. When they could, they continued to inch forward. When they were halted completely, they nevertheless held their ground and refused to retreat.

Ghonkaba was greatly impressed by the stand they were making, as was Colonel Morgan, who crawled up beside him. "We've got to blast the redcoats out of there before they get too firm a toehold," he said. "If that happens, we'll never get rid of them."

"The boys are doing their best, Dan. What do you suggest?"

Morgan scratched his head, then brought his long rifle up to his shoulder and put a bullet between the eyes of a British lieutenant who had moved up into the line to replace an officer who had fallen. "I reckon that's the best way."

"You mean we should kill their officers first."

"That's the idea, Major," Morgan replied. "The redcoats are first-rate fighting men, no two ways about it. They're well disciplined, and they're endowed with plenty of courage. Their one weakness is that—unlike our boys—their enlisted men have never been taught to think for themselves." He interrupted himself by raising his rifle again and disposing of a young British ensign. "Without officers to guide them," he concluded, "they're helpless, and we can force them back."

Ghonkaba promptly sent out word to his entire battalion to choose their targets well. Primary targets were commissioned officers, followed by noncommissioned officers, and only when no redcoats were left on the field except enlisted men were they to become targets. The same instructions were given to the Virginia regiment. The tactics quickly proved so successful that they became standard procedure for all American troops.

When no British officers or sergeants remained standing, the redcoat advance slowed and then ground to a halt. The soldiers, unaccustomed to wilderness fighting, failed to take adequate cover. Their losses were so severe that their front ranks were no sooner formed than they were riddled and forced to buckle.

Awaiting orders that never were forthcoming because no officer was on hand to issue them, the redcoats in the front ranks became uneasy and took several backward steps.

This was the moment that Ghonkaba had awaited. He fought with renewed fury, increasing the speed of his fire, and the scouts of his battalion followed his example. Again, Ranoga displayed exemplary leadership among the men, thus freeing Ghonkaba for more independent action.

Morgan's riflemen also fought with renewed vigor. No one on the American side issued or received any orders, but the pace of battle quickened, and at last the British division was forced to retreat.

General Burgoyne retaliated by sending forward two full divisions of his heavy infantry, men whose muskets had a longer range and who wore armored breastplates to protect them from enemy fire. They promptly showed that they did not expect to capitulate. Both sides demonstrated a stubborn courage that refused to admit even the possibility of defeat. After two hours—then three—it appeared that a stalemate was developing. Neither the Americans nor the British had the strength to deliver the final blow that would decide the battle. Both hung on grimly.

Unknown to the troops of the American army, Major General Benedict Arnold was in disgrace. He had disobeyed direct orders from General Gates, who had told him to hold firm, but not to advance. He had started to mount an attack when Gates, coldly furious, relieved him of his command and sent him off to his tent.

There he fumed in impotent rage, his tension and anger mounting higher and higher. Suddenly something within him exploded.

Gripping his naked sword blade, he dashed into the open and looked around wildly. His eyes lighted upon his stallion, tethered nearby, and he unlooped the reins, vaulted into the saddle, and, scarcely aware of what he was doing, waved the sword over his head.

"Forward," he shouted. "Let's go, boys! Let's win this fight once and for all." His stallion began to thunder toward the enemy.

The startled American troops saw the inspired figure of their second-in-command and heard his admonition to join him in charging the enemy. Immediately, they too began to race forward. In a matter of moments entire divisions were on the move, leaving their positions of relative safety behind trees and other obstacles in the forest and dashing out into the open to follow on Arnold's heels.

Fifteen thousand Americans were on the field at Saratoga that day, and fifteen thousand patriots reacted as one and advanced, uncaring what happened to them.

Among those in the lead were Ghonkaba's scouts and Morgan's Virginia riflemen. These troops had disliked being on the defensive, unable to move, and they responded readily to Arnold's summons.

Firing and reloading repeatedly as they raced forward, they resorted to the cold steel of their bayonets to drive the redcoats before them. No force could have withstood the fury of their attack.

Ghonkaba and his scouts had in fact been awaiting this moment for nearly two years—ever since they had volunteered their services to Washington.

During those years, they had endured hardship and suffering, humiliation and many defeats, but their pride as Seneca had never deserted them. Now, at last, they could prove their true worth, fight as they were accustomed to fighting, and show themselves as valiant warriors in their nation's tradition.

Following the example of Ghonkaba in the lead, the scout company sent flights of arrows into the midst of the enemy, who, having sought adequate cover in vain, were forced repeatedly to retreat. The scouts were at their best when on the offensive; they continued to sweep forward, gradually forcing the retreat of an enemy force many times their size.

Setting a magnificent example, Ghonkaba exercised caution as he moved forward, though he seemed to deliberately expose himself to danger as he pointed his unit toward the redcoat forces. The more the enemy fell back, the harder he drove forward, all the more determined to let no obstacle stand in his path.

The British, who had outnumbered the patriots by a scant two thousand men, did their best to halt the American tide, but their efforts were unavailing. They were ordinary, competent troops who in a normal order of battle would have fared well. As it happened, they were facing men who had been lifted to a high emotional state by an inspired general, and they formed a human tidal wave from which no escape was possible.

Arnold's charge began late in the afternoon. General Gates was so astonished that, by the time he recovered, it was too late to halt the avalanche. The Americans, in their finest exhibition of close-order fighting since the war began, were unstoppable, and the redcoats melted away in front of them.

Companies, battalions, and even regiments of British troops were surrounded and so severely mauled that they were forced to surrender. Before the sun had set, most of their divisional headquarters were captured, and General Burgoyne realized his cause was hopeless.

In an attempt to spare his troops needless bloodshed, he ordered a white flag run up above his headquarters. In a brief but significant ceremony shortly thereafter, he would have surrendered his sword to Benedict Arnold, but Arnold was not present. Wounded by a redcoat bullet in the final moments of his charge, he had been removed to the field hospital. Horatio Gates thus accepted the surrender of his enemy.

The rejoicing American troops knew only that they

had won a great battle. The long-range consequences became clear to them only later. The handwriting was on the wall for the redcoats. As Sergeant Muller of the scouts told the faithful Clem Dawkins, "Them redcoats are beat, but they don't know it yet. When they find out, they're going to skedaddle as fast as they can get ships to carry them."

Ghonkaba and his scouts, flushed with victory but exhausted by the prodigious effort they had put forth throughout the battle, headed back toward the bivouac area.

As they crossed a small meadow, they were suddenly confronted by a band of some two dozen warriors, who stepped from behind the trees of an adjacent wood. From their green and yellow war paint, Ghonkaba at once recognized them to be fellow Seneca. Their leader, who wore in his scalp lock the three eagle feathers of a war chief, was none other than his old enemy, Tredno.

Tredno now stepped forward and, in a voice trembling with barely controlled rage, addressed Ghonkaba.

"Your cowardly father and uncle dishonored the Iroquois nation by refusing to uphold their sacred obligations. Though bound by ancient promises, they refused to send their warriors to aid their British allies at the battle near Saratoga. They have besmirched the honor of our nation and are not fit to lead their people.

"I and my brothers came to offer our services in this battle, but the British officers—mindful of the Iroquois's cowardly disappearance from the Battle of Oriskany—shamed us by denying us the honor of engaging in this fight. But there is one fight I will not be denied—and that is combat with Ghonkaba, son of Ja-gonh!"

At this, Ghonkaba turned to his companions and quickly ordered them to stand back. His men obeyed without hesitation, realizing the manitous now demanded that Ghonkaba meet Tredno unattended.

Tredno likewise signaled to his followers that they should withdraw from the field of combat, and he now stood alone before Ghonkaba, his face filled with menace and hate.

The two antagonists—each armed with a tomahawk and a long double-edged steel knife—began to circle warily. As war chiefs of the same nation, they had known one another since training together as junior warriors many years earlier. Familiar with every trick in battle that the other knew, each man was prepared for any eventuality.

Ghonkaba at last was face to face not only with the man who had chosen to make him his personal enemy but with the reality of the poisonous hatred that had been pursuing him for so long. Belatedly, he recognized how mistaken he had been to dismiss Tredno as being of no major importance in his life. The familiar chill that he had experienced so frequently returned now in a gripping flash—and then, as suddenly, it was gone. Instead, he was suffused by the will to end the haunting, unreasoning bitterness that Tredno had brought to their relationship. He knew now, without question or doubt, that he had no choice but to strike with all his might against evil.

So committed, he also decided instantly against resorting to trickery. Instead, he would rely on straightforward fighting techniques.

Tredno, however, intended to use every device available to him, and feinted as he advanced. Ghonkaba caught his foe's knife on his own blade. Twisting his wrist as he had done in combat on countless occasions, he managed to disarm his opponent. Tredno's knife flew across the field and landed harmlessly many paces away.

Smiling to himself, Ghonkaba slid his own knife

back into his belt, refusing to use the advantage he had won. Now, each man carried only his tomahawk.

Ghonkaba's attitude infuriated Tredno, who saw it as condescending. They resumed their cautious circling.

Ghonkaba was determined to end the duel as rapidly as possible. In keeping with the Seneca adage that the warrior who seized the initiative in combat held a distinct advantage, he sprang forward and lashed out with his tomahawk. The blade caught Tredno in the shoulder, opening a severe gash that extended down the upper arm.

In a blind rage, compounded by intense pain, Tredno struck left and right repeatedly in an attempt to make effective contact with his opponent.

Ghonkaba backed off, waited patiently for a moment, and then stepped forward and drove the tomahawk's sharp blade into Tredno's head between his eyes.

The warrior fell to the ground, lifeless, and with him died his grandiose scheme to wrest the mantle of leadership from the descendants of Renno.

Ghonkaba stood for a moment over the motionless body of his former adversary. He refused to dishonor the dignity of a fellow Seneca by taking his scalp. For all the malign hate that Tredno had manifested toward Ghonkaba throughout his life, he had at least demonstrated unswerving courage and a zeal worthy of his ancestors. If these qualities had not been so twisted and misdirected, they might have worked great deeds for the Seneca and the entire Iroquois nation. As it was, Tredno had become another casualty of the great conflict being waged in America—the same conflict that had caused Ghonkaba to be driven from his homeland.

In Paris, the special envoy, Benjamin Franklin, made such good use of the American victory that he finally persuaded the government of Louis XVI to openly recognize the United States, to provide the infant nation with cash, arms and munitions, food and adequate uniforms, and all the other supplies necessary to win a major conflict. In addition, the involvement of France served to divert the British from what had been their main purpose, the recapture of the rebellious colonies.

A few months later, Spain, which had steadfastly refused to recognize the American claim to independence, declared war against Britain and thereby weakened Britain's hold on her former North American possessions that much more.

Never again would the British inflict a major defeat on their former colonies in America. They would cause considerable damage, to be sure, particularly in the southern states during the remaining years of the war, but they would never achieve a clear-cut triumph. Saratoga was the last major engagement of the war fought in the North.

Thereafter the Continental Army steadily grew stronger. New troops were properly trained, adequately armed and uniformed, and taught all that soldiers in the late eighteenth century needed to know.

George Washington knew that they lacked the strength to meet the full force of the main redcoat army, so he withdrew skillfully and refused to do battle for the American capital.

Once the British held Philadelphia, however, the Americans went to work with a vengeance, cutting supply lines between New York and Philadelphia. Thousands of Continentals engaged in these activities, and the redcoats lost far more munitions, weapons, and food than they were able to receive from New York.

The incessant activities of the Continental Army had an inevitable effect. The British had captured Philadelphia on September 27, 1777. On the following June 18, Sir Henry Clinton, following succeeded Howe, withdrew. He pulled back across New Jersey, and General Washington attacked him at Monmouth on June 28. The cowardice of General Charles Lee of the Continental Army made it possible for the British to escape to New York. But never again in the course of the war were the British able to put an effective fighting force together in the northern states.

A number of relatively small British forces continued to function in the South, where the fighting remained ferocious. But as the American alliance with France began to take effect and French warships aided in protecting the American coast—just as French money paid the bill for the Continental Army and French reinforcements strengthened the American regiments—no longer did American military men doubt the outcome. Victory was assured.

Chapter XIII

After the Continental Army reoccupied Philadelphia in 1778 and started north in pursuit of the retreating redcoats, Ghonkaba was promoted to the rank of lieutenant colonel, by far the highest-ranking Indian in the American field forces. He had much with which to busy himself, keeping the fleeing British regiments under close scrutiny.

When the British reached the relative safety of the city of New York, the Continentals spread a net across New Jersey and the Hudson Valley, bottling the redcoats in the city they had occupied since early in the war.

The powerful British fleet gave them access to the sea, but they were helpless by land, and they remained in that position.

Early in July, Ghonkaba was summoned to General Washington's field headquarters in New Jersey. He was informed by an aide-de-camp that he was expected to dine with the commanding general that evening. Surprised and pleased, he reported back shortly before dark to the farmhouse where Washington was making his headquarters.

A few moments later Ghonkaba was admitted to the presence of General Washington, who poured two mild drinks of rum and water. Handing one to his subordinate, he said with only a trace of weariness in his voice, "To victory."

"To victory," Ghonkaba repeated, and waited until Washington was seated before he took a chair opposite the one the general occupied.

Washington raised his glass and took a swallow of his drink. "In some ways," he said, smiling reminiscently, "it seems only yesterday that you came to me in Massachusetts and offered your services. I've thought of that day often. You had nothing but hope to bolster your conviction that the American cause might some day win. But that hope was enough to sustain you through the hard years that have followed."

"Freedom," Ghonkaba replied soberly, "is worth fighting for and is worth making sacrifices for."

"Indeed it is," Washington agreed, "and it's a lesson that I believe the whole country has now learned.

"As I see the present situation," he went on, "continuing French aid is making us stronger each day. French trade has made the Continental Congress solvent, and even their money has a positive worth these days."

Ghonkaba joined him in a laugh. It was unnecessary for him to comment that, until very recently, the pay he had received had been utterly useless.

"We're getting all the recruits we need and want," Washington said, "and we've established training centers all over the country for them. I can't foresee a time when we'll again be suffering a shortage of manpower, much less of arms, munitions, and food."

"You're right, sir," Ghonkaba agreed, wondering what point Washington was intending to make. "I don't think there's any question that we've turned the corner."

"Service in the Continental Army," General Washington said, "has been a great boon for some men who have made outstanding reputations as a result of their service. Others who have worked more or less anonymously have suffered great hardship." He looked intently at his guest. "I know of no group of soldiers who have suffered greater losses than you and your fellow scouts from the Seneca tribe."

Ghonkaba tried to make light of it. "I think you may be exaggerating somewhat, General."

Washington shook his head as he rose, went to the sideboard, and refilled their glasses. "You and your men," he said, "have suffered great losses, with no expectation of reward. You've endured cold, hunger, a lack of clothing, and above all, a lack of pay for years."

"Our situation is hardly unique, General. Everyone else in the Continental Army is in the same boat."

"No," Washington said. "The situations have not been in the least similar. Most Continentals have lived on hope—the hope they would some day be citizens of free states in a free nation. But you've been denied that very hope. As I understand it, your situation, with regard to your status as members of the Seneca nation, is completely hopeless. According to my information, you cannot be restored to a standing as full-blooded Seneca or members of the Iroquois League."

"Yes, sir," Ghonkaba admitted reluctantly. "I guess that much is true."

"You're free to settle wherever you please in the

thirteen states or in any of this country's territories,"
Washington said. "But all the same, you are Indians
without a homeland, without tribal affiliations of any
kind."

"We still think of ourselves as Seneca," Ghonkaba
said, "even though the nation no longer admits our
existence."

"I don't understand the principles on which Indian
nations function," Washington said, "but that's beside
the point. My understanding, or lack of it, is really
irrelevant. What matters is that you and your Seneca
scouts are being repaid shabbily for your great loyalty
to our cause."

"We don't see our situation in that light," Ghonkaba
replied firmly.

Washington was even more firm. "Perhaps," he
said, "you lack a certain breadth of vision. Be that as it
may, I want to give you every opportunity to create
new and useful lives for yourselves in peacetime.
Therefore, I'm willing to approve any requests that you
and your fellow Seneca may make for a release from
duty in the Continentals. Naturally, you'll be released
at your present ranks with honorable discharges."

Ghonkaba was so shocked he could only stare at
the commanding general. "Surely you're joking, sir,"
he said in a voice that was hardly more than a whisper.

"I've never been more serious," Washington assured him. "At one time during the war—a long period—
the contributions that you could make to our cause
were vital. That day has passed, and we have more
troops than we need to do what you and your Seneca
have done. I'm anxious," Washington said, "to give you
a head start on the road to successful, postwar lives as
civilians. Effective immediately, I'm granting leaves of
absence to you and to your Seneca. Confer with your
family and with each other. Make up your mind where
you want to go and what you want to do, what kind of

life you want to lead. Then report back to me, and I shall do everything in my power to help you establish yourselves where you wish to be."

Ghonkaba's Seneca scouts, all hard-bitten veterans who had served in more campaigns than they could recall, filed silently into a small grove in the familiar woods of New Jersey. Three warriors had won battlefield commissions and had progressed through the ranks to positions as high as that of captain; the others, without exception, were high-ranking noncommissioned officers. They had achieved their ranks on merit alone and were as realistic and as resilient a group as any comparable unit in the Continental Army.

They sat in a semicircle awaiting the arrival of their commander, and when Ghonkaba joined them he faced them all and began to speak in the language of the Seneca. They knew at once that this was no ordinary occasion. He had made a point of always speaking to them in English when relaying orders.

With careful deliberation, he traced the record of their unit from the morning they departed from the land of the Seneca. After he reached the present, he repeated his conversation with General Washington, including the general's insistence that the Seneca terminate their association with the Continental Army immediately.

When he was finished, a moment of silence followed before he added, "We have two choices. We can go our separate ways or we can travel together and make our new lives together."

They answered with one voice. "Together!" they shouted.

Ghonkaba was not surprised. "That coincides with my own view," he said. "We will venture into the world united, as we have been throughout the war. Now the great question arises. Where shall we go?"

The warriors replied in the order of their seniority. The first to speak was Ranoga.

"We have traveled far from the land of the Seneca in our journeys since we have joined the army," he said. "We have visited Philadelphia, the largest city in the New World, and also seen Boston and New York. I do not deny the need for cities to exist. I can say only that life in a city is not for me. In order to be fulfilled as a warrior and as a man, I require the wilderness surrounding me like a thick blanket. I need the solitary life it provides. I need the opportunity to communicate with the manitous. I love the sustenance that the wilderness provides me. And I require nothing else in all of the world."

The group broke into wild, sustained cheers.

Ranoga held up his hand for silence. "I do not know where we will find such a place in the wilderness, one which will be suitable for our needs, but I cast my vote in favor of our removal to such a place."

His comrades agreed with him so heartily that discussion of the point hardly was necessary. They then began to examine different locales.

Casno, a stalwart war chief, was the first to mention a specific area. "I well remember," he said, "a campaign we waged as Seneca against the Algonquian in Maine. The forest in that part of the world is thick and wild. The rivers are teeming with salmon and other fish. The forests are well stocked with deer and other animals necessary for us to sustain our lives. I propose that we go north to that land."

Ranoga leaped to his feet in protest. "It is well and good for Casno to speak of going north into the forests of Maine," he said, "but as a bachelor without family responsibilities he overlooks one important factor. Our children—and I am thinking particularly of the daughters— will one day grow old enough to choose mates. Whom shall they select? If we are living in the land of the

Algonquian, the women will be forced to choose braves of the Algonquian nation. As a true Seneca, I feel sick at my heart, and my stomach revolts at the thought of being compelled—if I have daughters—to greet men of the puny, cowardly Algonquian nation as my sons-in-law. Under no circumstances will I agree that we move to Maine."

Great candor marked their discussion of other sections of the United States. They ruled out the wilderness of the Ohio country. The warriors of the Miami nation, long envious of the power of the Seneca, were known to be extremely jealous, and it was assumed that they would be hostile.

In central and western Pennsylvania lived the Erie, and no discussion of any kind was necessary. The Erie were the implacable, traditional foes of the Seneca. No one needed to point out the absurdity of a dozen Seneca warriors trying to settle down and make new lives for their families in the midst of sworn enemies.

The Chickahominy lived in Virginia, and without exception, the Seneca spoke of this nation with great contempt. The Chickahominy were known throughout the Indian world for being shifty, untrustworthy, and ready to break their word whenever it suited them. They were immediately dismissed.

Farther to the south, in the Carolinas and Georgia, were the Choctaw, a mighty and prosperous nation that instinctively disliked all other Indians. They would have nothing to do with men from another tribe. Invading their territory with such a small force would guarantee that the men would be killed and their families enslaved.

Also in this same general area were the southern Tuscarora, a branch of the nation that was a member in good standing of the Iroquois League.

The Seneca scouts didn't know much about the southern Tuscarora, and life as their neighbors sounded promising. After all, as fellow Iroquois, they could be expected to greet the Seneca with considerable warmth. At this point, Ghonkaba found it necessary to enlighten his comrades. The southern Tuscarora, he told them, were envious of the prestige of their northern relatives as members of the Iroquois League, and as a consequence, they had nothing to do with them. On repeated occasions, they had ignored invitations to meetings and celebrations of the northern branch of their family. Undoubtedly, he argued, they would be very cold and rude in their treatment of the Seneca. He prevailed and the idea was reluctantly abandoned.

As a result of the cursory analysis, it appeared that nowhere in the United States would the small group be welcome. But Ghonkaba hastily reassured his comrades that such a point of view was false. America was a vast, constantly growing land, and he felt certain that somewhere within her borders they would find a welcome and a home. They would make a more systematic search, and then they would determine where they should go.

In the meantime, they would obtain their final pay from the Continentals, be mustered out of the service, and leave for the Philadelphia area to join their families. Of the twelve men, seven had wives and children. The five bachelors in the group would accompany the majority.

Ghonkaba said his farewells to his battalion and thanked the men for their fidelity and service to their country. Then he met with the four older sergeants, who had been his friends and most intimate collaborators. But the quartet refused to say good-bye to him.

"When you decide where you're going to be living in years to come, let us know," Sergeant Ginsberg told him. "We're not likely to be spending the rest of our lives with the Continentals, and there's no telling where we'll turn up once we go back to civilian life. We're most likely to wind up in the lands where there aren't too many people. City life isn't for us, any more than it's for you and your Seneca. So the odds are pretty good that we'll show up one of these days and say howdy, no matter where it is you're living."

. It was easier by far to part on that note, and Ghonkaba felt in his heart that he was not destined to lose sight of these close friends. Somewhere, in some way or another, when they least expected it, they would be reunited; he felt sure of it.

Young Renno and El-i-chi listened to their father in wide-eyed absorption as Ena frowned, but even though her mind was racing, she kept her thoughts to herself. This was an occasion when the young people of a Seneca family listened but did not speak.

No such restrictions applied to Toshabe, whose mind was filled with questions. "Do you approve of General Washington's decision in this matter?" she asked.

Her husband nodded. "My first reaction," Ghonkaba said, "was to refuse to leave the Continental Army at this point. But the general convinced me that we who are Seneca have done all in our power to help the American cause and that the time has now come when we must look after ourselves. I agreed only with great reluctance, as did the Seneca in my battalion. We have decided that wherever we go to make our new homes, we're going together. That is most important. In that way, our children will grow to manhood and womanhood knowing, we hope, a great deal about their heritage and the traditions of their people."

"But you don't know as yet where you plan for us to settle?"

"I'm afraid not," Ghonkaba said. "We had one discussion of the subject, and we found something wrong with almost every part of the country. We'll have to look at the question in far greater detail." He smiled at his children. "If any of you have any ideas, don't be afraid to express them. We shall need all the help we can get, regardless of its source. It's of vital importance."

At this point, Clem Dawkins arrived on his daily visit. He had been left behind when General Greene's division had moved north into New Jersey with General Washington, and consequently he called regularly on Ena.

They could hear Ena's voice in another room. She spoke at length, earnestly and persuasively. Then Clem replied in one short speech, and Ena appeared in the doorway.

"My father," she asked, "may Clem and I have a word with you?"

"Of course," Ghonkaba replied, and accompanied her to the adjoining room.

Clem rose to his feet, frowning in concentration, and looking very much concerned. "Colonel," he said, "I don't know if you're familiar with my present situation, but my physical condition is being held against me yet, and I cannot enlist in the Continental Army. I am finding the life that is permitted to me embarrassing and irksome."

"I can't blame you for that," Ghonkaba replied.

The youth was very much encouraged by his reaction. "As a matter of fact," Clem went on, "the war could be ended by the time the army is willing to take me. Ena and I are wondering . . . she tells me that you're leaving shortly to make your new home somewhere in America, and we wonder if you would consent to taking me with you."

Ghonkaba looked at the youth and then at his daughter, and he was struck by the anxiety in their faces. He recalled how difficult a first romance could be.

Toshabe came into the room and stood behind the young couple. It was obvious that she had heard the conversation. They did not see her, and behind their backs she nodded while smiling broadly.

Ghonkaba, however, was reluctant to be maneuvered into a position that he would regret. "I have no objection to your coming with us, Clem," he said. "You'll have to work, of course, as we all will, but you have demonstrated that you're not afraid of hard work, so I see no problems on that score."

"No, sir," the young men replied eagerly. "I'm prepared to work very hard."

"One aspect of this, however, causes me to hesitate," Ghonkaba said. "In our vote my Seneca brethren and I were agreed that we have no wish to settle in the large cities. On the contrary. We intend to go somewhere where we can find open land and suitable wilderness that will enable us to live the kind of life that is important to us."

"That sounds great to me, Colonel," Clem exclaimed. "I'm willing to go anywhere."

Ghonkaba peered at him intently. "You may be willing to go anywhere, Clem. In fact, I suspect that you'd make no complaint, no matter where you went, provided that Ena was there. But I'm not forgetting that you were city bred. You grew up in a large town and lived your whole life there until you went to Trenton a year or so ago. Even Trenton is a far larger community than we have in mind. We are intending to settle deep in the forest, in a place where our shelter will come from materials that we gather when we chop down trees. Our clothing and our food will come from the animals we kill for food, and from plants that we raise, such as cotton and flax. We will have very few of the benefits of civilized living. We do have iron pots and pans that make our cooking preparations much easier. And we have scissors and razors and burnished metal that we use as mirrors. We have blankets of fine wool. In the main, however, we shall be living close to the land and off the land. Such a way of life is alien to you. It is so strange, in fact, that I'm not certain you would be able to survive in it, much less attain happiness in it."

The young man looked crushed.

Ena interceded quickly. "For some months, my father," she said, "since both Clem and I have had little to do, I have been instructing him in the ways of our people and our customs. I am sure you will find that he is adept at living in the wilderness and at accustoming himself to the ways of the Seneca there."

Ghonkaba still looked somewhat dubious.

"Let us come to an understanding with you, my father," Ena said persuasively. "Give your permission for Clem to accompany us when we go to our new home, wherever it may be. If he should be unable to accommodate himself to our way of life in the forest, he will be the first to know it and will return to a city. But if he is at home—and I predict that he will be—then he may stay with us as long as he pleases."

She was so much in earnest that Ghonkaba's opposition melted away. If the two young people continued to feel as they felt right now, he could look forward to Clem joining his family as a son-in-law within the next year to three years. In fairness to the young man and to his daughter, he was called upon to give them a chance to prove Clem's worth, rather than simply dismissing him out of hand.

"Very well," he said, to their delight. "We will arrange the future accordingly, as you have just spoken it."

The expression of ecstatic happiness that Ena and Clem exchanged was reward enough for Ghonkaba.

When he and Toshabe were alone later, he told her of the objections that their fellow Seneca had expressed about the various parts of the country in which they might settle.

"You make it sound," his wife declared, "as though no part of the country is suitable as a home for us."

"Our common sense alone tells you and me," he said, "that that is not true. Some appropriate stretch of wilderness where we can be happy surely can be found. We must be patient. The right place will be revealed to us at the right time."

"Of course," Toshabe replied. "The manitous have been good to us for many years, as they were good to your ancestors before you, and we must have faith in them now to guide us."

Later that night Ghonkaba had difficulty in getting to sleep, attributing his insomnia to his featherbed. He had not used it during his entire time in the field with the army.

After he drifted off, however, he fell into a very deep sleep.

Suddenly the pungent odors, sharp but sweet, of a pine forest assailed his nostrils, and he knew he was dreaming. That knowledge grew into certainty when the scent became stronger still, and he found himself standing in a small clearing in the midst of a wilderness. He was alone, but gradually a figure, transparent at first, then increasingly opaque, took shape in front of him. He was not surprised to see his distinguished ancestor Renno.

They greeted one another in respectful silence, each raising his left arm stiffly in the Seneca style of greeting.

"You are troubled, Ghonkaba," the shape of Renno said solemnly. "I have watched you wrestling with a problem, and you need assistance in order to solve it."

Ghonkaba acknowledged the truth of what was said by inclining his head. He did not need to speak in words to someone who had no difficulty in reading his innermost thoughts.

Renno reached into a pocket of his buckskin trousers and withdrew a single sheet of very soft, flexible birch bark. "I have here," he said, "a spirit map of your life on earth."

Feeling as though he had been struck by lightning, Ghonkaba automatically reached out a hand toward the birch bark.

Renno withdrew the sheet, holding it beyond Ghonkaba's reach. "Those who still live in your world," he said gently, "are not permitted to read the spirit maps of their own existence. It is enough that their lives are unfolded as they live them day by day."

In his dream, Ghonkaba obediently folded his arms, lowered his head, and waited.

"Take heart," Renno told him. "Your problem is not so great that it is insoluble. Indeed, a solution lies at hand for you."

"Are you hinting," Ghonkaba asked eagerly, "that I may be welcome once again in the land of the Seneca?"

"Never!" Renno replied flatly. "You made your choice and there is no looking back. You may not look back now. The life you lived previously is behind you, but a new life, useful and full of glory, awaits you and our mutual descendants, who will follow you."

Ghonkaba found it so difficult to speak in the dream that his throat ached. "Where would you have me go to find contentment and glory, my grandfather?" he asked humbly.

"You were wise," Renno said, "when you decided to stay away from the territory that adjoins the land of the Erie. The same is true of the land of the Chickahominy, the Choctaw, and the Tuscarora."

"Where else can we go?" he cried.

"Follow the arrow," the shape of Renno intoned.

"The arrow? What arrow? I don't understand!" Ghonkaba could feel a note of frenzy come into his voice.

"Follow the arrow," the shape of Renno said softly

but with great force. "You will find it in the land where the god of the sun sleeps. Do not doubt your destiny. Trust the hawk."

Ghonkaba's bewilderment grew, and to his horror the image of his grandfather began to fade from view.

"Wait! I beg you, wait!" Ghonkaba called frantically. "Your meaning is not clear!"

The last thing he saw was Renno's strong, wise face. His grandfather was smiling at him and offering him silent encouragement as he faded completely and disappeared from view.

Ghonkaba awakened with a start, and Toshabe woke up, too. He poured out the story of his dream to her, repeating the exact words of Renno.

The message made no more sense to Toshabe than to her husband. "This is no time of night to trouble your brain," she said. "Wait until morning, and perhaps all will become clear to you."

They went back to sleep, postponing a solution until morning, but when daylight came both were as uncertain as they had been in the middle of the night.

Ghonkaba sent his sons to summon the other Seneca warriors to a meeting. An hour later they had all gathered in the yard outside Ghonkaba's dwelling.

He joined them there and related his dream of his grandfather in full detail, repeating word for word what Renno had said to him, including the statement that they were wise not to try to set up their home in the wilderness near the lands occupied by other nations.

They were at a loss to explain the phrase "follow the arrow," and the reference to a hawk also seemed meaningless to them.

But Casno, the senior war chief, tried to shed light on the rest of what Renno had said. "The god of the sun," he said, "sleeps in that direction." He pointed toward the west. "We see the sun disappear in that direction over the horizon every evening. But we must rule out some portions of the West, as your grandfather told you, Ghonkaba."

"What portion of the West does that leave for us to explore?" Ranoga demanded.

After a long silence as all the warriors pondered the question, Ghonkaba spoke up to offer a solution.

"I know of only one region that might be suitable," he said at last. "It lies across the mountains, west of North Carolina, and it is a wilderness where the mighty Cherokee nation dwells. Some of the early settlers are calling it Tennessee, after the great river of that name which flows there, while others call it Franklin, after Doctor Franklin of Philadelphia."

One of the bachelors rose to his feet. "I say we migrate across the mountains to the land near the home of the Cherokee," he said. "We can let the riddle of the arrow and that of the falcon wait until some later time when they will become clearer to us."

The others shouted their approval, and the issue was settled. The homeless veterans of the American Revolution would cross the mountains into the wilderness of Tennessee and plan to settle in those lands, even though the Cherokee, one of the mightiest Indian nations in all the land, made their home in the forest there.

The great adventure was about to begin.

Coming in October 1984 . . .

BOOK X IN THE WHITE INDIAN SERIES

CHEROKEE

Donald Clayton Porter

Now that he has led a brave band of his Seneca in victorious campaigns under General George Washington, Ghonkaba must pay the price for supporting the American Patriots—banishment from his own land. With his family and a dozen loyal followers, he sets out with Washington's blessing for the open, untamed country across the Appalachians. His daughter, Ena, and sons, Renno and El-i-chi, again distinguish themselves in the difficult trek. Meanwhile, Ena finds the romance of her life in the midst of tragedy. In Kentucky, Daniel Boone cautions them about the Cherokee tribe which they are soon to encounter. Ghonkaba, as well as Ena and her brothers, daringly take up this challenge and succeed in winning a decisive role in the Cherokee nation. Their heroic efforts climax in a perilous but triumphant battle against Creek and Tuscarora enemies. And even then one more grave crisis looms, with Ghonkaba as the nation's sole hope.

(Read CHEROKEE, on sale October 15, 1984,
wherever Bantam Books are sold.)

**FROM THE PRODUCER OF WAGONS WEST
AND THE KENT FAMILY CHRONICLES—
A SWEEPING SAGA OF WAR AND HEROISM
AT THE BIRTH OF A NATION.**

THE WHITE INDIAN SERIES

Filled with the glory and adventure of the colonization of America, here is the thrilling saga of the new frontier's boldest hero and his family. Renno, born to white parents but raised by Seneca Indians, becomes a leader in both worlds. THE WHITE INDIAN SERIES chronicles the adventures of Renno, his son Ja-gonh, and his grandson Ghonkaba, from the colonies to Canada, from the South to the turbulent West. Through their struggles to tame a savage continent and their encounters with the powerful men and passionate women in the early battles for America, we witness the events that shaped our future and forged our great heritage.

☐	22714	White Indian #1	$3.50
☐	22715	The Renegade #2	$3.50
☐	22716	War Chief #3	$3.50
☐	22717	The Sachem #4	$3.50
☐	22718	Renno #5	$3.50
☐	20559	Tomahawk #6	$3.50
☐	23022	War Cry #7	$3.50
☐	23576	Ambush #8	$3.50